SHAKESPEARE'S
Sister

SHAKESPEARE'S
Sister
A NOVEL

Doris Gwaltney

CYPRESS CREEK PRESS
DISTRIBUTED BY

HAMPTON ROADS
PUBLISHING COMPANY, INC.

for Atwill

with love and gratitude

For information write the distributor:

Hampton Roads Publishing Company, Inc.
134 Burgess Lane
Charlottesville, VA 22902

Or call: (804) 296-2772
FAX: (804) 296-5096

If you are unable to order this book from your local
bookseller, you may order directly from the distributor.
Quantity discounts for organizations are available.
Call 1-800-766-8009, toll-free.

ISBN 1-57174-041-4

Printed in Canada

"Let me imagine. . .what would have happened had Shakespeare had a wonderfully gifted sister, called Judith, let us say. . .as adventurous, as imaginative, as agog to see the world as he was."

A ROOM OF ONE'S OWN by Virginia Woolf

PROLOGUE

Marriage, her father had said. And then he had shown her a paper, a contract, as if he were selling a horse.

"Nonsense," Judith had told him. "I have no wish to be married."

"This is not a matter of wishes," her father had said. "It is a matter of necessity."

Judith had grabbed for the paper but her father was too quick for her; he had slipped it cunningly inside his jerkin beneath his armpit. And so she had turned to her mother, who sat watching from her place at the chimney piece.

"Mother, please speak to father about this. I cannot marry the man."

"Judith, dear, what can I say more than the words of our blessed catechism?"

And then Mary Shakespeare had quoted the words Judith had memorized some years before and spoken to the priest through clenched teeth.

"Love, honor and succor your father and your mother. Submit yourself to all your governors, teachers, spiritual pastors, and masters. Order yourself lowly and reverently to all your betters."

"Order myself? Submit myself?"

Judith's voice had grown louder with every word. She had stamped both feet. She had thrown a glass bowl straight into the empty fireplace and shattered it. She was reaching for a small bottle on the overmantel when her father said he had had quite enough.

"Give me the key to the cupboard," John Shakespeare had said to his wife.

Mary Shakespeare had twirled her ring of keys, long ones and short, rusty ones and shining new, until she came to the cupboard key. She had twisted it free and held it out to her husband.

"Now," said John Shakespeare. "I will show you what it means for a girl to disobey a father."

He had taken Judith by both shoulders, the key projecting from between the thumb and forefinger of his right hand, and he had lifted her off her feet, and marched through the length of the parlor and the kitchen. Into the back passage where stood the cupboard. He had kicked the door open, pushed Judith inside, and turned the key in the lock.

"You are an ungrateful girl," he had said. "And you will stay inside this cupboard, meditating your sins til you are ready to ask forgiveness."

PART
I

CHAPTER I

In the darkness of the cupboard, where only a sliver of light came through the locked door, where there was not space to stand erect or to sit with any degree of comfort, Judith sobbed quietly, covering her mouth with both hands so that her family would not hear her. Though she did not think anyone was listening.

Judith pushed at her sleeves, untied the strings of her cap. She felt that she was suffocating, dying here in this dark airless place. She extricated her right foot from beneath her, and then her left. She jammed her shoulders against the back of the cupboard and in the small space in which she could manipulate her legs, began to kick against the cupboard doors.

"Come your ways, Judith Shakespeare," she could hear her mother saying from inside the kitchen. And further mumbled conversation between her parents and Old Sallie the cook. Judith grew quiet, listening. She could make out a sprinkling of words. "The man has a thousand pounds," said her father. "Six painted cloths," said her mother.

"But he is old," Judith shouted. "Old and ignorant."

"A man is not ignorant who has a thousand pounds," said her father. "And Henry Wilcome furthermore is a justice of the peace and owns more acres of land then you could count."

"Nevertheless, I will not marry him."

"You have no choice in the matter," her father called back to her.

"You wait and see," she whispered into the darkness.

Judith's troubles had not begun with her father's announcement of the marriage to Henry Wilcome. On an ordinary day, her mother would chastise Judith for an inventory of faults that would have taken up a copy page in any notebook, except for the fact that, of course, Mary Shakespeare could not write. For Judith did not possess the womanly arts which were prized in Elizabethan society. Her embroidery knotted to a whickerpucker. Her custards clotted;

her comfits shattered like powder. Her manner was not comely. She had reportedly been seen alone, wandering the highroads and hillsides. She spoke too loud, bothered into things meant only for men to know. She held traffic with the poor and lowly, stopping often at the hovels of the cunning women, of the ancient, doddering uncles.

Besides this there were constantly stains and rips in Judith's clothing. She was unpleasant whenever she was interrupted from reading her papers.

"You must think of your position," Mary Shakespeare would say. "You are an Arden. By our lady, when I was your age. . .no less, much less, I was known for my seams and for my puddings."

"I shall not be known for puddings, mother," Judith would reply.

Then Mary Shakespeare would crook her small, fat finger in Judith's direction, and nod her head.

"It is only because you will not exert yourself. For you are like me, Judith. . .Very like me."

"I am not like you, mother," Judith would say. "I am not like anybody."

Yet Judith did bear a physical resemblance to her mother. She was short like her mother, but unlike her mother, as flat in her breasts and her buttocks as a boy. And like her mother, she had long yellow hair, curled in ringlets, yet tangled as her mother's could never be under the tight cloths she bound about her head.

When pressed to do so, Judith would comb at her temples and down the sides as far as her ears. Then she would tie her cap on to hide the tangles. She had no time for arranging hair. Nor for sewing and cooking dainties. And sometimes not for talking with her family, not even her brothers. Sometimes words poured into her mind so that she could think of nothing else. Poems and plays every bit as good as Will wrote. Whereas her poems were bound in a knot beneath the settle while Will was paid for his. And they were performed upon the London stage.

Yet she could bear no malice toward her brother, for Will was her only support. He had taught her to read and write when she was no more than five years old. And now when he visited Stratford, usually in August of each year, he brought her sheets and scraps of paper to write her poems on. He asked her to read them to him. He read his plays to her. And sometimes she thought he changed a word or two at her suggestion.

Judith rested her head against the splintery wood and closed her eyes. And then she remembered the lines which had come to her in the back garden. She had been running into the house to write them down when her parents called her into the parlor.

"O, it came o'er my ear like the sweet sound
That breathes upon a bank of violets,
Stealing and giving odor!"

But then her father's voice broke through.

"There is no need to discuss the matter, Mary," he said to his wife. "My need is too great. The marriage must proceed."

"Enough, no more!" said Judith. "Tis not so sweet as it was before."

Judith knew precisely the chronicle of her father's rise in the world and of his sudden fall, though much of it she was not yet born to see. She had pieced it together from the chance remark of a neighbor, a sudden view from behind a half-closed door, and most of all from her mother's veiled hints of the delights of John Shakespeare's courtship.

"It was shameful to him to lie so far below me, I being an Arden, and so he took to leather work to come up a little higher in the world," her mother would say. And then she would nod and smooth the worn silk of her skirt, for she never wore less than silks and velvet though it be as old as Doomsday. And she would laugh aloud, and perhaps take a sweet from the silver box she kept beside her chair.

"Your father was an ambitious lad. And though I never minded his humble state, he would not bring me down to the disgrace of marrying a tenant farmer."

For Judith's paternal grandfather, old Richard Shakespeare, had rented land at Snitterfield from her maternal grandfather, Robert Arden. Which was not the only property Robert Arden owned. And though he had been blessed with seven daughters, her mother even though the youngest, received as her portion the farm called Asbyes with house and fifty acres, and an interest in the farm at Snitterfield as well. It must have seemed great wealth to John Shakespeare, though not so marvelous a thing as the fair skinned, dimpled, dainty Mary Arden.

"He had no choice but to turn to leather work," Mary Shakespeare would murmur again.

And then she would tell how John had faced up to his father, who had nothing in the world but two old mares, both with a case of the bots, two plows, a dull scythe, five pigs, ten chickens, one old cow— and one remaining son, Henry, as shiftless a man as was ever made— and spoke into his father's very teeth, "I am away to Stratford, there to make my fortune."

"He had no choice," said Mary.

John Shakespeare had apprenticed himself, all on his own, to learn the ways of leather. To tie the animal to a tall post and slit its throat. To peel away the skin from the flesh, to scrape off hairs and bits of meat, to pound in oil and sometimes the brains of the slaughtered animal. To pound and soak, to soak and pound until the leather was as soft as silk and yet as tough as iron. And after months of this slitting and scraping and pounding and soaking, when he was master of his craft, he had set himself to make a tiny pair of gloves, paper thin, unstained white, and these he took to his sweetheart, Mary Arden.

In the good times after his marriage, John had bought two houses side by side in Henley Street. He kept his shop in one house, and his growing family in the other. He bought another house in Greenhill Street with a garden and cottage. He invested in wool, malt, and corn. He made gloves so fine that Robert Dudley, Earl of Leicester, sent his steward to buy a pair for the Queen. John, it must be said, was inordinately proud to think that the leather he had pounded and soaked and stretched for so long would grace the hands of her Royal Highness, Queen Elizabeth.

He boasted. Already elected to the council of the town of Stratford, his fame took him to greater heights. He was made ale taster, then one of the four constables, then assessor of fines, and finally Chamberlain. He held that office for four years. He marched resplendent in black robes, carrying the mace.

And then in the year when he had invested heavily in corn, the crop failed. One by one his investments went astray. The Earl of Leicester sent no more to buy gloves for the Queen for he had lost his place in her regard.

"There was never a man so put upon," her mother would say. And she would cry bitterly.

John Shakespeare had mortgaged Asbyes for forty pounds to

his brother-in-law, Edmund Lambert. He sold the interest in the farm at Snitterfield. It was not enough. He neglected attendance at council and stayed in his shop, making more and more pairs of gloves. Hounding his two apprenticed boys to cut faster. Pushing his way to the best stalls on fair day.

All this Judith knew with the clarity of her own memory. And all this she saw every day that passed as her brother Gilbert hurried about from farm to farm, buying up the cheapest animals for slaughter. She watched her brother Richard, bloody from the constant killing of the animals. And poor little Edmund, sweeping hairs and scrubbing up blood. Yet knowing all this, she still resolved she would not marry the rich old man her father had chosen for her. How dare her father come to her with this cruel idea of a husband?

Henry Wilcome was so old that even his cane had become importunate. Daily it begged the earth to lie flat before him and not to dimple into potholes to make him stumble. Begged his house floors not to sag to the corners and speed his weaving steps. His velvet doublet hung to his shoulders, flapping mightily against his rib cage where the bones showed pointy beneath the little flesh that clung to them. His poor withered legs inside puddled hose were no more than sticks. He had rheumy eyes. A red nose. No teeth at all. His breath stank. As did his arm pits. And the odor that rose from his shriveled codpiece was beyond all thought.

Yet John Shakespeare had contracted with this man because he had no choice. He had canvassed the town's wealthy, marriageable males, and in every case he was greeted with a chorus of nays.

"Marry Judith Shakespeare?" said one young man. "I am sure I should starve to death."

"I could never trust a woman who reads," said another.

Henry Wilcome's wife had been dead a fortnight of gasping sickness. He was too proud to take a serving girl to his bed, and so he sought a wife.

"I will take her," he told John Shakespeare.

And though John Shakespeare understood well what the wrath of his daughter would be, he shook hands on the agreement. He had to have the money. He had to pay his debts. For his wife was an Arden. It would not do to bring embarrassment to an Arden.

That very afternoon old Henry Wilcome rode to town on his

trusty mare. Some one of his grooms had put him on at Wilcome Place, and turned the horse's head toward Stratford. Upon arrival, he sat in the saddle before the house door, bawling and shouting until John Shakespeare himself came to the street to take him down. They sat in the front parlor drinking port until Henry was revived enough to whisper.

"Now. I want her now. The house needs direction. I'm cold o' nights. We'll go to the church on Saturday."

"But the banns. . . ."

"It's done. I paid the money. The marriage must be on Saturday. Now bring her out. I want to see her."

And so John had gone to the cupboard and got Judith. She protested that she was blinded by the sudden light, that her right foot was permanently injured. She had shouted that she would not be displayed to a death's head so that John was forced to gag her. Then she had kicked and scratched until he tied her hands. And then her legs at the ankle.

Gagged and tied, Judith was paraded through the room. Since Henry's vision was failing, he accepted the explanation that she was wearing a new fashion sent from London. A gift from Will to Mistress Anne. Anne had taken on flesh, so she had given the outfit to Judith.

Yet all of John's fabrications would have been revealed had Mary Shakespeare not gone on her knees beside the old chest in her bedroom where she kept her treasures, and brought out an intricately worked shawl to drape across Judith's shoulders. It fell nicely to her waist and covered the ropes. One corner was drawn carefully up across Judith's mouth to cover the gag.

"Complements her figure, wouldn't you say?" asked John.

"Ay, indeed. A beautiful maiden. A touch thin, but when I have had her through a full moon, she will begin to plumpen."

When they had managed to drag Judith through the room and back again into the kitchen with the door closed, John Shakespeare set Henry Wilcome on his horse, turned its head to Wilcome Place and gave her a whack on the rump.

"Saturday," the old man said.

"Saturday," John replied.

Later that afternoon, Judith stood at the parlor window, staring into the street, trying vainly to shut out the sound of the women's voices. Her mother could speak of nothing except the wedding feast. "A banquet on the lawn would be a fine thing," she said. Her sister Joan was already planning a visit to Wilcome Place. "Judith will not know how to arrange the furnishings nor how to direct the cleaning of so many painted cloths." Will's wife, Anne, spoke only of the space Judith would be vacating. "I think Susanna can sleep in the middle room with you, Joan. That will give us more room in the back chamber when William visits," she said.

Judith shivered. The sky was darkening. It would be twilight soon and then pitch dark night. And though she had made the decision to run away to Will in London, she had not devised a plan as to how it could be done. She leaned her head on the window sill, turned to look toward Rother Street, and caught sight of Launcelot Gobbo, the slop boy. Holy Jesu, she and Launcelot could be twins. By a measure he was her height. He had no more buttocks than she. He too was flat downward from his chin to his knees. His hair was lank and dark and his face pocked, but that was no matter. There was no measure to a face. Her own head could protrude from his collar as well as his.

Judith slipped quietly from the room and out the side door. No one called after her. Nor did she wait to hear them. She ran to Launcelot where he was walking down Rother Street, and grasped him by his bony arm.

"Take off your clothes," she said. "I must borrow them."

The lad's eyes blazed like the fire which the east wind had blown up some years before, and burnt half the town. He was already unbuttoning.

"No, wait," she said. "Not these clothes." For Judith had caught the full force of Launcelot Gobbo's odor. "You have better clothes than these. I have seen you in church in an old jerkin and hose. Go home and get them for me."

"When will you give them back?" the boy asked.

Judith had to nerve herself to look into those fluttering brown eyes and tell him a lie. How trusting he was. How devoted. Yet the truth of the matter was that he was simple minded.

"I will not need them long," she said.

"Can ye give them back tomorrow morning? I need them tomorrow because tomorrow is Wednesday."

"Wear your best clothes of a Wednesday?"

"I'faith, yes. Don't ye know tomorrow is Midsummer's Eve?"

"By the world," she said.

"And this Midsummer's Eve is not just any Midsummer's Eve. For this Midsummer's Eve, I be leaping the fire with Jane Bigsby."

Judith stared so hard at the grinning boy that she counted the rings of dirt around his neck bones. How could she take his clothes at such a time? Yet how could she remain another day in Stratford?"

"What is the reason you cannot leap the fire in these same clothes you have on?" she asked him.

"Well, for meself, Mistress Judith, I could do so. But Jane Bigsby that is my sweetheart says she will not have me stinking. Ye know what manner of work I do."

"Indeed," said Judith. Nor would she need to be told even if she had not seen him all these years mucking about in every variety of excretion known to the versal world. "I tell you. At midnight o' Midsummer's Eve, bring them to me at Clopton Bridge."

The boy was beginning to look belligerent. He was taking small steps backward, away from her.

"O come now, you must do it for me," she said commandingly.

"What will ye give me?" the boy asked.

"I will give you money. I promise."

"How much money?"

"I will say this, Launcelot. I will give you all that I have."

"Very well, mistress. And I won't fail ye neither."

"Be sure you do not."

Meanwhile, in London, Will Shakespeare was toiling manfully at the writing of Henry VI, Part III. He wrote at the theater as he was waiting to go on stage. He wrote in his solitary chamber til his last candle guttered out. He wrote at his meals. He wrote as he lay with his wench.

"Ah-h-h-h God," said he, turning away from the woman and starting to rise.

"Are you done already?" asked the wench.

"Not at all, but I've made a fine speech in my head and I must write it down."

He clambered from the bed, a very fine bed, wide and tall, and when not in use covered with a splendid woven-work bedrug. He made his way in the darkness to the rough table where he had left the manuscript.

"You cannot see, Will Shakespeare," said the wench.

"I can light a candle then, can I not?" he replied.

"Words are not worth the cost of the candle as far as I can see," she said. "I know nothing about words, neither having the power to read them nor write them, as it befits any decent woman not to know, but it does seem to me they are a great waste of time and money."

"Then why do you waste so many in speech?" he asked.

"In speech? Why, what do you think? When you speak a word, tis over and gone. Requires no space to put it. No paper. No ink. It's all that writing down I find so wasteful."

The sound of a pen scratching against paper could be clearly heard. Tiny bursts of speed, then pauses which grew longer. And longer.

"Od's Prittikins," said Will. "I forgot it."

"Did I not tell you? No need in the world to write things down, for if a word is not worth remembering on its own, tis worth nothing at all. Come back to bed. I can make you remember things much better than words."

"No, I will not. Not now."

"Bloody hell," said the wench.

There was a stretching sound, as of the ropes moving and shifting under the straw mattress. The wench was rising from the bed.

"To reconstruct," said Will. "King Edward says, 'So, lie thou there. . . .'"

"I will not lie back there for no man," said the wench.

"For Warwick was a bug. . . ."

"Which bites me ever and anon."

This time the scratching sound was the wench's fingernails on her bare butt.

"Then Warwick, asking who is nigh, who victor, then. . . ."

He drummed with his fingers on the table.

"My blood, my want of strength, my rich heart shows, That I must yield my body to the earth. . . .Yes, yes, and so on. . . Ay God. . . Thus yields the cellar to the ox's edge, Whose arms gave. . .home?"

Will lifted his pen to his chin. The quill feather tickled at his ear.

"No," he said. "It will not do. Should I say place?"

He wrote in the air, making words into exaggerated circles.

"No. That will not do neither. Whose arms gave. . . ."

"I'd rather sleep in the street than shelter longer with a madman," said the wench.

"Shelter. . .ah, God, yes. . . Shelter. . . Whose arms gave shelter to the princely eagle."

The door slammed and the sound of the wench's shoes struck each step a severe blow as she descended. Then another door as she went into the street.

"Under whose shade the ramping lion slept."

Will Shakespeare filled the page and started on another. Two hours later he turned toward the bed and was greatly surprised to find that he was alone.

Back in Stratford, Judith lay sleepless on her pallet. Her legs were prickling. Her elbows itched. Her eyes burned. She could not be still. For her mind was in a turmoil.

Beside her, Joan slept peacefully, breathing little puffs of gentle breath. There had been a time when Judith was jealous of her sister Joan. Joan was a beauty. Joan was dutiful. She was always in her mother's good graces. Indeed, she had spent her whole life preparing to be married to some worthy man. And Judith had never once considered that such a thing could happen to her. Nor did she now believe that it would.

Yet lying sleepless, her brain churning, she did consider what it might be like to be Henry Wilcome's wife. Would the old man try to mount her? Or would he lie like a feather beside her on the bed? Oh, Jesu, she could not bear the thought of either.

She turned her face away from Joan. She closed her eyes. But there was no difference, for the room was already as black as pitch. She thought of London. Of all that Will had told her about the Theater. About the inn where Will lived in Bishopsgate. Likely he would have a trundle bed. If not, she would sleep on the floor. Nothing could be worse than Henry Wilcome's bed.

She turned again. Joan stirred but did not waken. But how was she to get to London? Alone, on the highroad. A young woman. But she would not be a young woman on the highroad. She would be a boy.

Again she felt she must turn back toward the wall. And knew equally well she could not sleep. O Holy Mother of God, would this night never end?

On that Wednesday morning, June 24, the Vigil of St. John the Baptist, otherwise known as Midsummer's Eve, Judith was still awake at four o'clock, her usual rising time. The kitchen was just below the small chamber where she and Joan slept on their straw mattress and boards, and every morning at that hour she heard the small bumps and scratches as Old Sallie, Nancy, and the spit boy began their daily cooking.

Judith would slip quietly out of her chamber and down the curving steps, past the dark kitchen windows and straight to the fireplace. There to take a seat on the settle, and draw from beneath it a packet of papers, tied with a tattered ribbon, once white, now a dim shade of gray. These papers were her poems and her plays, the extent of which was unknown to her family, but shared openly with the cook, the scullery maid, and the spit boy. They would not betray her. They could not, for she knew things about them which they would wish hidden.

There was great love between Judith and Old Sallie so they had nothing to fear from each other. But Old Sallie's secret was dark indeed. She had not given up the old faith when the queen made her proclamation and John Shakespeare announced the protestantizing of his household.

"How could a poor woman own beads nor cross, Master John?" she had said.

And yet one day Sallie's cross had belied her and fallen into the soup as she bent over it to take a taste. Judith did not remark on the cross, but she had watched the movement of Old Sallie's lips and read the words she whispered. "Hail, Mary, mother of God, and forgive me that I did let thy son fall into the soup."

Judith knew also the secrets of the scullery maid Nancy. For Nancy would lift her skirts to any man, and sweat and wage with him to fruition. And take into her chapped, red hands the penny she felt was her due. And though the spit boy was innocent of any venial sin, yet he failed each day at many of his appointed tasks, and often ate the little cakes meant for his mistress' silver box.

They were comfortable, the four of them, in the early morning kitchen with its smells of rising bread and warming beer. And on this day, Judith worked with great urgency. Some poems would need to be copied over, and plays and poems alike be rolled carefully together. For when she arrived in London. . .God's mercy, she shivered to think of it. She, Judith Shakespeare, in London. Yet not Judith neither, for Judith could not be a player and she was bound to be one. Til she could make her name with her writing.

"Mistress," said Old Sallie. "Not wanting to bother ye thoughts, but do ye have a hand to slap the boy? He have gone to sleep and me own hands be mixed somewhat in the bread dough."

"Gladly," she said.

Judith leant forward to the hearth and whacked the spit boy a good knock against the back of his head. And went back to the copying of her poem.

Before she could complete her work, the house awoke. First her brothers, Edmund and Richard, came lumbering down the stairs half asleep, and pushed in beside her on the settle. Next came her father who stood at the window and silently drank his morning mug of ale. Judith knew no way to hide such a roll of papers, and so she held them in her lap, cradling them in her hands.

Nancy brought each boy a mug of ale, and as they swallowed they began to unroll themselves, to open their eyes and stare about. After some moments, Richard focused on Judith and scowled.

"I say, Judith, what have you there? Is it some of Will's plays he has sent you?"

"No," she said, and bent over them.

"Don't tell me you have been writing poems again. Father, did you see this? Judith has been writing poems again."

He grabbed at them, and Judith slipped them inside the bodice of her dress.

"Jesu Christ," Richard howled. "Judith has got bosoms for her marriage. Old Henry Wilcome is going to be mad for them."

Judith reached to the hearth and grasped a long handled fork from the spit boy's hands. She turned to her brother, and pointed the tines straight at his throat.

"Richard, I am warning you. Say one more word and I shall spear you."

"In God's name, Judith, I was only teasing. Father, do you see what Judith is doing? Can you not control her?"

John Shakespeare set his mug on the table, and had taken two steps toward the settle when Mary Shakespeare's head appeared around the turn in the stairs.

"Good morning," she said cheerily. "I trust you have all had a pleasant sleep. And now, I have no time for further pleasantries. Judith, come this way. Immediately. For I have just the idea for your dress."

"What dress?" asked Judith.

"What dress? Why, Judith, what dress could I mean?"

"I have no idea."

Though of course she did. She handed the fork to the spit boy, then drifted across the room. She hid the papers behind the dough tray and winked at Old Sallie. Old Sallie looked blank for a moment, then shook her head and smiled.

"The mistress do likely speak of ye dress for the marriage," Old Sallie said.

"But there is no need. . . ."

"Mistress Judith," Old Sallie whispered, "If ye wish not to spend ye last hours in this house lodged in the darkness of the cupboard, go ye to ye mother and take what dress she give ye."

Judith glared at her brothers as she walked past the settle, nodded to her father. She lingered long over every step, dawdled past her own chamber, and came at last to her mother's door.

"Judith," said her mother, and clasped her hand and drew her into the room. "I have remembered a treasure from my chest. Oh, my dear, you have nothing to fear for a wedding dress."

Mary Shakespeare smiled broadly, then fell to her knees beside the old carved chest. And pulled Judith down beside her. She lifted the lid and there were laid out all of Mary Arden's greatest treasures. A swirl of ancient silks and lace, rich embroideries, parti colored shawls and scarves, swaddling clothes, woolen capes, and a few gold chains. Mary rummaged gently among the stuffs until she came to a white bodice, embroidered down the front, across the shoulders and down the back. She lifted it, held it to the early light now streaming through the windows.

"Judith dear, I want you to wear it," Mary said.

Judith stared at the bodice as if she feared it might mount upward like smoke and smother her.

"A maid needs a white dress to be married in," said Mary shyly.

"But, mother. . . ." Judith felt she was suffocating, just as she had the day before in the cupboard. Again she loosened the string of her cap. "Mother, I cannot wear it. Truly. This bodice was for your confirmation. I have seen it many's the time."

"There is nothing else," Mary said. "And you are tiny as a child."

"No," Judith said. "I cannot wear it."

Mary leaned her head on the trunk and her shoulders moved ever so slightly. It came to Judith that her mother was crying, and her heart softened.

"Mother," she said. "Do not cry."

Mary's sobbing stopped and she lifted her head.

"If you will not wear this dress, Judith, what then would you have me do?"

"Do nothing, mother. Let the day pass. Let me not go to this man."

Judith felt amazed that she had spoken these words, yet never before had she felt so close to her mother.

"Do you understand my feelings, mother?" she asked.

"Oh, Judith, you know I do. I, and your father as well, we have waited, watched til you showed favor toward some young man. We knew you were not like other girls. You never cared for womanly things. Nor followed womanly inclinations. I always thought the trouble started when your brother taught you to read and write. It is not seemly for a girl to know these mysteries. But let that pass. Still, marriage must come, for a maid goes heavy through life. So that if love does not come, then an arrangement must be made."

Mary reached out to take Judith into her arms. Judith hesitated. She looked down at the bodice, imagining how it might be to love someone, to see a man she did not scorn. A man who read poems, and spoke brightly. A man who saw humor. And spoke wisely.

"Judith, a woman must marry. It is not right that you should make a burden on your brothers when your father and I are gone."

"But, mother, I could care for myself."

"Doing what? You can not sew in silk. Nor cook dainty foods. There is nothing else for a woman to do. Would you be a scullery maid? Or milk the cows?"

"Oh, yes, mother, any of that. Except not to marry that stinking old man. Why, he is half dead. . . ."

"Exactly. And when you are a widow, you will be mistress of a fine place. A fine place."

"But I would wish him dead, mother. Every hour of the day I would think of it. 'Die, old man.' It is not right. I shall not do it."

Judith grabbed the bodice out of her mother's hands. She took both shoulders as if it were occupied and she would shake the occupant. Instead she pulled as hard as ever she might. There was a great ripping tear, and Judith did not stop until she held the two pieces in her hands, severed from top to bottom.

"Judith," said Mary.

And hesitated. For Mary felt a very pall, a stillness, a coldness as if a death had been visited upon her. It was the sadness as when a servant came into the garden at Asbyes to say that her father had died, that came with the death of the little girls, her babies, who died almost as soon as they were born. The sadness as when John had told her of the queen's law and snapped the chain with the small gold cross from around her neck.

"Come your ways, Judith."

And paused again. For why should she of all people, an Arden, an heiress, if truth be told one that should have a coat of arms emblazoned on the very door. . .why should she be asked to suffer the indignities of this life, the travail, the sorrow. . .

"I will have none of this," she said. And with these words, her anger flared. Judith would be punished. She would not be allowed to tear and ruin and have her own way in everything.

"Stand here, I say. Judith."

"I will not stand," Judith shouted back.

Again there was nothing for it but to put Judith in the cupboard with the whole family standing by watching. She shivered as she heard her father turn the key.

CHAPTER II

In London, there was great anxiety among the city fathers concerning the celebration of The Vigil of St. John The Baptist. For Midsummer's Eve was a time of riotous celebration. Bonfires would burn at night at every cross within the city. Greens would trail from every house front. There would be singing and dancing in the streets. Much drinking of ale and beer. And most menacing of all, the apprentices in their blue coats and wool hats would be turned loose to commit what mischief they could in this afternoon of freedom.

By two o'clock, the Theater, where Will Shakespeare served as player, was filled to overflowing with these apprentice lads. They had trudged through the fields outside Bishopsgate, penny grasped in hand, to take their stand in the pit and watch the play. Now the groundlings, as these penny customers were called, would have had an excellent view, for the stage jutted out so they could stand on three sides of it. Except that the apprentice lads pushed tight together around the apron, and shoved about, and gouged eyes and throttled necks and twisted arms of anyone unfortunate enough to get in their way.

Besides all this, vendors plied their wares, threading through the crowd with trays and baskets throughout the entire presentation of the play. In the midst of a great battle scene, with death and bladders of sheep's blood exploding across the stage, the orange girl might yet be calling, "Oranges. Fine oranges." Others would be selling nuts and cakes and gingerbread. A constant eating as long as there was a penny in any purse.

And joining the apprentice lads had come droves of younger sons up from the country, rich merchant's wives with their serving maids, young men from the universities, all kinds, and these with money to pay the second gatherer at the stairs leading to the galleries. For the great "wooden O," the tall circular building was flanked right round to the stage with three tiers of galleries, fitted with joint stools so that the richer and more elegant might sit to watch the players. These galleries were thatched with roofs as was the stage. It was only the pit left open to the wide, blue sky. A sudden rain would drench the groundlings, the stinkards as they were aptly called.

The stage itself was a marvel of mechanical skill. There was a trap door, from which could appear demons and other apparitions that might be thought to reside in the lower regions. There was an inner chamber with curtains which could serve as a cave or other private apartment. A balcony. The roof housed ropes and pulleys to launch whatever bird, goddess, nymph, or flying creature which might astound the audience.

Yet on this midsummer day, the audience had found more astonishment in the performance of one Thomas Notbright, an apprentice player late come from the countryside around Chester, than at anything flying from above or appearing from below.

The boy so mixed his lines in the beginning that he had come to the end of the play halfway through the second act. He would speak no more regardless of how he was coaxed and then cursed by the other players. Richard Burbage, chief of his father's company, at last had lifted him bodily and carried him to the back curtain. There he remained like a stone til the play was over, and on through the dancing which ended the performance.

Some half hour after the Theater had been cleared of spectators, the boy stood in the selfsame spot, still dressed in the long white gown required for his role, though now the bodice was untied and the train was tangled at his feet. His gaze was still transfixed on the rushes that covered the floor boards.

"A stick," thundered Richard Burbage as he paced the stage grimacing and growling.

Burbage was a handsome fellow, much adored by the ladies. He played the leading roles day after day, memorizing whole pages of speeches at the time and never forgetting a line nor an entrance. This day he had played a king, father to the princess portrayed by Notbright. He yet wore a circlet on his dark curls though he had changed out of his royal robes.

"You are a very stick," Richard Burbage continued. "No. A stick could do more. A stick could snap, could break, could burn. You are a very stone."

"Fie, Richard, fie. Tis a good lad," said his father, Old James Burbage.

Old James, stooped now and somewhat doddering, walked toward Thomas Notbright as fast as his bowed knees and trembling ankles would carry him. He fit his arm neatly across the boy's shoulder.

"The lad has but lately come to us, tis true. . . And true tis, he do pause in his speech a bit. . .Have patience, Richard. Patience, my son. For if the boy do pause a bit. . . ."

"Pause a bit? Father, this boy has spoken his lines with the speed of light. He would have us done with the play in half an hour. Do I lie, Will Shakespeare?" he asked, and turned toward his friend. "Were you not beside me on the stage? Can you testify to my father who calls me a liar that this boy is incompetent?"

Will looked up from his papers where he was hurriedly inking in the lines he had so lately composed. It often happened that new lines would come to him while he was on stage and in the middle of one of Richard's speeches. And then Will must speak one set of lines in reply to Richard while memorizing the new set, and must hurry off stage to write them down. This afternoon in all the confusion a perfect sonnet had come to him. And so his pen raced line on line down the folded paper scrap he had found in his pocket.

"One moment, Richard," he said and dipped his pen.

"Ay God," said Richard. "Is a man to live?"

"You may find, my son,. . .that is, it may prove. . .If Will Shakespeare do not write his plays. . .We may all go hungry."

Richard reached for his coronet, grabbed it from his head, and had started to dash it in the pit.

"There," said Will. "There. Quite finished. Now what do you say, Richard?"

"I say the lad is a loggerheaded rascal. He has memorized his speeches, but he has not the brain to grasp their meaning. And now I think he is dead and left behind by the grave diggers."

The boy came out of his trance at last, burst into tears, and threw himself at Will's feet.

"You will have no sympathy from Will Shakespeare," said Richard. "When he has written lines of beauty, of power, of grandeur. . . ."

A sound of applause came from the far door of the theater. Then, "Bravo. Bravo."

Will and all the remaining company turned to look for the solitary voice.

Standing on the far side of the pit, a wash of late evening sunlight splaying a diadem across his head, stood a young man, attended by no less than fourteen ushers, they dressed all in scarlet, and he, the young man, attired in doublet and trunk hose of peacock blue.

But then the sunlight faded, the color neutralized, as a gentleman attendant stepped forward, cutting off Will's view of the resplendent figure. After a significant pause, the usher rapped his staff sharply on the packed dirt and bawled.

"The Honorable, Sir Henry Wriothesley, Third Earl of Southampton and Baron of Titchfield."

When the usher had stepped back and fallen on one knee, Will's eyes were again drawn to the finest figure of a man he had ever seen. Far nobler than the Lord Robert Dudley, Earl of Leicester, or of the Earl's brother, Lord Ambrose Dudley, Earl of Warwick, both of whom he had seen as a child in Warwickshire.

Yet this was a youth of no more than eighteen years, tall, with brownish curls falling down his right shoulder. Full of thigh with gently tapering limbs down to a perfect ankle. His sword belt gleamed as did his resplendent clothing.

Even Thomas Notbright stopped his crying. There was no sound from any quarter save the gentle tap of Sir Henry's sword against his comely knee. With bowed heads Will and the others watched, straining their eyes so as not to miss a single footfall. And the Earl strode through the pit as if he were dancing. His attendants matched their steps to his. And though none was dressed as splendidly as he, now they too gleamed and sparkled in the falling sunlight.

"James Burbage," the old man whispered when the youth had reached the stage. "And this is my son, Richard Burbage. At your service, my Lord."

The Earl spoke as if he had heard nothing.

"Will Shakespeare," he said. "Which of you is Will Shakespeare?"

"I. . .I am, my Lord."

Will did not know what to do. Must he fall on one knee, both knees? In his panic he lifted his hand to genuflect.

"Bring a stool," the Earl said. "I want to talk to Will Shakespeare."

He waved his hand in the direction of the Burbages.

"You may retire. And do take the offending maiden with you. You, Will Shakespeare, may read me Talbot from your play of Henry VI. Retire, I say."

Will could not watch as Richard led off his old father with one hand and Thomas Notbright with the other. He only heard their footfalls on the rushes. Heard the closing of the stage door.

He himself found a stool and offered it to Sir Henry. And since he always had a copy of his work about him, reached into his doublet and pulled out the manuscript. With faltering voice he read to Sir Henry Wriothesley, Third Earl of Southampton and Baron of Titchfield. But he could not stop his brain from conjuring up pictures of riches, honors. I shall be a knight, he thought. I shall be the greatest poet in all England. Better than Marlowe. He read on and on. And when he had read everything he had on his person, the Earl called for more.

Will Shakespeare could not say no to Sir Henry. He started to read over a piece he had already done.

"You have read that," said Sir Henry, and waited.

In his panic Will could think of nothing on earth except a poem his sister Judith had written and taught him when he was last in Stratford. It was not a bad piece for a girl to have written. He smiled wanly and began.

"And when the one I love shall die,
Take him and cut him out in little stars,
And he will make the face of heaven so fine
That all the world will be in love with night."

Will paused and Sir Henry sighed and mopped his forehead with his scented handkerchief.

"By the world, Will Shakespeare, that is the best you have done yet. You must write more poems in this vein and bring them to me. I will send for you at my convenience."

"I thank you, Your Lordship. I will do my best."

Will's hands shook so wildly that the silken purse tossed to him by Sir Henry's attendant slipped through his fingers and fell to the rushes. Will scooped it up. And bowed thankfully and profusely.

In the dark hours which Judith spent in the cupboard that day, she gave serious consideration to the idea of death. Her father had vowed to leave her locked in, day after day until Saturday morning, until time to leave for the church. In which case, she would find some method to dispatch herself. She searched the flooring and the walls around her, longing to feel the cold comfort of a knife. Or a rope to hang herself. Pausing in her search for some lethal machine, she heard footsteps, and then a voice.

"Are you sorry, Judith, and will you promise me there will be no further outbreaks?"

Judith put her ear to the keyhole. She could hear her mother's quick breathing. Then she put her eye to the keyhole and saw a mountain of dingy silk skirt.

"Mother," she said. "Indeed. I will do anything you ask of me."

"And will you go on your knees to me?"

"Oh, yes, mother. On my very knees."

"And will you tell your poor sister Joan you are sorry you have screamed so loud in the cupboard that you have given her a headache?"

"Tell Joan what?"

"Tell Joan you are sorry you pounded the cupboard walls til you gave her a headache."

"I never shall," said Judith. "I never shall tell her that."

"Then in you stay."

Judith could hear her mother's soft shoes padding down the passage. She burst into tears.

"Stupid," she reproached herself. "You are a stupid girl."

Yet it was not long before she heard other feet approaching.

"Mistress?" she heard at last. "Mistress, it is me. Old Sallie. If ye could stop ye mewling now and listen."

"I will not apologize to Joan. Do not ask me."

"Now, Mistress, listen to me. Ye have already missed the early festivities. The lads and maids have long gone to the woods and brought back all the greens in the world ye could want."

"I do not care about greenery."

"And Mistress Anne has helped with hanging the doorways while poor Mistress Joan had her paining head."

"I hope her head kills her."

"And the bonfire is laid in the crossways. And the pipers is blowing and the lads and maids is took to playing at blind man's buff."

"I do not want to play blind man's buff."

"But ye do care sommat to get out of the cupboard. Now tell me, what matter is it to fall on ye knees and pray ye sister's forgiveness? For if ye would agree to do so, ye mother would go that minute into her reticule for the key and have ye out."

There was a long silence. Then, "Never."

"Then ye must spend the three nights in the cupboard and come out only to go to the church for the marrying."

"But. . . ."

"Mistress Judith, hear me. What is a word to ye sister? What do it mean?"

"It means. . . ."

"It means if ye do not, ye shall marry the old Master is what it means."

"Holy mother of God. . . ." Judith said.

And put her head in her hands. There was nothing she could do. She was not strong enough to tear the doors open, and did not truly want to kill herself even if there had been a weapon. If only she had not waited for Launcelot's breeches. Yet how could she go without them? A woman could not travel alone on the high roads. A woman could not buy food in an inn. A woman would be raped and left to die.

"Old Sallie, it is not right that I should have to do this," she said.

"But do it all the same, mistress."

"Very well. Bring mother and I shall do as she bids me."

Judith could hear Old Sallie's bare feet pattering off to the parlor and two sets of feet returning. Then she heard the grating of a key and saw daylight.

"Mother," she said, and fell upon her knees. "Mother, forgive me." She touched her head to the floor. "I am changed, mother. Nevermore will you hear me shout in anger. Nevermore will I murmur at your requests."

"And will you repeat this to your sister?"

"Yes, mother."

"Then get up from your knees and wash your face."

Mary turned and was off to the door.

"Joan. Joan, dear. Come down so that your sister may make her manners."

Judith closed the door to the cupboard firmly.

"Nevermore," she said.

Judith scarcely breathed or moved the rest of that afternoon, for she feared she might offend some family member and be locked once more in the cupboard. She smiled til her face hurt. She agreed to anything. Indeed Anne did have a way with greenery, and indeed the house front had never been decked finer. Joan's hair was the model for all hair in the kingdom. She was unable to see any of the stitches which her mother had made to the bodice she, Judith, had so willfully torn earlier. Indeed she would try it on, and indeed it was a perfect fit.

And when it was time for the bonfire and festivities down at the Rother market, Judith thought her mother wise to suggest that they two should remain at home. A bride did need her rest.

Judith sat with her mother in the upper chamber, nervous as a cat, sometimes wanting to laugh and sometimes to cry. What would she do if Launcelot failed her? God's wounds, she would go to London in her skirts. And what if she were raped and killed on the highroad? Would that would be better than life with Henry Wilcome? Yes, it would be better, but surely it could not happen. No, it could not happen. She would darken her cheeks with charcoal, and paint on pock marks and scars. She would hobble like a cripple. And babble like a madwoman. All the way to London.

"Go to the window, love," said her mother. "See if the fire burns brightly at the crossways."

Judith rose from her chair, smiling pleasantly all the while, and went to the window. There was a lightening in the sky where the bonfire burned brightly, too brightly now for jumping, but before the night was gone even the old people would join hands and sail across the dying embers.

And then it seemed to Judith that she was watching a vision of the festivities, the fire, the gathered crowd. Outlined above the flames a familiar set of breeches. And very sticks for legs arched above the smoke. Up leapt Launcelot Gobbo, up, up, and sailing out across the flames, his hand tightly grasping that of Jane Bigsby. Judith followed those shafts of legs, soaring upward, seeing virtual destruction, seeing no way that he and Jane would clear the lapping flame. And watched those pitiful extremities top the roaring tip and make their descent. And at last to touch down onto a cow chip on the other side.

Judith looked up to see her mother leaning forward, staring suspiciously into her face.

"There is something. I know there is something that has happened. Tell me, Judith. Tell me this instant."

"No, mother, there is nothing. It is just that I was thinking of the day I shall be married."

Judith paused, as if she were overcome with joy.

"Ah," said her mother. "I can tell you much of the joys of being a bride. Now that you have come to your senses and see the great honor that is done you."

Judith bowed her head to cover her face. She was tired to death of smiling, and limp from anxiety. But she hoped against hope that Launcelot had proved a leaper and had not singed his garments in the flames.

Some hours later John Shakespeare returned from the bonfire, smelling of strong drink, bleary eyed and somewhat shambling in his walk, but nevertheless shepherding his remaining family as though he were a dog trained for the purpose. He had hardly set foot in the bedchamber before he announced that Judith must sleep there with her parents that night and every night until the marriage.

"I cannot sleep except in my own chamber," Judith said.

"It is the cupboard or here at my feet," replied her father.

So Judith went into her chamber, where she had a quarrel with Joan in spite of herself, and dragged her board through the doorway to rest at the foot of her parent's bed. In one fell swoop she lay down on it, all in her bodice, skirt and shoes, and started to snore.

"Not so fast, young lady. Out of your clothes. Down to your shift. Hurry."

Judith's heart sank as she had not felt it before. For there stood her mother with arms outstretched, waiting to collect shoes, hose, bodice, skirt, everything down to the shift. These she took to her own bed to sleep with or upon.

"Now," said John Shakespeare as he set the candle on the stand and took his place in bed. "Go to sleep. But do not fear. I shall be watching."

The candle would gutter, would burn out, and then she could go. Even if her father did not sleep. Though he would sleep, she knew, from all the spirituous liquor he had drunk at the bonfire.

But in some two hours time, when indeed the candle began to smoke and flutter, John Shakespeare sprang from his bed, secured another candle and lit it.

"I cannot sleep, Father, with so much light." Judith told him.

"Your mother is sleeping well enough."

As if that were a measure of possibility. What her mother could do.

"But I cannot," said Judith.

"Then you are like me," said her father. "I cannot sleep with the light neither, and so I shall watch you throughout this miserable night. And I will watch you on Thursday night and Friday night and that will be an end of it. After that it will rest with Old Henry Wilcome."

The two lapsed into silence. Silence that dragged on and on. Judith had no idea what time it was, but if the sun had risen and peeked through the window at any moment, it would not have surprised her.

After a time, when Judith thought she would scream if she did not do something, she rose on one elbow, making no sound, and stared upward to her parent's bed. She could hear the whistle of sleeping breath. All through the house a very seizure of sleeping breath. And when she had risen high enough to see her father's face, Holy Mother of God, his eyes were closed. His mouth was slightly open. A whistle of breath could be heard escaping from it.

She sat up and thrust her feet to the floor. And waited.

She stood. And still waited as her shift whispered down around her ankles. She hardly dared to breath. She took one step and then another. She was raising her foot to take the third when her father leapt from his bed, took two further jumps and grabbed her by both her wrists.

"Aha," he said. "Then, Judith, you are not to be trusted. Just as I thought. It is into the cupboard with you. And no one is to have the key except me. And it shall remain in my pocket til morning. And each night until the marriage you will be required to sleep in the cupboard."

Mary Shakespeare, being a sound sleeper, had managed to sleep through all this, but even she roused awake when Judith began to shriek and cry.

"What is it?" she moaned. "Is it robbers? Come your ways John Shakespeare."

Mary pattered behind the two of them as they wrestled and thumped through Joan's chamber, down the steps and into the kitchen.

"Lud, Master," said Old Sallie, who had dropped off to sleep on the settle, still holding a pan of rising dough. "What do ye mean to knock about so in the middle of the night?"

But neither Mary Shakespeare, nor Old Sallie, nor Joan, nor the brothers all spilling down the steps together could deter John. He pushed Judith into the cabinet and slammed the door. He kept his weight firm against it til he could insert the key into the lock and turn it.

"Now," he thundered. "We all may sleep. And on Saturday we will be rid of her. Not another word, I say. To bed."

Judith sat flat down on the floor of the cupboard. And sobbed. The sun would be rising soon. For it seemed to her this night had been going on forever. And again she contemplated death. This time it would have to be death. She would find some way. As soon as her father let her out in the morning, she would ask for bread and a knife to cut it. And there would go her throat. Failing that, she would throw herself into the Avon. Or she would find some poison herb. Or she would. . .

But then she heard footsteps, heard a key turning in the lock, saw the door opening, saw above a short stump of candle the wrinkled face of her dear friend.

"Old Sallie," she said.

"Quiet, mistress. Ye must not make a sound."

"But I must know how you were able to get the key from father."

"Which I never did, mistress, nor needed to."

She held up a rusty key in front of Judith's eyes.

"Do you mean that you had a key all this time and never before let me out?"

"And if I had, would I still have it now when ye need it worst? Do ye think I did not read ye thoughts and know ye would run off this night to Master Will?"

"O, Sallie, how can I thank you?"

"Then never ye try to. Ye must be off. Quickly. Here is ye

little packet o' papers. Ye little poems and things. And mistress, ye must be careful now. For it would rest sore on me conscience if I sent ye off to be murthered."

Judith embraced Old Sallie, then stood back.

"I thank you for all you have done for me, but most of all for minding my papers. Keep well. I will get word to you somehow when I have reached London."

"Bless ye," said Sallie. "But go quickly. And I pray to our Lord's Mother I shall be still alive when ye come home again."

The night air came fresh into Judith's face, and she was outside. Then she was running down Henley Street on the way to Clopton Bridge.

She waited for an hour, expecting every minute to see the sunrise. What if Launcelot Gobbo had come and waited and gone? What if the morning came to find her standing on Clopton Bridge in her shift? Her father would come and drag her home to the cupboard and this time there would be no extra key. He would not let her out until the very hour of the wedding. And she would marry Henry Wilcome barefoot in her shift.

"That I shall not," she said aloud. "O, I shall not."

Judith leaned over the bridge and listened to the current running strong below. She stood on tiptoe. She lifted her skirt and then her bare leg, and delicately dandled it over the railing to Clopton Bridge.

"That I shall not marry him," she said. "I shall drown myself in the Avon, and then they shall see how they cry and moan."

"Mistress," whispered a sleepy voice close beside her. "Mistress, wait. Do not harm yeself for a lack of breeches and jerkin. I have them here and ye may have the borry of them until Sunday. Though what a bride would do with breeches. . . ."

"Oh, Launcelot," she said as she drew her leg back and planted both feet firmly in the roadway. "Oh, Launcelot, I shall love you all my life."

"Is that so, mistress? And ye being married to a rich man too."

"Oh, yes, Launcelot, for you have saved my life."

"All to the good, mistress. Here are the clothes ye asked of me."

The breeches, shirt, and jerkin were rolled together in a tight ball which he quickly proffered to her.

"Oh, thank you, Launcelot. And now. . . ."

She released the clothes for a moment when she realized she felt no shoes.

"Where are the shoes?" she asked.

"Shoes? I have no shoes but the one pair which I presently have on me own toes."

"But I must have shoes."

Judith was frantic. How could she walk so long a way without shoes?

"If I had the second pair, I would as leave give them to ye as any man alive. I would. But I cannot do me job of work without shoes, mistress. When I would tell ye what messes me shoes saves these poor toes from when I am at me job of work. When I would tell ye what these two shoes has stepped in. . . ."

"Launcelot."

Her voice was stern. She knew she must outface this poor, ignorant boy. She must steel herself to do it.

"Launcelot."

"Do ye see, mistress, for that I have Jane Bigsby to think of now. And still I have me old mother too."

"O, Launcelot, your poor mother. . .How can I do this thing?"

But even as she was handing the breeches, shirt, and jerkin back to Launcelot, a scene came stealing before her eyes. The vision of Henry Wilcome asleep in his bed. He barely made a place in the covers with his thin, measly body. But there was his face and head. Laid out on the feather bolster. His mouth was opened in a very circle and he made a noise like a whistling kettle through his bony nose. And there she was beside him, dressed only in her shift. And her eyes were open wide. She would never sleep again. Never.

"Laun-ce-lot."

She could feel the boy shaking as she grabbed the clothing once more from his hand and pushed him backward to the ground. She removed his shoes, slapping at him at every movement for he would not lie still. And then off with his hose. She hit him once again, this time so hard that his shoulders fell flat to the ground and he did not move. And then she hugged the clothing all to herself until her arms were overflowing.

"Then if ye have beat me and taken my clothes, I hope ye will not forget the money ye promised," he said in a trembling voice.

"O, Jesu," she said, and she was crying too. "Launcelot Gobbo, you are a good lad."

She took one step away from him. And when the vision of Jane Bigsby and Launcelot's pitiful mother sought to eclipse Henry Wilcome, she blinked. And took another step. And recalled the rankness of Old Henry's breath wafting across his rotting teeth. And stepped again. And smelt his armpits. And stepped two steps. And saw and smelt his miserable codpiece.

And then she turned and started to run.

"Then can ye give me the money when ye return my clothes o' Sunday?" he asked.

"O' Sunday," she called to him over her shoulder. "I will do what I can o' Sunday."

Judith knew she would have to change into Launcelot's clothing before the sun rose. When she had run as far as she could, she turned to look behind her. For though it was still dark, she knew she would be able to see a figure if Launcelot had chosen to follow her. There was no one.

She quickly stepped into the next field she came to, and crawled beneath a bush to dress. She pulled the breeches up on her legs and tied them at the waist and flexed her knees.

"God's Body, what a strangeness," she whispered to the darkness.

The hose felt no different to her than her own, nor the shoes either except that Launcelot's feet were longer than hers. She pulled them off, pushed a wad of leaves in the toes and put them on again. Off came the shift, and on went the shirt and jerkin.

"Why did I not ask him for a cap?" she muttered, then pulled her tangled hair behind her ears. It would have to do.

When the sun rose, Judith was far enough from Stratford that she recognized neither house nor barn, nor hedge nor wall. She plodded on, setting Launcelot Gobbo's shoes straight down the track dug out by a farm cart some hours before. The horse dung steamed below the morning mist. On her right hand there was a broad field of Runcival peas. On her left a stand of bread wheat. And just ahead a farmer on horseback, trotting steadily toward her.

Judith reached up with both hands and pulled her hair tight behind her ears. And tried to think how her brother Richard walked. He held himself very straight. And took long strides. And slung his arms forward and back.

"Halloo," she called in a false voice, low and growling.

The farmer trotted closer. He bent his head, stared quizzically, then broke into a laughing whinny.

"Halloo," she called again, only this time her voice broke and ended on a treble.

The farmer reined his horse to a complete stop even as he stifled his laughter.

"What is the matter, boy?" he asked. "I fear your voice has already cracked, but I hope better for your head which you hold so tight by both hands."

"O," said Judith, once more low and growling. "I have no problem with my head. I was merely being companionable. You see, I am on my way to London to see my brother, and I wanted to be sure I was on the right road."

"A lad so youthful and alone? And traveling all the way to London?" The farmer clucked his tongue. "Tis a danger to you, boy, to be alone on the highroad. For there's many a robber and murtherer here about."

"Truly?"

"Oh, yes, lad. You should go back to wherever you came from. I, being on the way to Stratford, could give you a ride. Hop up behind me."

"No, I thank you all the same. I must go on to London. I have no family except my brother, but never fear, I will be well when I meet him."

"Yes," said the farmer. "If you meet him. You are a brave, pretty lad, I hope with not a great purse to have stolen."

"Oh, no. No purse at all."

"Still you have a throat to be cut."

Judith lifted her hand to her neck. Launcelot's shirt was a bit tight. She loosed the top button and still felt a great pressure as she swallowed.

"I will be fine," Judith said. "Do not fear for me. Truly, I fear nothing for myself."

"Well, then, if you will not listen to reason, I must be off. I missed the fair yesterday due to a sickness in my shoats, but I must ride on today. Still, I am loath to leave a lad so young on the highroad."

"Do not be fearful on my account," Judith said, this time ending once more on a high pitch.

The farmer laughed again, them forced himself to look stern.

"Now you must be careful, lad. Do not take up with thieves. And wherever you sleep, keep your back to a wall."

"Thank you, sir, for your kind advice. I will remember that."

Judith watched the horse and man as far as her eye could see. She wondered if the man would happen to see her family. Or Old Sallie. And would he tell the tale of the lone boy, walking to London? She set out to run as best she could in Launcelot's shoes. They would be a sore burden on the journey.

She walked for perhaps an hour, and with every step her eyelids drooped lower. For two nights she had scarcely slept at all. And she was hungry. And thirsty. She placed one foot before the other, staring at the ill-made shoes, willing herself to step, willing her eyes to stare.

And through this fog of sleep, she gradually made out a gabble of sound. Voices. The clop of horses' feet. When she had plodded around a sharp curve in the roadway, she lifted her head, still willing her eyes to stare, and gradually she came to focus on the figures of two men on horseback. Holy Jesu, she recognized the two horses. The mare had eaten oats from her hand not three days ago. And the man who rode her, Adrian Quiney, a neighbor on Henley Street, had set out to ride to Oxford on the same day. She did not give herself time to recognize the other man though she felt sure it must be George Whateley, the warden of Clopton Bridge.

Judith leapt into the ditch at her right hand, then clambered up to a thick hedge of hawthorn and dog roses. She pushed her way through the brambles and lay down, careful to keep her back close to the woody trunk. The men rode past, laughing, talking together.

When they had passed out of sight, Judith thought that she must get to her feet and set off in the opposite direction. Toward London. But her head was so heavy. Her shoulders were like rocks and her feet like small tree trunks. She promised herself that if she were able to rest for a few moments, not to sleep, but only to lie staring at the road in front of her, then she would be able to walk faster. She could make up the little time she would spend here.

Judith's eyelids fluttered; the road danced. Her eyelids closed; the dust dwindled to a shadow. Judith was asleep. Nor would she waken til the following morning.

At daylight Judith was wakened by loud shouts and curses proceeding from some distance down the high road. As they grew closer and louder, she realized there was only one voice shouting the same words repeatedly.

"Melikes it not, old man," the voice argued. "Melikes it not. Tis some odd humour pricks thee thus to such accord. Tis some odd humour. . .Melikes it not. . . ."

Judith peaked from beneath the hedge, but there was nothing to be seen as the curve in the roadway hid the thing that could be so loud at daybreak in the morning.

"Melikes it not, old man. . . Melikes it not. . . ."

Judith lay as still as she could, but her legs had begun to shake uncontrollably. She thought of the robbers and murtherers the kind farmer had warned her of.

"Tis. . .some. . .odd. . .humour."

The man evidenced an odd love of these same several sounds. Judith, contrary to her nature, was beginning to take a great distaste to them.

"Melikes it not, old man. . . ."

Judith peeked again, and just at the center of the road's curve, she saw a formidable figure. It was a man on a horse. But such a horse and such a man as she had never seen before. The horse was so swollen in the mouth and jaw that she looked like she had two heads, which must have prevented the consumption of grain for she was a perfect rack of bones, her back a half-moon, swelling tumors on both front legs and a shoulder so out of joint she seemed to be walking up a stair.

The man was no improvement on his horse. His jerkin had come loose from his right shoulder so entirely that it flapped off down his back. His stockings were rags. His breeches though made of velour were yet as mottled as old ivory. His shirt was torn open to the waist. And his eyes gleamed like a madman. A robber. A murtherer.

"Come your ways," she whispered. "Come your ways."

And proceeded to shake so pitifully throughout her whole body that she lost her place in the hedgerow, rolled down the incline, and into the road at the horse's feet.

"Ah, God, melikes it not," the apparition said.

And tugged the reins so tight the poor horse stopped still, one foot pausing in air somewhat above Judith's torso.

"Melikes it not," said the man. "Come, dagger, let me clutch thee."

Judith opened her eyes to see the point of a wretched dagger aimed straight at her very throat.

CHAPTER III

Judith prepared to die. The dagger would descend. The man would slit her throat with no more feeling than her brothers showed in killing an old cow. Her blood would drain out all over Launcelot Gobbo's tight-necked shirt. O God, why had she run off to London alone? Why had she dressed herself like a boy? It was punishment from the Almighty, that now she was to be murdered in the highroad.

"Methinks. . ." came the voice, "you are an unarmed lad. Methinks. . .you do not wish me harm."

"Indeed, sir, you are right. I do not wish harm to you or any man alive. And as you can see, I have no weapon. I am all alone and on my way to London to see my brother, Will Shakespeare, and be a player."

"Will Shakespeare? Your brother is Will Shakespeare?"

"Yes, do you know him?" Judith replied.

"No, but I want to," said the man.

He sheathed his dagger, and being so near the road due to his horse's half-moon back, he merrily stepped down. Instantly the horse crumpled in a heap beside Judith in the highroad, and its bones rattled so loud she hardly heard the words addressed to her by the ragged murderer.

"I am Arthur Amboid," he said. "A famous player, and greatly sought after by every licensed company in the realm."

The said Arthur, with a great flourish, reached out his hand and pulled Judith to her feet.

"And what is your name?" he asked.

"I am. . . ." Judith looked down at her soiled breeches and sighed. She must be careful, for now she was forming a true personage, an identity. And this time she must speak naturally. No more growling and squeaking.

"Your name?" asked Arthur Amboid somewhat impatiently.

"I am. . .I am Richard," she said at last. Without a quaver. "Richard Shakespeare."

"And do your friends call you Dick to shorten it?" asked Arthur.

"Well. . .some do."

Never in her life had she felt such uncertainty. Being a boy did not prove to be an easy task. Yet Dick sounded fine to her. Not exactly the same as her brother Richard, yet near enough. It gave a little slack to the personality she had chosen.

"Yes, some people call me Dick," she said.

"Excellent. Then I shall call you Dick and we shall be friends, and ride to London together on the back of this noble steed."

Arthur reached down and patted the head of the poor crumpled animal.

"Ride together on her?" said Judith. "I scarcely think either of us could ride that poor animal to London."

"Who, Jasmine? Not ride Jasmine to London? Now, Dick," and he whispered behind his hand, "that is the very kind of remark that hurts poor Jasmine to the bone."

Jasmine shook her head and gave a rattle all along her body. And rose to her feet, straightened her back and held her head high.

"Jasmine has Arabian blood," whispered Arthur. "She is very proud. Like all Amboids."

Arthur brushed his ragged clothing and flexed his muscles and his excellent knees, straightened his shoulders and puffed out his chest. And lo, he was the handsomest man Judith had ever seen. His eyes were a brilliant blue, his hair gold as sunshine. His facial features were chiseled fine, as was the symmetry of his entire person. Yet Judith read in his eyes the word liar. Pay no heed to what he says. Or what he does. The man is a vacant house. He would bear watching, this Arthur Amboid.

"Dick, old lad, Jasmine and I would be most honored to take you for a traveling companion. We will share our sustenance with you and expect the same in return."

Judith nodded.

"Is it a bond? Are we brothers?"

"Yes," Judith said. "Brothers. If only we can get to London."

"If? Without doubt we can get to London. So let us sit beneath the hedge you rolled out of, and share your breakfast."

"But I have no breakfast."

"Then let us count over the coins in your purse and set out to find a farmer who will sell us milk and bread and, perhaps a few raspberries. A little honey. A fish or two."

Arthur was smiling broadly and patting the spot in his rags where one would expect to find a stomach.

"But I have no money."

"No money? Then shall you plan to starve on the road to London?"

Judith shook her head sadly.

"Then you are a liar," said Arthur, "for no brother of Will Shakespeare would be so great a fool as to start out on so long a journey with no food and no money."

Arthur leaned down and stared straight into Judith's upturned face.

"Aha," he said, "you have run off from home, am I right? An apprentice lad from Stratford who had once heard the name of Will Shakespeare, and that is all."

"It is not all. Will Shakespeare is my brother, and I am. . .Dick."

"And have no purse?"

"I have no purse."

"Are you hungry?"

"No, I am not hungry. And you can take your windgalled, spavined, shoulder-shotten horse and ride to the moon for all I care. I will go to London on my own."

Judith had nothing to throw or she would have aimed it straight into Arthur Amboid's laughing face. Lacking that, she turned abruptly and started down the highroad.

"You are off to Stratford, Dick, old lad, back to your master's arms."

She whirled and set out in the opposite direction.

"Only jesting, Dick. You were right the first time."

"You whoreson cur," Judith shouted.

And reached into the dust of the road and took handfuls of the loose dirt and threw it hard against Arthur's face and shoulders. He laughed down at her.

"You three-inch fool. You jolt head," she continued.

The light sand fringed Arthur Amboid's eyelashes, sifted down his cheekbones, and lay piled along his shoulders, yet he laughed uproariously. The sky rang with Arthur's jollity.

"Ah, Dick Shakespeare, what a good lad."

He shook himself heartily, and snatched up a saddle bag which lay in the road beside Jasmine's prone body, drew out a feathered hat with which he further beat about himself, then set upon his head.

"We must find a tavern, an inn, an alehouse. Ah, Dick Shakespeare, what a fine lad. I shall buy you a breakfast for a king."

Breakfast for a king or even a commoner was not within the grasp of Arthur Amboid on that sunny June morning. They walked onward mile after mile, saying little. They eyed each other with sly glances, then quickly looked away. And walked faster still until Jasmine stopped and would not budge til she had cropped a little grass at the roadside.

"God's mercy, Dick," said Arthur. "This grass is starting to look good. Methinks I shall make a salad of it if nothing else turns up."

Judith laughed, then turned aside and covered her mouth with her hands. It was decidedly a female laugh. And Arthur Amboid was, after all, a man. A young and handsome man. She must look like Dick Shakespeare, talk like Dick Shakespeare, act like Dick Shakespeare, and think like Dick Shakespeare. No more Judith. Not til she was safe with Will in London. And maybe not then. God's Body, maybe not ever.

"I say, Old Dick," said Arthur.

He paused, staring intently at Judith's face.

"I say, Old Dick, are you truly not hungry?"

"Truly I am," Judith replied, somewhat unnerved at Arthur's penetrating look. "Indeed, we must look for berries. There should be something growing wild which we may take and eat in good conscience."

"In good conscience? Dick, lad, do you have troubles with your conscience?"

"Why, no. It is just that I should not like to be caught stealing."

"Stealing? Dick, my lad, do you think an Amboid would steal?"

"No," she said. "Of course not."

Arthur continued to stare down at her. And Judith grew increasingly uneasy. Until he began to laugh again, as loudly as before when they had first met.

"No, Dick my lad, an Amboid would not steal. However, there are certain debts owed my family, and since I am the last in my line, it is my duty to collect."

"Oh, then, you know people hereabout?"

For some reason, this idea gave her great comfort, but it was not to last long.

"No, I cannot say I know anyone on this very length of highroad. But there are those who owe others who owe my family. Do you understand me?"

"No. I do not."

"Ah, Dick, lad, and you so sharp a boy as to be Will Shakespeare's brother?"

"But I am. I swear it."

"Indeed, yes. I believe you. And you must believe me that I am owed."

Just as they had reached that impasse, Jasmine gave a loud snort and turned into a path between tall hedges of hornbloom. Til that moment it had not been visible to either Arthur or Judith.

"Ah, Jasmine. Always the one to search out food."

Arthur turned into the lane behind her.

"Are you coming with us, Dick, my lad?"

"Is that the way to London?"

"Tis the way to breakfast, and I advise you to follow us."

They walked single file through the hedged pathway until they came suddenly on a fair-sized manor house built of close timbered oak beams and quarried stone, with grassed yard and garden, and a jumble of outbuildings in back. Jasmine ambled toward a round stone structure, a dovecote, as if she were heading to her own stable. Her feet lifted high, and, as she got closer, she broke into a run.

"Who could have believed she could run like that?" Judith said.

"What? Jasmine? Why, on appropriate occasion Jasmine is a very racer. Or, to put it another way, she can dance a jig if the price is right."

"What is she doing now?"

"She seems to have uncovered a cask of Pomewaters."

Under a ledge built onto the dovecote, there was a heap of bright red apples. Jasmine began to gnaw ravenously, and Arthur too ran to the ledge, pocketed several, bit into one and handed one to Judith.

"Is it stolen?" she asked.

"Owed," said Arthur.

Before either had got half through to the core, a surly yard man with a growling dog nipped round the corner of the dovecote.

"Ah ha," he said. "Thieving, apple eating knaves."

He gave a loud whistle and instantly they were surrounded by dairy maids and stable boys, with finally, the master approaching.

"Thieving rascals, sire," said the head man. "Would ye set the dogs onto them?"

The master walked into the circle, his sword drawn, a perfect picture of a fighting man home from the Flemish wars.

Judith stood with the half eaten apple in her hand, shivering at the prospect of the monstrous dog presently straining against a leash in the servant's gnarled fingers. And at the master's sword, flashing and glinting like a live thing. She reached for Arthur's arm, and felt nothing but air.

"Arthur," she called out.

And was answered by a voice such as rose up from graves at midnight.

"Mercy," said this creaking voice, the voice of an old palsied man, one whose body shook with such violence that his words came quaking out, shuddering and shivering.

Judith turned toward the sound, and there stood an old man, shoulders stooped, body sagged, and with eyes sightless as gourds staring up at the sword point of the master.

"Mercy," the old man croaked again. "Alms to the blind beggar with blind horse in attendance."

For Jasmine's eyes now gave the appearance of being as sightless as the old man's.

"Blind, all blind," he continued. "My grandson here, brave Dick, I call him, he is blind too. We beg our way and pray blessings from God on all those who provide. It is God's curse that we cannot see, yet God's blessing that whole men do give us alms."

The master stepped closer to the sightless man.

"The lad is blind as well?" he asked. And he rose on his tiptoes the better to peep downward into the beggar's staring eyeballs.

"Look at him. Judge for yourself. If the lad an't blind, ye can whip him to his death for he has deceived me mightily," the old beggar replied.

The master stepped to Judith now. He began the same minute scrutiny he had made on the old man. Judith was unnerved to say the least, and she cursed Arthur Amboid to all eternity. For the blind man was Arthur or else Arthur had turned into a ghost. For Arthur was nowhere else to be seen. And Judith had not the faintest notion of how to appear to be blind.

"Blind at birth," the old beggar, Arthur Amboid, went on. "When he was but a babe, tottering to the house door, he would stand staring toward the light, and could see naught in the world, neither tree nor flower. The little fool would look toward the warmth of the sun. So sweetly he would twitch his face."

Judith stared toward the sun, twitched her face, thought of darkness, and prayed not to be beaten to death. The master passed his hand before her eyes and she did not blink.

"Blind at birth, do you say?" the master asked.

"At very birth. Hath never seen his mother's face. Can do no honest work nor nothing in the world save begging."

The master passed his hand before her eyes again.

"Blessed Jesus," he said, "Blind as a newt. And has been from birth, do you say?"

"Yes, master," said Arthur. "And to compound it he cannot speak neither."

Tears came to the eyes of the master. He put away his sword and motioned to two of the serving maids.

"Lead them inside the hall," he said with a tearful voice. "They shall eat their fill this one time before they go on their way."

"God's blessings rest upon ye," said Arthur. "And since it be late of day, we shall not hang at breakfast, but should it please ye, we could dine freely."

And freely they did. When it came to locating the loaf of bread and the rack of lamb, the blind beggar was able to whisk his knife from his belt and hit home at first try.

With full bellies, for Jasmine too had been given a bucket of oats while Arthur and Judith dined in the hall, they walked through the lovely afternoon sunlight. And this time both Arthur and Judith had much to say to each other.

"I could have been killed," Judith said first.

"And you could be a liar too. Wouldn't a brother of Will Shakespeare know how to appear blind? I thought as much. A brother who is going to London to be a player?"

"But, I am Will Shakespeare's brother," she said.

"Perhaps. And so the master believed you and no harm came to you. What do you have to complain of? A full belly?"

"Very well. But don't let such a thing happen again."

"And don't you lie to me," replied Arthur.

After that, they walked in silence. And when night came, they crawled beneath a hedge and went to sleep with only Jasmine to stand guard for they were both so tired they could not stay awake.

The first finger of light, the first song of the ouzel bird resting in the branches above her head, wakened Judith. She was lying close against Arthur Amboid, where one or the other of them had turned in the night seeking warmth. She shivered to be so close to this man she knew to be a liar and possibly a thief. She must get away from him. Quietly. In the early light. Off down the highroad by a mile or two before Arthur and Jasmine wakened.

She slid away from Arthur, making no sound. The grass she lay on scarcely moved. One more inch and she would sit up and put on her shoes. And tiptoe off. One more inch.

"Melikes it not," Arthur thundered.

And then he rolled from under the hedge, sat up and gripped her arm tight with both hands.

"Melikes it not, old Dick."

He drew his dagger, and still with one hand holding her tight, he brought the point to rest at her breast.

"Who are you?" he asked. "I feel in my bones you are something other than you say. And though you are young, there are younger murderers on the highroad. Have you been sent by my enemies, boy? For a player you are, and could be apprenticed of Lord Worcester's Men and sent here to spy me out."

"I have come to spy no one out," Judith said, trying hard to remember she feared neither spider, newt, nor toad. Neither ghost nor fiend nor hobgoblin.

"I shall kill you at this moment unless you tell me your true name and mission. Whoever you are, if you tell me true, you shall live."

Judith looked hard into Arthur's eyes. She thought she saw that he would kill her, and so she opened her mouth to tell him the whole story of her life, of old Henry Wilcome and the marriage, of her poems, of all she had suffered in the cupboard.

"Tell me false and you shall die."

"I. . .I am Richard Shakespeare," she said, surprising herself mightily that she should say this, "whom some call Dick, and I am running away from home to see my brother Will and be a player."

"Aha! Running from home. I knew there was something strange about you, Dick Shakespeare. So, the question lies in this. Is there greater reward to take you home to Stratford or to press on to London?"

"O, please, Arthur Amboid, do not take me home to Stratford."

Tears came to Judith's eyes. Angrily she wiped them away, and glared in Arthur's direction.

"Do you swear Will Shakespeare is your brother?" he asked.

"I swear."

"What proof can you give?"

Judith considered what she might say. What would Arthur Amboid believe? And then she knew exactly what proof she could give him.

"I have copies of some of my brother's poems, never seen by anyone but Will and me. If I should read them, you would know that only Will Shakespeare could write such words."

"Fair enough," said Arthur.

And so she drew the rolled packet of poems out of her shirt, loosed the dirty ribbon and straightened the pages across her knees. As she read, Arthur's face lightened and broke into a smile.

". . . .what envious streaks
Do lace the severing clouds in yonder east.
Night's candles are burnt out, and jocund day
Stands tiptoe on the misty mountain tops.
I must be gone and live, or stay and die."

"None other than Will Shakespeare," Arthur said, his voice hushed and reverent. "No one else could have written such words. Let us proceed, Dick Shakespeare. To London. To find your brother Will."

Late that afternoon, the day being a Saturday, Arthur decided he would change into the attire of a prosperous merchant. He untied the rags from his legs to expose canary yellow hose, and these he cross gartered, wrapping and tieing them smartly below the knee. He then stuffed the rags into his bag and drew out a yellow doublet and black trunk hose which he slipped behind a blackberry hedge to tie himself into. When he stepped out again into the highroad, he was transformed into a man of fashion.

"Arthur," said Judith. "I would never have believed. . .that is, are you the same Arthur Amboid who went behind the black-berries?"

"The very same. And now, Dick Shakespeare, watch how I shall provide for us this night."

They had not long to wait before a prosperous looking farmer, his wife and three daughters, all crammed into a ponderous cart came creaking down the highroad. Arthur reached into his bag and pulled out his plumed hat and swept them a low bow.

"I wonder, sire, if you could point out to me the way to Wodstock. This is my nephew Dick, you see, and we are off to my wedding which will take place in three days time at Canterbury in the cathedral."

The farmer drew up his horse and gestured off in the distance.

"You cannot miss it," he said. "You have only to keep on as you are going."

The farmer flicked at his horse to move on, but Arthur stepped quickly to the cart and leaned both elbows on the sides which were made of willow work and thus exposed baskets and tubs of every variety, all covered with cloths and shawls.

"God's body," said Arthur, eyeing the covers and imagining each full to the brim with some valuable commodity. "I am all atremble, for my bride is passing fair and heiress to a fortune in grazing lands. I am a made man if my poor horse holds out to get us to Canterbury."

He paused for the farmer to look at Jasmine. To admire her sunken back, her swollen joints.

"To look at this horse," Arthur continued, "You would hardly believe that until two days ago, she was the swiftest runner in the kingdom. Ay, God, the jingling coins I have won on old Jasmine."

"What happened to her?" grunted the farmer.

"Tis a strange story," said Arthur, "which I will not bore you with the telling. But you may trust me, Jasmine was a racer."

The farmer's eyes narrowed.

"Tis a pity," he said. "Nothing I like better than a race."

"Nor I," Arthur said. "Winning plays a small part with me. Tis the sport alone that draws me to it. I dare say I would wager today though any man can see I would lose."

The farmer laughed, then turned to his three daughters wedged into the cart behind him.

"What do you say, daughters? Shall we challenge the young gentleman?"

The girls giggled and nodded.

"Very well," said the farmer. "Consider yourself challenged. What wager would you be willing to make on so poor an animal?"

Arthur paused a moment in consideration, smiled, but then grew stern.

"Am I to believe that you will run this splendid horse which presently pulls your excellent chariot?"

The farmer nodded. His daughters poked each other and giggled louder.

Arthur paused to study his audience. He counted the fingers of both hands, winked at the daughter who sat closest to him and whose breasts strained so tight against her bodice that they appeared to be climbing out through the top lace, and then he sighed.

"Here goes good money after bad," he said, "but I am a man driven to gamble. I cannot help myself. What do you say to a wager of a golden guinea?"

"Tis a dangerous wager," said the farmer. "I am not used to such high stakes, but since I cannot lose. . .I accept."

"Excellent. Now if your lovely wife and your beautiful daughters will alight from the vehicle, my nephew will make short work of the unharnessing."

"Me?" asked Judith. "Why should I do such menial work?"

"Menial work? How can you call the preparations for a race menial work? Nevertheless, now that I have reconsidered, I am sure Master. . .and by the by, sir, I did not catch your name."

"Chapman, sir. Simon Chapman."

"As you will. I am sure Master Chapman would sooner trust to his own devices in preparing for such a race as this is to be."

The ladies clambered down and stood in a line along the edge of the highroad. The daughters watched Arthur's every movement, every gesture. The farmer grunted and groaned as he unfastened straps and lowered the cart shafts to the roadway. When he had finished, he led the horse out, reached back into the cart and retrieved a saddle.

"I knew I should have brought a groom along," he said, "but no, you ladies would give up no inch of space."

"Here," said Arthur, "Let me help you. If you trust me, that is."

The farmer nodded, and between the two of them, the horse was soon saddled and ready to begin the race."

"Now," said Arthur, "It is your turn to set the course. How far do you wish to run? It matters little to me since my poor Jasmine will scarcely make it across the finish line."

"Can you see that great leaning oak tree which hangs its branches across the path? I would say that would make the run a half mile."

"Ay God," said Arthur. "It would take Jasmine half a day to run so far. But it is even as you wish. To horse."

As the farmer and Arthur took horse, Judith stepped closer to the three daughters.

"What do you think of this racing?" she asked.

The plumpest of the three plump sisters rolled her eyes and sighed.

"I think nothing at all of the racing, but I would wish in my heart that your uncle had not contracted to marry so soon. He is a very pretty man, and he has elegant manners. What do you say, sisters?"

"I am in agreement," a second girl answered. "His eyes are most unusual in their color. I could wish they would linger a while on me."

"And his hair," said the third. "I have heard spoken of a golden fleece, and though I know not what that could be, I think it might be this gentleman's curling hair. I dare say he has had his choice of ladies wherever you have traveled."

"I cannot say," said Judith. "We have not been among ladies in our recent travels."

"But what of his betrothed? He is to be married in three days time. He said so."

"Ah. . .yes. He did say so. And he is."

Judith was saved from further explanation by a loud halloo from the farmer, and the racers were off. The sisters squealed and jumped up and down. The mother wiped her face and huffed and stood on tiptoe the better to see her husband and his mount.

Judith stood amazed. How could it be? Jasmine had left the farmer's horse in the dust. She held her head high and forward. Her hooves were scarcely visible. And Arthur, Judith had to admit, cut a fine figure as well. In short, he and Jasmine had passed the leaning oak tree and turned to meet the farmer when he arrived at the finish line. The two men rode slowly back toward Judith and the ladies, arguing wildly all the way. Judith could hear the farmer's nasal tones mixing freely with Arthur's practiced elegance. When they were closer, she could make out the words.

"You are a cheat and a dissembler," roared the farmer. "I will not pay you. You misrepresented that horse though I cannot say how it was done. She appeared as near death as any horse I have ever seen. I thought she would not live til dusky dark today, and here she takes off running. You are a cheat."

"I resent those words, sir, I truly do. I plainly told you Jasmine was the fastest horse in England."

"Until three days ago, you said. And so I will add liar to the list. You, sir, are a liar. I will not pay good money to a cheat and a liar."

The two men reined in the horses even off with the cart and the ladies.

"If there were not ladies present," said Arthur, "I would add a few words to my list too, sir. As their gentle ears are even now trained on our conversation, I will say nothing more than this. I have won the wager. You, sir, must pay me."

"That I will not. And if you say another word, I will reach into my cart for my hunting horn, and give a good blow. My property lies not half a mile along this road. When my servants have heard the call, they will hasten here armed with daggers, broadswords, and with dogs trained to tear a man into naught but several body parts."

"You expect me to believe this?" Arthur asked. "I was not born a fool."

The farmer walked his horse to the cart, leaned down, and drew forth the horn. He put it to his lips and blew. Judith covered her ears with both hands.

"God's Prittikins," she said. "We shall all be deafened. Arthur, perhaps. . . ."

"Do not fear this man, good nephew," said Arthur. "He is many miles from home. I am sure of it. Now, sir. Open your purse and pay me. I shall give you, perhaps, five more minutes, and then I must take action."

"I will not need five minutes, you wastrel. In much less time than five minutes you and your greedy nephew will be run through and bleeding in the highroad. If the dogs do not devour you."

"Arthur, let us be off," Judith said.

She ran to him and climbed up behind him on Jasmine's back.

"Please, Arthur," she said.

"I shall not be moved," said Arthur. "I give you five minutes. And then I will have to ask the ladies to avert their eyes while I take my wager. Nothing can deter me."

The farmer laughed aloud and then he drew his own small sword and brandished it over his head.

"I hear the jolly boys making ready. There go the dogs barking. Clear as matched bells. You will see them shortly."

"I hear nothing," said Arthur.

"Then you are deaf to add to your other iniquities," Simon Chapman said. "For I tell you I hear my boys."

"Arthur, look," said Judith.

She pointed far off down the highroad to where a cloud of dust was blowing up around five mounted figures. And as Simon Chapman had said, there were dogs. Great jowled, long legged mastiffs straining at the ends of the leashes the frontal riders held.

"Arthur, you do see, do you not?"

"Dick Shakespeare, I do. Ay God, I assuredly do."

"Then in the name of God, let us go."

"Yet a golden guinea is not to be walked away from casually."

"Please, Arthur," Judith shouted.

"You may be right," Arthur said as the riders drew closer yet and he could see their faces. "You may be right.

Arthur swept off his hat and bowed toward the three sisters and the mother.

"If you will excuse me, ladies. I am sorry to leave you of a sudden. But I have remembered me of an infinite deal of business I must attend to. . .now. It was good to make your acquaintance. And yours too, sir," he said to the farmer.

He turned Jasmine's head, and dug his knees into her side.

Jasmine took off like the wind, and never stopped til they had passed five wagons of families and twelve men o' horseback. Never stopped til they had come to the town of Wodstock. Never stopped til they had run straight down the one street there was in the village. Past the smithy, the butcher, the mercer. Past the stone church. And straight into the courtyard of the inn. There Jasmine dug in her heels and stopped.

"Thank God you were not lying about Jasmine's speed," Judith said when she had got her breath.

"Nor about anything else," replied Arthur Amboid. "But neither have I provided funds to buy our dinner."

He jumped to the ground and looked about him.

"Ay God, I must begin again to feather our nest. What measure shall it be tonight?"

"I hope it will not be a lie this time," Judith said.

Arthur took two steps toward the inn door, then came back to stand at Judith's knees.

"Remember, Dick old lad, it is only liars who expect to be lied to."

Judith blushed scarlet, and could think of no reply.

"Then let it pass. I shall speak no more of lying if you do not."

Judith nodded.

"Very well. And now I shall call forth the landlord and make some settlement, for it is here we will sleep this night."

The landlord of the inn, Ben Doyle, was not a man to be bargained with easily, for he had lately married a rich Puritan widow and was now a zealot of that church.

"No music," he said.

He wiped at his hanging jowls with a clean, white cloth, then tied it around his mountainous stomach.

"You shall not sing, nor pluck a lute, nor beat a drum. Music is the devil's own instrument in this world, and a man must resist it."

"Then if you will not accept our music," Arthur continued, "perhaps you would be pleased to hear my young brother lisp out some tender verses of poetry. Or I myself have often enacted biblical scenes. One of the apostles. Or perhaps old Daniel in the lion's den."

At this Ben Doyle grew so angry he could not speak with any degree of intelligibility. He slammed his thick hands upon the bar, and stamped his foot, and showered spit down the front of his jerkin.

"Indeed, sir, you do make your point well," said Arthur. "Never before in my life has the sin of plays and players been so graciously shown to me. You may believe me, sir, that in the future, I shall refrain from playing as long as I live."

Arthur drew Judith aside for a whispered conference.

"I am done for," said Arthur. "The man would not have me

shovel his dung pit. But you, old Dick, are a clean slate. If you will provide this once, I will see to our welfare from here on. What do you say?"

"Very well. But I don't see what I could do here."

"Never mind. Trust me."

Arthur returned to his position at the bar, this time humming a hymn tune, and with his face as solemn as Job.

"Mine host," he said. "You have met my test, and so I have no qualms to put myself and my brother in your hands for the night. For indeed, though you see me decked in fine clothes, my heart is pure. You see, I have lately become a Puritan and I am saving my money to buy proper black. I hope you will understand me."

Ben Doyle nodded. His manner changed completely. He shook Arthur's hand and poured him a glass of ale which he intimated would be his treat. And so they fell into conversation, sharing another pint of ale and comparing their conversion experience. Judith was left standing at the door, staring about at the cobwebs and dust balls that hung from the ceiling beams and scudded across the floor rushes. Yet she was listening to the conversation too. And in the midst of a story concerning the disappearance of the cook's daughter and the tapster that very afternoon, Judith heard the name Dick much bandied about. And then she heard Arthur saying this same Dick was apt for the position.

"Tis a good lad, Ben Doyle, as ye shall find this night," said Arthur expansively. "There was never a lad so young who could twist taps and carry trays, and do anything which lies about. Am I right, Dick?"

"Ay," Judith said merrily, for she did not yet know what was required of her.

And it was settled.

It was not long before Judith suffered a change of mind and heart. For she was kept busy running back and forth from public room, to kitchen, to cellar, to pantry, while Arthur lounged at the table, emptying his saddle bag of various objects, sorting, dusting, and redistributing them about his person and back into the bag.

"Is it possible you shall sit the whole night at the table drinking ale while I work my fingers to the bone?" she asked him.

"Ah, Dick, lad, but I have no vocation. It is your good fortune to be provided with so many benefits."

"Dick."

And it was Ben Doyle calling from the chambers above to say that covers were wanted in the fourth apartment. So off she ran to the shelves where they were stored, and up the winding stairs and down the hall to where he stood shouting.

"Hurry," was the only word Ben Doyle the Puritan had for her as she arrived panting. And she had scarcely begun to put the covers on the bed when he was calling from below.

"Dick. Cook is asking for ye."

Judith stopped off in the public room on the way back and whispered hurriedly with Arthur Amboid.

"It would seem to me," she told him, "the job of tapster has been greatly enlarged. Tapsters, to my mind, serve spirituous liquors. I have run my feet off."

"And isn't that the very meaning, Dick, old lad? Tapster. To tap. That is, to walk, to step, to noise oneself about. Now if your shoes were three sizes smaller, you would not be fit for the job. Do you see, lad? You must be our salvation. And from this night, I promise you, I will take on our provision. Yet you must see that here my hands are tied because my shoes do verily fit my feet."

Just at nightfall it had started to rain, and the warmth of the day drifted into a coolness that called for a fire on the hearth. Judith was given that job as well, hauling in logs and running with the coals from the kitchen until the flames leapt high and bright.

"Ah, Dick," said Arthur Amboid from where he sat at the table across the room. "You are a very Prometheus."

Judith shook her fist at Arthur and ran back to the comfort of the kitchen. She preferred the company of the cook, a greasy soul, strong in the shoulders from much lifting of pots and kettles. Strong of limb, which she generously exposed to the world by catching up her skirts by a string around her waist. And red of face, perhaps accented by blackened teeth. She talked without ceasing, punctuating her speech with slurps from the stock pot, and a smacking of the lips at small tastings she took of every dish cooking at the wide hearth and oven. She interspersed culinary comment with household gossip, leaving the listener to sort it out to his own designs.

"A nab salty," the cook would say even as she reached for the water jar. "And that same runnion did make off with the wench to his own destruction. Good. Good. All to the good."

By which Judith understood that the meat stock and the tapster's carrying off of her daughter were both to her liking. And by following this devious, puzzling talk, Judith discovered that Ben Doyle, he of the fat stomach, lived in fear of his new wife and her brother, the church warden. The two of them owned most of the property in the village, and thereby kept the villagers in their debt and under their thumb.

"Then it was better for your daughter to leave no matter how," said Judith.

The cook stopped her stirring and embraced her.

"Ay, what a lad. Ye've got brains, I can see that. And are ye hungry, lad? For ye do look somewhat thin and stringy."

Talking all the while, she poured Judith a bowl of broth, broke a loaf of bread in half, cut it and buttered it, cut cheese, polished a large apple. And as Judith stood close beside her chewing ravenously, the cook rehearsed her of all the names of drink she would serve this night, and of every meat and soup and pudding and vegetable. Had Judith wished to make her living by writing receipt books instead of poems, she would have been well provided. And so the time passed and it was pitch dark, and all was made ready against the arrival of guests.

On her next return from the kitchen, Arthur was standing, greeting a party of wet and hungry souls as if he, himself, were the owner of the premises.

"Welcome," he called out. "Are you weary then and cold and hungry? But you must join me here at my table." He snapped his fingers. "Dick, lad, we have here a merchant prince, nay, three of them. One a tinker. One a seller of ratsbane. And one a dealer in old clothes. A fripperer."

He gestured from man to man, and each nodded with some degree of embarrassment.

"Bring on a cup of Spanish sack, a bottle of French wine. Bring on a. . .What? You will have a tankard of ale, sir? Very well. Step sharp there, lad."

The room was small so that when the tinker and the other two merchants had brought in all their baggage, there was little space left over. And since there was only the one table, Arthur's invitation was perhaps superfluous. After an abundant shaking of cloaks and a few moments spent dancing before the fire, rubbing their hands together, shaking off droplets from their beards, scraping mud from their shoes onto the hearthstones, they did indeed seat themselves on joint stools around Arthur's table.

Judith came running with ale, and in only a moment more Ben Doyle was bowing to the company and laying out suggestions for such viands as the cook was even then slurping and tasting in the kitchen. The decision was for broth of capon, roast of mutton, cheese, bread, and more warm ale. Arthur ordered straight along with the merchants, as if he had money in his pocket.

The food was brought, drink poured, and the room grew quiet. There was audible chewing, little snaps that were the twisting of joints, sucking of marrow from bones, followed by great belches from all except Arthur who ate daintily, cutting his meat into small pieces with his dagger, lifting it to his mouth with two fingers only, and chewing with his mouth closed.

Judith watched Arthur in amazement and admiration. How had he learned such manners? Such elegance? His hands were as smooth and white as a Lord's. And he had a ring on the middle finger of his right hand with a stone the size of a peach pit.

"Dick," called Ben Doyle. "You are wanted in the kitchen."

When Judith returned, carrying a bowl of pudding, she distinctly heard a clicking sound of bone which was not from the joints of meat. It was the rattle of dice. For Arthur had taken from his doublet an excellent carved pair, and invited the tinker to a game between courses. She watched the little cubes dance across the table, watched Arthur's elegant hands dip them up, shake them and throw again.

She glanced toward the fireplace where Ben Doyle sat drowsing. What if he should wake and see Arthur at his sport? They would both be in the street.

"Arthur," she whispered. "Do you think it wise? Gaming in a Puritan tavern?"

Arthur laughed uproariously.

"Quiet," Judith said.

She looked toward the hearth. Ben Doyle slept peacefully.

"Dick, lad, do you mean to insult our guests? My friend here, the illustrious tinker, has, by the fates, lost no small sum in the game. Would you deny him the chance to make up his losses?"

"But you know that Ben Doyle is. . . ."

"Asleep," countered Arthur. "Now if you will bring my companions a pitcher of ale."

Arthur frowned deeply and gestured toward the taproom. And Judith, so tired she could scarcely exert herself to keep Launcelot's shoes onto her toes, nodded and turned toward the door. But she had taken no more than four or five steps when she heard a sudden noise from across the room. She turned to see a joint stool crashing down on Arthur Amboid's head, flung by the tinker who was shouting: "Thief. Cheat. Your dice are heavy."

Arthur ducked at the last moment, and the stool hurtled past him to strike the fripperer full in the face, causing him to pitch backward onto the floor turning the table onto himself and the seller of ratsbane, smashing china, and causing the fripperer's dagger to fly sideways and lodge in the shin of the tinker who collapsed at the pain, hitting his head violently on the floor. Arthur stepped back and brushed his hands together as if finishing a long and difficult task. Then quickly put the dice into his doublet.

Ben Doyle was at once on his feet, wide awake and calling for silence, calling for explanations, calling for payment for damages.

"Damages?" quoth Arthur in accents befitting a king. "What do you mean damages? Only to think that my brother and I trusted ourselves to your hospitality, and were set on by ruffians. I'll have the law to you, Ben Doyle."

"You shall have the law? I shall have the law to you. . . ."

The three merchants lay pale and palpitating on the floor. "If you have killed a man amongst them. . . ."

"Self-defence," said Arthur. "The fat one came at me with a joint stool. The two others were wounded in the general disorder."

There was a groan from the tinker and then from his companions.

"Not dead, I see," said Ben Doyle, "but still I cannot have a rumpus. Mistress Doyle cannot abide a rumpus. You must leave at once, Arthur Amboid, though your brother may stay. He is a fine lad and as good a worker as I have seen."

"What are you suggesting, Ben Doyle? Would you separate a family? Would you drive a wedge between me and the last living Amboid?"

"T'would be a service to the lad to rid him of such as you. Now, be on your way."

Arthur drew a large handkerchief from his right sleeve and mopped his face of several tears he had forced from his eyelids. His face contorted, and he sobbed audibly.

"D-Dick," he said. "Can you not speak for me? I am too.. too full for speech."

Judith hesitated. Should she rid herself of this man? She looked around the room. Which of the others would see her on her way? Which one would understand her desire to go to London and be a player?

"I. . .I can only say. . . ."

Arthur put his handkerchief back inside his sleeve. He picked up his satchel and started for the door.

"I can only say. . . ."

Arthur looked back at her sorrowfully, and waved his hand.

"I can only say that if my brother is ordered forth from this establishment, I will go too."

"Then out, both of you. Out of my door this instant," said Ben Doyle. "You are a troublous duo as I have yet seen. Out."

Arthur and Judith joined hands, coughing and moaning, both turned to shambling invalids. But Ben Doyle could not be dissuaded by their performance. He turned them out into the rainy night.

Throughout the night the wind never ceased to blow, and the rain fell heavy all through the village. Nowhere did it vent its fury louder than about the walls of the stone church. Nowhere was the cold felt more pitifully than on the cold stones of the church floor where Judith and Arthur Amboid lay together, Judith with her back against the rough wall.

On the previous night, when the innkeeper had so vilely driven them into the storm, Arthur had knocked at every house door in the guise of one character after another and was turned away as every one. Soaked to the bone, he had led Judith into the darkened church, where they had stumbled and fallen in a heap and had been too tired to rise. They lay together as spoons in a chest, to save whatever warmth could be found in two sets of soaking garments.

Arthur, who had sobered up quickly in the downpour of rain, found sleep impossible, but Judith, at his back, could not be kept awake even by the hard stone and the wind, and her discomfort at the feel of Arthur's body against her own.

There was little light inside the church, but enough to suggest that day had dawned. The storm had passed and all was quiet.

Judith opened her eyes to see that Arthur was gone, and in his place wafted about the hem of a long, black garment, and a pair of long, black shoes with pointed toes and silver buckles.

Judith turned onto her back and looked the long way up the black figure, the priestly robe. Up to the black wig, the curly beard, the spectacles set on the nose.

"Wake up, lad," said the tall man. "Tis time to don your acolyte robes. Tis the Lord's day, Dick, and we must be about our accustomed duty."

Judith lay quite still, staring up at the tall stranger.

"Slugabed," the man continued in a high pitched voice. "Up, up, I say."

And then the man frowned and grimaced and winked until the spectacles flew off and his beard slipped sideways, and she could see his true resemblance.

"Od's Prittikins, tis you, Arthur. Why are you dressed in a preacher's robe?"

"Ah, Dick, my lad."

Arthur stooped and pressed his hand tight across Judith's mouth.

"Have you wakened out of your senses? You know well this day is the sabbath, and," Arthur paused a moment, cleared his throat and went on, "as you know, when our robes and, yea, our every belonging was swept away in a flood of water from the heavy rains, that we made our way straight, stopping nowhere along the way but coming straight, to the sanctuary of our Lord's house."

Arthur stood up, all the while shaking his head and grimacing.

"Have you come to your senses now, lad?"

"O yes," Judith said, pinching her nose back into shape, "quite to my senses."

"Then up at once and into your robe, for our brothers of this church have need of us. Master James Parker here," Arthur gestured toward a dark figure, a pinch faced man in black hose and doublet with a black cape thrown lightly across his shoulders, "our church warden and our brother in the Lord has contracted us to have charge of preaching here this day. Brother Hotbreath Hounder, til yesterday beloved parson of this beautiful church. . ." Arthur rolled his eyes across the rough stone walls fringed with mildew, across the altar bravely set with spidery cloth and chalice not cleaned this twelve month, a cross with arms set slightly askew, and a pulpit with one broken tread to the stairs, "a glorious church. . .has passed to his maker. God the Father Almighty. In heaven."

Arthur made a fist of his left hand, on the side where Master James Parker could not see.

"Do not ask another question, lad, else you shall have reason to fear retribution. . ." He gave a few downward plunges of the fisted hand. "From above."

"Indeed, sir, I think you must beat him," said Master Parker. "Indolence is not to be taken lightly. You should fetch blood to so cockering a young lad. Nay, I shall insist that you lay on."

"Yet he is a good lad," said Arthur. "And he is penniless, orphaned, often hungry."

A tear rolled off the end of Arthur's nose.

"Would you show pity?" asked Master Parker, his eyes wide with wonder. "Then you are not a man fit to preach the gospel."

"But I assure you. . . ."

"Beat him. Draw blood before my very eyes."

As Arthur leaned toward Judith, he drew his dagger quickly and slit a place in his own finger. And then he proceeded to heap skillfully artificial blows on Judith's head and to smear her nose with the blood from his own veins.

"Is that enough?" asked Arthur.

Master Parker pulled back the corner of Arthur's robe for a better view. Judith lay in a heap, rubbing her eyes and smearing the blood across her upper cheeks.

"More blood."

And so Arthur leaned down once more, and once more drew his dagger, and this time cut a vein in his own hand, a thing he had not meant to do, and so the blood poured across Judith's cheeks and into her tangled hair. She screamed and babbled and prayed until Master Parker said it was enough.

"I shall home to break fast," Master Parker said, "and shall return at quarter to the hour of eleven. Be ready or our contract shall be not honored."

"I shall be much in prayer," Arthur said.

Judith and Arthur waited stock still until the door closed on their erstwhile benefactor. Then Judith jumped to her feet and grasped Arthur's hand tight in her own.

"God's mercy, Arthur," she said, "you will bleed to death."

"Fetch me a rag then. You will find one in my bag."

"Those dirty rags? They would never hold together."

Judith untied the right sleeve of her shirt, still damp but whole, and wound it round and round Arthur Amboid's wound.

"There," she said. "Is that better?"

"Much better."

Arthur frowned, perhaps from pain. And he stared hard at Judith. At her bloody hair. And then at her body.

"Dick, old lad, you are. . .most unusual. Most unusual."

Judith blushed again. Almost the color of Arthur Amboid's blood.

By eleven o'clock, there were assembled on the five benches that fronted the pulpit perhaps twenty people. Or indeed there were nineteen because Master James Parker had once again tiptoed to the back door to look into the street. Judith counted them from front to back and then from back to front. And counted James Parker again when he seated himself in his place on the front row, making sure to save space beside him for two more communicants. Mistress Doyle, he had told Arthur, had never in her life been late to church until her recent marriage. And in a few further whispered words he had revealed his distaste for his sister's new husband.

After another hurried trip to the street door, Master Parker seated himself and motioned Arthur to proceed with the service.

Arthur clambered up the steps to the pulpit, and stumbled on the missing tread. He grabbed the lectern to steady himself, leant toward the minuscule congregation, and gave a mighty groan.

"Let us pray," he said.

And then he did. For every flower of the field, and every animal of the forest. For every rock and tree in the realm of England. Minutes went by and still he prayed. For the queen, the entire peerage, every yeoman farmer. And at last came to amen.

Judith meanwhile, was seated on a joint stool beside the altar, waiting to grasp the alms basket and, as Arthur had instructed her, to linger long before the prosperous and to waste no time on the poor. She had washed the blood from her face and hair as best she could in the baptismal font, had dragged her fingers about in the tangles, and so was not altogether disreputable. Arthur had found a pair of spectacles for her in his voluminous saddle bag, and with the acolyte hat, her disguise was accomplished. She felt easy that neither the tinker, nor the fripperer, nor the seller of ratsbane would recognize her. And there they sat with their patched heads, and the tinker with a great rag tied about his shin. For Ben Doyle was required by law to see that the guests of the inn should attend church.

Arthur's amen was her signal to begin the circuit with the alms basket. She carried it in outstretched hands, peering slyly to watch the bounce of each deposited coin. Master Parker's offering was an avalanche of dancing silver. The tinker's something less. But every adult contributed. That too was the law.

When every pocket was turned out, every possibility of sacrifice made, Judith brought the basket to Arthur to be blessed. She could see that his hands were shaking, and he swallowed endlessly, licking his lips, taking deep breaths. At last he whispered gratitude for the ears of the Almighty alone, then gave a loud amen.

When Judith had placed the alm's basket on the altar, she returned to her joint stool and waited for Arthur to begin the sermon.

"Ahem," he said loudly. "My sermon today is titled The Yellow Ruff, for it is in such a ruff, sixteen inches wide and colored with that abomination beyond all abominations. . .yellow starch. . .it is in such a ruff that I see the sins of the realm of England. Allow your mind to rest upon such a ruff, and the white, stiff neck inside such a ruff. . . ."

Judith could not imagine why Arthur had chosen such a topic. Yet after a few minutes she could see in James Parker's face that he approved of the sermon. As did every other peaked face man and women seated about him, even the raft of fearful children, all listening in trained silence to the preacher.

"God's grace is proved to thee by the abundance of thy wealth," Arthur was saying. "To every man as he deserves. And by this token, the beggar in the street deserves not alms but to be cuffed and kicked."

Judith could see that the congregation was greatly moved by the thought of kicking and cuffing beggars. There were murmurs of assent from every bench. Master Parker gave his full attention to the preacher's words and did not look toward the door again.

"For perfect goodness is to turn thy face to God. To chastise thy neighbor who would dare to smile. . .Dare to sing. . .Nor unthinkably, to purse his lips to whistle. . . ."

"Amen," said Master Parker.

"Amen," said all the rest.

"And those that would stoop so low as to paint themselves, to deck their bodies in silk, to wear the ruff. . .the yellow ruff. . . They shall end their days in the depths of hell. . . ."

Judith noticed now that Arthur was carried away with his own fire and brimstone, lost in his violent ranting. He pounded the lectern, and the people said amen. He shook his fists and stamped his foot, and the people sat forward on the benches. He shouted out a call for repentance. And so a stir had begun among the people even before the door opened, and Mistress Doyle entered, followed by Ben Doyle, her new husband, in his best doublet.

But Arthur was unaware of their approach, for when he had pounded the lectern a final time, the Bible was dislodged and began to arc toward the floor below. He had reached for it, stumbled, reached again, and thus torn his glasses from his face, stumbled again, reached again and dislodged his curly black beard.

Halfway down the aisle, Ben Doyle locked eyes with the wild preacher who stood now silent and clean shaven, and recognition was instant and complete.

"Thief. Cheat," called Ben Doyle. "His dice are heavy."

Which refrain was taken up by the tinker, the fripperer, and the seller of ratsbane, and gradually by the whole congregation. But Arthur Amboid did not waste a moment. With the alms basket under one arm and Judith under the other, he nipped across the altar space and leapt out of a back window. By a miracle never to be explained, Jasmine stood beneath, and Arthur, Judith, and the alms basket lodged on her back and off they went.

They raced across the village green and into the highroad. Past the great forest that lay close beside the village. And out of sight before Ben Doyle and Master Parker could saddle their horses to follow them.

Through the long afternoon they raced. The priestly robes billowed and floated behind them like small clouds attached to this fiery steed, this swift empyrean. There was no further threat of pursuit. And yet Jasmine would not be reined in during all through that shivery Sunday afternoon.

As night approached, they came to a village larger than Wodstock, and to an inn finer than Ben Doyle's. Jasmine clattered through the inn yard and stopped short at the stable door.

"Jasmine, my good girl," said Arthur, as he slid to the ground, "you have saved our lives this day. And now we are free to spend the fruits of our labors on supper, and drink, and a fine bed to rest our bones."

Judith dismounted and looked into the alms basket. It was not a fortune to be sure. Only some hammered shillings, a groat or two, and a handful of milled sixpence pieces.

"I would not want to have trouble with the law," she said. "You don't think James Parker will send after us, do you?"

"No, Dick old lad, I am sure there is not enough money to warrant that," Arthur replied. "And you must remember that I preached a fiery sermon for Old James Parker. And would have preached more had circumstances permitted."

"True, but. . . ."

"And though my extreme modesty should prevent mentioning such a thing, I did, after all, shed blood in your behalf."

Arthur waved his bandaged hand before her eyes.

"So, what do you say, good Dick? Shall we call the hostler to stable Jasmine and proceed to a fine dinner?"

"Very well then," she said.

Judith had not taken two steps toward the stable before she saw a sight that froze her blood.

"O, Arthur," she whispered, "I see my father's horse. In the middle stall. . .and mother of God. . .coming towards us. . .Tis my father."

CHAPTER IV

Judith would have made a run for it had Arthur not grabbed her arm and held her.

"Quiet," he said. "And do what I tell you."

In a twinkling he had stripped Judith's robe off her back, turned it here, twisted it there, and returned it to her as a cowled cloak which covered Launcelot Gobbo's shoes, clothes, and her own face and hair. She heard rather than saw the meeting of her father and Arthur Amboid.

"Good day, sire," said Arthur. "We are fairly met in my new happiness."

"Good day," replied her father in a voice so low and mournful her heart failed her.

"Tis my young wife here, too shy to show her face," Arthur said brightly.

Her father grunted, and then replied, "Your young wife, do you say?"

"Even so," said Arthur. "And my heart burns to show you her lovely face, her hair freshly combed, her breath sweet as Cytherea's."

Judith trembled so hard that she very nearly dislodged one of Launcelot's shoes. And cursed Arthur Amboid along with her father and Henry Wilcome and every other male she knew except Will.

"Yet my wife has whispered to me that she will keep herself for me alone. So, though she is a vision, you may not see her."

Judith sighed with relief. For this moment she was safe. But she did not feel secure in what was to come. Ever in her mind she heard Ben Doyle's words. "He is a thief, a cheat. His dice are heavy."

"Are you alone?" she heard Arthur asking now.

"Yes. I am alone," replied her father.

"And where are you coming from and going to?"

"I've been to London, riding day and night, and all for nothing.

I must rest tonight for tomorrow I ride on to my home in Stratford."

"Even so?" asked Arthur. "Then we must share our meal. For my bride has chosen to dine alone on bird wings and slivers of cates. But I myself am famished. Come, I will gladly stand you a fine supper."

John Shakespeare groaned.

"Go to, sire, cheer yourself. For I will stand for no melancholy on this, my wedding night. Say you will be my guest."

"What can it matter now?" John Shakespeare said. "It is all beyond remedy. Very well. I accept your invitation."

"Aha." Arthur pranced with excitement. "Then I shall bestow my young wife in the finest chamber in the inn, and we shall be merry, what say you?"

"Ah-h-h-h-h-," her father sighed.

Judith followed the men at some distance, her head down, her hood pulled forward lest her father should turn and see her face. Already Arthur was asking leading questions, questions that if her father should answer, she would be done for. She had half decided to slip out of Launcelot's shoes and run when Jasmine whinnied ever so softly. Holy Jesu, what chance would she have to run off with Arthur and Jasmine in pursuit?

"Sweeting?" Arthur said even at that moment. "This good gentleman will proceed to the public room while I make arrangements for your comfort. Come this way."

Arthur grasped her arm again, tighter than before, and led her up a step and into a dark, narrow hallway.

"In God's name, Arthur, why did you take up with my father? You needn't have spoken a word beyond good day."

"Not speak to your father, Dick, old lad? What do you think of me? I am not completely without manners."

"But. . . ."

"Ah, mine host, how good to see you after this many a year. But you must excuse my young bride. We were married this very day, and she knows little of the world."

He thrust Judith behind him and shook hands jovially with a broad faced man, tied up in an apron so that only his arms and legs were visible around its exterior.

"Well met," said Arthur. "It has been many a year since I stayed within these walls."

"Ay God, it has, Master Arthur," the host replied. "And now you have a wife, do you? Then let me have a look at her. By God, let me call the mistress."

"Not. . .at this moment. For it is a fact that my bride is shy to discomfort. She will not look at any man save me. Not even her own father. But, I am sure I can bring her around to it in time. When next we pass through, I promise you may see her and admire her beauty."

"There is no doubt of that," said the host. "I have never seen a wench you could not bring around."

"Ahem," said Judith.

Arthur glared back at her.

"Ah. . .true," he said, turning again to the host. "But, this paragon of shyness, my wife, must have the best room in the house for our wedding night. Could you lead us there forthwith? There is a fellow who awaits me in the public room, and I must not keep him."

The host went at once to the stairs and began to ascend, all the time laughing and shaking his head. Judith wanted to kick him, wanted to kick Arthur, and considered even now that she might bolt and run. But Arthur pushed her ahead of him, forced her to walk between him and the host until they had climbed the stairs and turned into a large room, the finest in the house, or so said the host.

"Excellent," said Arthur.

Beneath the cover of the hood, Judith could see him take one of their precious coins from his pocket and give it to the host. Could see the two of them leering and winking. And then Arthur led her into the room and closed the door. But not without one final grimace toward the back of the retreating landlord.

"Arthur Amboid, what do you mean by all this. . .this stupidity?"

"Quiet, my sweeting. You would not want your father to hear your voice."

Judith subsided. Indeed she did not want her father to hear her voice. But neither did she want Arthur to hear what words her father would surely say to him.

"Arthur, I think it were best you did not go."

"And I, good Dick, think I must be on my way."

Without another word he was out the door and gone.

Meanwhile, in London, Will Shakespeare was bid to Southampton House at eight o'clock that Sunday night. He was to read a number of scenes from his new play, and he was also bid to prepare a sonnet on the subject of music. He had sat himself down in the early morning to write and had got as far as: "Music to hear, why hear'st thou music sadly," when up out of the versal world had come his father pounding at the door and shouting like a madman.

"Ruined," his father had called at the top of his voice. "Forty pound owed in a civil suit and she has run off. I am ruined."

Will, unable to think of anything except the gratitude he felt that he had sent his wench off at daybreak, pulled his father into the chamber, closed the door, and barred it with his body.

"Ay God, father, what is the matter?" he asked. "What is this ruin you speak of? Who has run off?"

"Judith. Your sister. I have ridden day and night to London, searching every way, every ditch, every inn and tavern. She has disappeared, your sister."

"But why would she to do such a thing?"

"Why? Why indeed? There is no reason for it. No excuse for such an action."

John Shakespeare clenched his fists, lifted his face upward as if he could thereby draw closer to the canopy of heaven. He moaned. He ranted.

"Father, you must calm yourself and give me an explanation. Here, sit down. All this shouting will bring no remedy."

And so John Shakespeare allowed himself to be led across the room, and to be seated on Will's only chair. After a few pointed questions from Will, he proceeded with the tale of Henry Wilcome. Of the marriage. He hurried past the disadvantages of the match, and embroidered the extent of the land and the money which would come to Judith at the old man's death.

"This talk of money leads me to think you have sold my sister against her will."

"Against her will? What does her will have to do with marriage?"

"Yet, father, you could have chosen a younger man."

"A younger man? You know Judith would not be accepted by a younger man. Or by any man with good eyesight and proper use of his faculties. Judith is a trial, Will. I tell you, this marriage was to be her salvation. And ours."

Will shook his head. What could he say to his father? This man who had been his secret ally when he had run off to London, burning to be a player, burning to write out all the words which lodged in his brain, that prodded and taunted him til he thought he would go mad. "Leave Anne and the children with us," John had whispered. "You will have no peace with that woman looking over your shoulder. I will pacify your mother."

Yet with all that, he did not think his sister should be forced to marry old Henry Wilcome.

"Father. . . ."

Before he could go on, his father dropped his head into his hands.

"Ay God, Will, what is to become of us?" he said.

"Tis a troublous time," Will replied, "I will grant you that. But the problem of the moment is my sister's safety. Are you quite sure she is not hidden away in the countryside? She has many friends among the poor thereabouts."

"No, my son, she was seen on the road to London. A peddler spoke to me of a boy he met on the way. . . ."

"But a boy, father. That would not be Judith."

"Yes, it would. Do you remember the slop boy, Launcelot Gobbo?"

"The one who cleans out dunghills and. . . ."

"The very lad. He has confessed that he lent his clothes to Judith. Or as it falls out, she took them from him and beat him for thanks. Besides that, your mother had a confession out of Old Sallie. It was she who opened the cupboard door with a rusty key we did not know was in existence."

"Judith was locked in the cupboard? Father, why would you. . . ."

"Say no more about the cupboard. If you had been there, you would have done as I did. Judith is an unruly, disrespectful girl. She deserves worse than locking in a cupboard. But, the matter of it is that she has run off. To London, as I believe. Your mother thought she would come to you."

"And if she had come to me, father, I would hide her. . . ."

His father rose from the chair and held out his hands.

"But she has not come," Will told him. "I swear it."

At this, John broke down completely. Will could not bear the pain of watching his father sobbing, so he got out a bottle of his best sack, poured two glasses and forced one of them into his father's hand, guided it to his mouth, tipped it and poured the contents into John Shakespeare's open mouth.

"Ah, Will," said John when he had swallowed. "Then you think you can help us in this matter? That is, could you find Judith and bring her home?"

"If Judith is in London, I will find her. And since she cannot stay here with me, I will arrange passage back to Stratford. But, father, you must learn that Judith is not like other girls. She cannot be bullied. Perhaps if you tried kindly persuasion. . . ."

"You may be right," said John. "Yet I owe forty pounds in a civil suit, and I must have it no later than a fortnight."

"I will do my best to send you the money," Will had said. "As soon as I have it in hand. Now, we must be off to church. The vestry is watching most carefully at this season of the year, and I have missed one Sunday of late. Then we will dine below in the public room, and you must be off for Stratford."

All of which took time, and so now Will sat at seven o'clock with the one line of the sonnet written.

"It is not possible," he said.

And rose from the table to don his new velvet doublet and be off. And since it was too far from Bishopsgate where he resided to Southampton House in the Strand, he must call one of the grooms to saddle his horse. For it would not do to be late before Sir Henry Wriothesley, Third Earl of Southampton and Baron of Titchfield.

In the failing light, Judith surveyed the chamber. There was a very large bed with carved posts and hangings patterned with strange, exotic birds. The bed rug was a stiff, woven fabric, no match for the hangings but adequate. There was a table by the window, and two stools close beside it. The rushes were clean and sweet smelling. On the wall opposite the bed, there was a painted cloth of Samson pulling down the pillars of the temple. A fine room. A room which any bride would rejoice in. But Judith was no bride, and she trembled to think what might happen before this night was over.

From the moment she had been left alone in the room, her position became clear to her. Below stairs, she was reined in by fear of her father, of being dragged home to Stratford to marry Henry Wilcome. Once this fear became less immediate, she realized there were greater dangers in this quiet place. She had run to the door, only to find the latch string was pulled through to the other side. She could not open the door. That whoreson dog, Arthur Amboid, was even then on the stairs, hurrying to join her father below in the public room. In the next few minutes her father would be telling him of his runaway daughter. And in a few hours, after the household was asleep, Arthur would be pulling the latch string, stalking into the room and threatening her very maidenhead.

For Judith knew well the ways of a man and a maid. She had seen Nancy, red in the face as an apple, straining with the butcher behind the large vat in his slaughter yard. And the old cunning women had told her enough of it beside. Of how a man would thrust his member into the hidden part of a woman. How this thrusting would bring pain at first, but then great joy. And after joy a baby would grow inside you. And then shame. For the rest of your life you would be forced to provide pleasure to any man who would buy you a crust of bread. Judith would rather die than live at the behest of one ragged man after another. She stamped her foot. The monstrous shoe rattled across the floor. She grew angrier, and kicked off the other.

Then she would not wait here in this chamber until Arthur Amboid came to do his monstrous deed. She would not be dishonored in such a way. She would face him down. And in that moment she vowed, whispering to the ceiling, that she would remain a virgin all her life, even as the blessed Queen Elizabeth had done. She ran to the door and pounded with both hands. And called as loud as her trembling would allow.

"Arthur. Arthur Amboid."

And pounded and called again and again until she heard feet running toward her down the passage. The door flew open and there stood Arthur in his preacher's robes.

"Are you mad?" he asked. "Do you want your father to find you? Dick, lad, you do verily act like the young wife I called you."

Judith searched that muddle of lies, Arthur Amboid's face. What did he know? What had her father told him thus far?

"Leave off, Dick, or I shall call you a shrew."

Arthur smiled now, and walked into the room and closed the door. Judith backed away from him til she was standing close against the bed. She could feel the feather mattress against her thighs.

"Ay God, Dick, you are trembling. What ever can be the matter?"

"I. . .I fear my father will discover me. I. . .I do not want to return to Stratford."

"And this you called me up the stairs to tell me? Dick lad, I was quite aware you did not wish to be discovered. And who was it draped you in your acolyte robe and made it up that you were my young wife? Dick, I am amazed at you."

Judith blinked and looked away. And remained quiet until she could see that Arthur's boots were moving away from her to the door. Ay God, she must do something. Now. Before her father revealed her identity.

"Arthur. Wait. Let me go down with you, and slip past the tap room door and be off. That would be much the best, I am sure."

"And I am sure it would not. I have promised that I will take you to your brother in London, and that I will do. You may be very sure, Dick, that I will not lose my chance to meet Will Shakespeare."

"But, Arthur. . . ."

Once again, Arthur had turned to go.

"Do not leave until I tell you this," she said.

"What is it now?"

"It is that I am hungry. I have had no food today."

"Hungry, you say? Then if hunger is your problem, you have not a worry in the world. The cook is even now fixing you a tray. You shall have dainty messes to eat this night, old Dick. And I shall pick your father's brain if it takes til midnight."

Judith watched Arthur open the door and walk through. And could think of no way to save herself. He had started to close the door, but then he turned and opened it wide again.

"He is a close lipped man, your father."

It was not long before the door opened again, and a serving girl walked in, bringing a tray.

"Good evening, mistress," she said.

And smiled slyly as she set the food upon the table by the window. Judith pulled her cloak more closely around her. For truly she did not know what role to play. If the girl thought she was a boy, there might be gossip in the kitchen which could come to her father's ears. O God, what was she to do?

"Tis a splendid meal your husband has provided you," the girl said. "And a splendid husband too. If I was provided with such a one as he, I can tell you I would not be here in the chamber and he in the tap room. Holy Jesu, I never saw such a pretty man before. Yet the cook says she has seen him many's the time."

"Truly? How was that?"

"She never had time to explain herself. There's much eating and drinking tonight. A great body of travelers. And when the cook heard that Arthur Amboid was about, she bestirred herself to cook beyond anything I have seen in the weeks I have been here."

"What is your name?" Judith asked.

"Phoebe is what I am called. And I believe I hear my name being sounded even now. So I will leave you to enjoy your repast. Mother o' God, if your husband have not sent you French wine."

Phoebe stared longingly at the tray. Judith stared too, at the tray and then at Phoebe.

"Phoebe," she said. And waited. "Phoebe, could you do something for me? A small favor?"

"If it can be done quickly, mistress. I hear my name louder and louder."

"It will take no time at all. It is just that I. . . ."

Before she could speak another word, the door opened wide and in came Arthur, smiling broadly.

"Sweeting," he said. "I wondered what was keeping Phoebe so long. Is there any problem?"

He strode across the room and took Judith in his arms. He pulled her so tight against his chest that she could not speak nor hardly breath.

"Leave us, Phoebe. My sweeting here is filled with such love for me that she will scarcely allow me to tear myself away from her. Go at once. I have left a penny for you in the kitchen."

Phoebe walked backward to the door, unable to take her eyes from Arthur's person.

"Quickly," Arthur said. "My sweeting has become somewhat violent in the expression of her love for me."

Judith struggled against him, unable to move her upper body, but aiming a kick at his shins.

"Close the door, Phoebe. That's a fine girl."

When the door was closed Arthur let Judith go. But when she raised her hand to slap him, he took her arms again.

"Dick," he said, no longer playful. "What are you trying to do? Have you no reason? No judgement? I am beginning to lead your father to speak his mind. And that is important, Dick. We need to know his plans. I know already that he has been to Will in London. The rest will follow, I am sure."

"But, Arthur. . . ."

"I will hear no buts. You must be quiet and eat your meal. Tis quite a lovely mess if I do say so. French wine. A lovely pudding. What do you say, old Dick?"

Arthur did not stay to listen. He pushed her back from the door, leapt through it and closed it behind him. And again, the latch string was pulled through on the other side.

Judith stared at the tray for some time, thinking she would not taste a mouthful of it. But then her stomach began to roil and gurgle. And when she paced to the table, wringing her hands and moaning, when she bent down to look out of the window with an eye to jumping to the courtyard below, she smelled the pudding and the enticing fragrance of the French wine.

"I shall eat nothing," she told herself.

And bent further to see what might be just below the window.

"Ay God," she said. "Such aromas. And I will need my strength on the highroad."

And so she seated herself on one of the joint stools. And took first the wing of a small fowl. And began to eat. She ate the whole fowl. She ate bread. She ate an apple. She ate nuts. And the delicious pudding. And in between each course, she drank the French wine.

"Ummmm," she said, looking into the cup of wine. "Good. Good. It bites the tongue ever so slyly, and yet it soothes the throat. And warms the stomach."

And so she drained the cup.

"Now," she said. "To make my escape."

But when she stood and leaned across the table to survey the ground below, the window panes swirled like a glass bottle before her eyes. And since the darkness had descended while she was busily eating, she saw nothing but blackness.

"Well," she said. "Tis dark."

She reached for the single candle which Phoebe had left burning on the table. Her eyes blurred. She saw two candles. And then two window latches, and neither of them would open.

"O God," she said. "There is something amiss here. My stomach churns, and I am so sleepy. O God, what if I am poisoned? I must lie down."

Judith pulled herself up. She lurched to the foot of the bed. She reached for the bed post. And held to the mattress and guided herself along the side until she reached the headboard. She lifted one knee and then the other. And collapsed headlong across the mattress.

Judith struggled to open her eyes. Her father was calling her name. Over and over. "Judith, wake up," he said continually. But her eyes would not open. It was so pleasant sleeping on her parent's soft mattress.

"No," she said. "No, father."

But he would not leave her alone. He shook her. He called her name. And finally he grabbed her shoulder and turned her onto her back. And leaned down to look at her, lowering the candle until it was at her chin.

"Judith love, you must wake up now. We have much to discuss, you and I."

And finally Judith opened her eyes and stared straight into Arthur Amboid's face.

"Ay God," she said. "Arthur."

"Indeed, Judith love, Arthur Amboid, minstrel, player, and poet. But it seems that you are something different than you professed to be."

"Arthur, I had no choice. I. . .In God's name, take that candle away and let me sit up."

"Sit up? Why, Judith love, you have no need to sit up. With all this downy marriage bed to hold you. No, I insist. Lie where you are. I want a good look at you. For as I told you, I have much to decide."

Judith tried to sit up, but Arthur would not have it. He pushed her back on the bed, and leant down, holding her shoulder with his free hand.

"Yes, Judith love, I have many choices. Number one, and simplest of all, I can walk to the end of the hall and rouse your father. 'Master Shakespeare, I cannot go on with this charade. I have within my own bed chamber you own daughter, the beauteous Judith.' How would you like that?"

"Arthur, you wouldn't. Say you wouldn't."

"Not at this moment, no, I would not. For I have other choices. I could drag you out in the night's chill, saddle Jasmine, and be off to see Henry Wilcome. It seems the old man is disconsolate since you have run off from him. He might be willing to post a tidy reward for your return."

"I will not go."

"I could simply wait until morning, and after your father has ridden off, proceed to your brother in London."

"Much the better plan," said Judith.

"Or. . .Or. . . ."

Arthur took her chin between his thumb and forefinger. He turned it from side to side. Then he brushed her hair back from her eyes. All the time staring at her as if he were memorizing her every part. And then he touched her throat, her shoulders, and finally her breasts.

"Arthur, please, I beg you. Do not dishonor me."

"Dishonor you? What is there to dishonor? You may not be a boy, but you have the body of one. Besides which, do you think I would take pleasure of my companion on the highroad? Do you think I would not sooner make my way to the kitchen where awaits me the plumpest dumpling, who would give herself willingly? Very willingly."

"Then go, for God's sake. But before you do, tell me this. Did you put some potion or other in that French wine? I thought at first that I was poisoned. And then I grew so sleepy I had to lie down."

"Judith love, you know I cannot tell a lie. I am guilty. I did put a simple sleeping potion in the wine. But it will do you no harm. I had to be sure you would not slip away. You are my introduction to Will Shakespeare, remember?"

"How could I forget it? You remind me of it often enough."

Arthur laughed softly.

"Never mind, dear child, you will be rid of me soon enough. Tomorrow we will be in London. I will take you to your brother. And all your troubles will be at an end."

Arthur left her then, and she drifted back to sleep. And wakened some hours later to sounds in the passage. Footsteps passing, and morning coughs, and much blowing of noses. Sounds from below.

Crockery and tin knives and tankards. And sounds from the courtyard below her window. Hees and haws from the grooms, and hoof clatter on the cobblestones as they led the horses forth to their masters. The house was awake, alive with noise and smells of baking bread.

"I must be up and about," she said.

She sat up and looked toward the window, then grimaced and lowered herself into the channel she had made in the feather mattress. She had remembered that Arthur Amboid had come to her in the night with the knowledge that she was not a boy. He had touched her here and here and here. And she touched herself, her throat, her shoulders, and her breasts. She ran her fingers down her rib cage. She squeezed at her hip bones which seemed to be rising from Launcelot Gobbo's breeches in perfect peaks.

At this moment she heard a crash in the passage outside her door. Then giggles. Then running feet. Then Arthur himself walked into the room, a broad smile covering his features.

"Good morning, wife, and how do you fare this day? Why, I would call you a slugabed. The sun high in the sky and you still within."

Judith sat up quickly.

"Phoebe and I brought you bread and good ale, but we met with misfortune. However, fear not for your morning repast. Phoebe has gone below for more."

Arthur raised his arms above his head and stretched himself luxuriously.

"When you have eaten, my sweeting, you must make your toilette. We will be off shortly with a company of travelers for London."

"I see no reason why we should ride with a company of tiresome people. I refuse to hurry myself."

"Then I will go without you. I have no desire to have my throat slit by a robber in Watling Street."

Arthur started for the door.

"Wait, Arthur. Please wait. And tell me what you have seen of my father this morning."

"I have seen very little of your father this morning. He is somewhat discommoded by strong drink. Remember to dress yourself in your disguise before you go below stairs. He might rise up at any moment. You would not want to encounter him."

"No, I would not," Judith agreed.

"Very well, my dear, as long as you are forewarned. I shall see you when you get to London. If you get to London."

"Wait, Arthur. Perhaps I will go with you."

Arthur grinned and danced the rest of the way to the door.

"Judith love, I feel we will be successful, you and I. Players, poets, and singers. Greatly sought after throughout the realm. And I will be back for you when I have made my tearful goodbyes to the host and his wife. And to the gentle Phoebe."

In less than five minutes Judith had risen, completed her bodily functions, and eaten the repast which Phoebe had brought. When Arthur came for her, she stood quietly as he turned the acolyte robe once more into a cape. She followed him circumspectly down the stairs and out the door, where she was greeted by a company of prosperous merchants, all of whom were dressed in solemn black. Each of them had a splendid horse saddled and waiting.

"Where is Jasmine?" Judith whispered.

Arthur lowered his head and whispered back.

"I was hoping to bring up the rear of this magnificent cortege. For if Jasmine stares at the hind quarters of these splendid animals all the way to London, she will somewhat improve her gait."

"Are you ready, Sir Arthur?" shouted a fine old gentleman from the lead of the pack.

"Ride on," Arthur shouted back. "My mare is even now being saddled."

When the hostler brought Jasmine out of the stable, Judith could not believe her eyes.

"What has happened to Jasmine?" she asked.

For there she stood with neither swellings nor tumors.

"A simple matter," Arthur replied. "The heavy rains did somewhat melt the painted mudpacks. This morning the groom was able to remove them with little effort. Tis a trick I learned some years back when I had need to disguise both myself and my horse. But here, the company stays for us. We must be off."

Arthur was right. By the time the company came to Uxbridge, Jasmine looked like a champion.

"She is a very chameleon, is Jasmine," said Arthur Amboid. "I cannot imagine how she came by her talent."

"She does look fine," replied Judith.

Once again Arthur pulled the drapery of her cowl close across her eyes. Each time Judith had let her hood slip, the better to see the passing scenes, Arthur had enveloped her. Thus, she had no inkling of the road to London. At Chipping Barnet, she had glimpsed a tavern front. And she had seen a winding river twice in passing.

They rode on. Arthur regaled the merchants with passages quoted from the Bible. For the men were all Puritan, though more congenial than Mr. Parker had been back in Wodstock.

At the gallows at Tyburn, Arthur had pulled her hood aside long enough for her to see a purple faced man swinging from a rope.

"Let that be a lesson to you, wife," he said loudly. "Know your place and walk in it."

Down came the hood. And Judith's stutters were completely eclipsed by the chorus of amens from the merchants.

At St. Giles in the Fields, Judith and Arthur parted company with the merchants. There were many proffers of hospitality should Sir Arthur and his young wife deign to accept it, but Arthur, preening and bowing, said they were indeed expected that day at court.

As soon as they had lost sight of the merchants, Judith put her head back and let her hood drop and then the folds of the robe fall down across Jasmine's withers.

"I hope never to be cooped up again," she said.

She leaned sideways so that she could see past Arthur's shoulder. Newgate stood before them, with the wall stretching as far as could be seen to left and right.

"Arthur," she said. "Is this London? Have we arrived at last?"

"Yes, Judith love, tis London. What do you say we enter in style?"

Without waiting for answer, he dug his heels into Jasmine's side, and she was off running. Judith would have her first view of London in a rushing whirl of tall buildings and stone castles, crosses and wells. Of dancing plumes on the elegant gentlemen's hats, of their mounts with braided manes and silver buckles and chains. Of their attendants dressed all in scarlet or green or brilliant blue. And they were blessed with outrunning the contents of a chamber pot emptied from a third story window by a laughing serving girl. As they passed St. Paul's church, a tall stone pile to their right, Judith twisted her head for a lingering glance. All the books in the kingdom, Will had said. For there in the churchyard the booksellers had their stalls, and many printers had their premises close by.

"Ay God, Arthur," she said. "Tis better than fair day in Coventry."

Arthur laughed.

"I agree with you," he replied. "And the best is yet to come. Shortly we will turn Jasmine's head to the north and make for Moorfield."

"The Theater?"

"Ay, Judith love, to the Theater."

When the Theater came in sight across the field, Judith could scarcely keep her seat on the horse. For there it was, the very rounded O which Will had told her of. "There is magic inside that wooden O," Will had said. "A royal circle where all are kings and knights and ladies. Where fairies dance, and all is gold and precious gems."

"Your brother is within," said Arthur. "They fly the flag on performance days. Luckily, within my purse, two pennies rub together for our admittance."

Arthur leapt from Jasmine's back and reached up to take Judith's hand. But Judith, now that they were close to the building could only sit staring. Her brother had lied to her.

"Arthur," she said. "Tis no more than a rack of sticks."

"Inside, Judith love, is where the magic lies. Come, let us go within."

The company of groundlings, apprentice lads, prostitutes, poor housewives crept off to one afternoon of ease, small merchants, idlers who had slipped through the hands of the watch, and poor relations from the country, all stepped two steps to give place to the handsome gentleman and the dirty lad.

For the dirty lad, Judith, had pushed and thrust her way forward, stepping on toes with Launcelot Gobbo's formidable shoes and jabbing elbows, until at last she could see the stage.

"It has begun already," she said to Arthur.

"But still there is much to see. Look at the handsome actor who plays the duke. Tis Richard Burbage."

"There?"

Judith pointed toward a figure seated on a joint stool to one side of the stage.

"No. Toward the back. Do you see him?"

But Judith could not look beyond that one player, a young man with back straight as an arrow. With strong legs, well shaped beneath his hose.

"Ay, God," she whispered.

"Judith love, look at the back of the stage. You are missing the greatest actor in England. See how he gestures, how he turns his head."

Her eyes would not move from the long brown curls, draped forward across the young player's left shoulder, shining in the sunlight. His velvet doublet sewed in pearl work, with great, colored stones scattered down his sleeve. The wide yellow ruff at his throat. His gloves dangling from long, elegant fingers.

"Judith love, your brother Will is making his entrance."

Will stepped from the wings, suited in gleaming armor. Her heart rose within her, and she knew she was safe at last. Yet in a moment, her eyes shifted back to the player on the joint stool.

CHAPTER V

Will Shakespeare strode onto the stage in his new armor, bought that morning from a second hand dealer in Bridge Street, and paid for in gold from the purse of Sir Henry Wriothesley. Though not a proud man, he was somewhat puffed up on this occasion. For there sat the Earl resplendent on a cushioned stool at the left side of the stage. Will turned his head, caught his Lordship's eye for a brief moment, and paused.

Ay, God, what the previous night had been. The Great Hall at Southampton House aglow with a hundred candles. Half the queen's courtiers in attendance. Enough jewels and gold chains on every chest to ransom the king of the Russians. Every dainty food set about. Liveried servants passing to and fro. And after some half hour of dainty chewing and quaffing, the Earl himself, dressed in scarlet, shimmering with jewels, rose and spoke.

"We have here the greatest poet in England."

"You do me too much honor," Will had replied.

But the Earl was insistent.

"The greatest, I say."

Will sighed. But then he felt an insistent, pressuring nudge at his elbow, and knew he had missed his cue. Thomas Pope, as Oxford, stood beside him, and it was the part of both of them to be staring at the pitiful dying body of Montague, cow's blood congealed about his mouth and beard. Richard Burbage had spoken his line twice already.

". . .live how we can, yet die we must."

"Oh. . ."quoth Will. "Oh, Warwick, Warwick, Wert thou as we are. . . ."

And then the words rippled off Will's tongue even as they had flowed from his pen. He could feel the Earl's gaze, those intelligent eyes agleam, his lips in a half smile. Ay, God, Will knew he was a made man. He would write poems such as no man in England had ever written. He would draft plays such as were never seen in the known world. The Earl would lift his hat to the balconies, and the audience would shout, "Bravo. Bravo." Will's eyes swept the galleries, top to bottom, and in a moment of compassion and gratitude he looked even into the pit.

And groaned.

"She has come," he whispered under his breath, recovered himself and went on. "Ah, Warwick! Montague hath breathed his last. . . ."

Yet his brain knew not the words he spoke, for it was filled tight up with the vision of Judith. For the first moment he felt great relief that she was safe in London. But then he looked at her unkempt hair, and her face dirty out of all reason. One sleeve lost and gone. Her right arm bare and hanging out. And Launcelot Gobbo's jerkin which Judith now wore must have belonged to his grandfather and been passed on through the generations.

With shame, he realized he would have to rebuff her, to hide her for a time. He knew that he dare not discover her to Henry Wriothesley, Third Earl of Southampton and Baron of Titchfield.

When Richard Burbage had spoken the last words of the last act. . .

"Away with her, and waft her hence to France,
And now what rests but that we spend the time
With stately triumphs, mirthful comic shows,
Such as befits the pleasure of the court?
Sound drums and trumpets! farewell sour annoy!
For here, I hope, begun our lasting joy. . . ."

Judith pushed forward in the press, calling all the while for her brother Will. Yet she could make no headway for Arthur was holding tight to her shirt collar, pulling her backward.

"There is more," he said. "You must wait for the dancing. And even then, you must not go to Will yourself. Do you wish him to greet you as sister Judith?"

"O no, for I will tell him straight away that I come as Richard."

"But if he has called you Judith before you speak. . . ."

"Ay God, Arthur, you are right. Then you must go to him and prepare him."

"With all my heart," he said. "Now, watch the dancing."

A consort of music began to play at once. Several flutes, a

drum, a horn, and a viol. And then the whole company came on the stage and began to dance. Seven couples, matched in height except that Richard Burbage was taller than anyone.

Judith smiled and clapped.

"I have never seen such," she said.

"Tis the dancing which brings out the rich widow ladies. And the courtiers who learn from the common players to be approved at court."

Judith still watched the handsome player who rose now from his stool, and lifted his hat high above his head. The clapping and shouting grew louder and louder, til Judith could hear no word that Arthur spoke to her or she to him.

A small man jigged onto the stage in a plumed hat with scarves flying off his shoulders, a dozen of bells sewed on each leg of his baggy trousers. The audience clapped louder and called out, "Will Kempe," and the little man went into such a frenzy of dance that he almost bobbed off the stage. And never ceased for a half an hour. Judith, weary as she was, would not have cared had the little man danced all night. She could have stood by the hour, gazing upward at the stage and nodding in time to the music.

When the dancing was over, when the crowds had abated and gone, Judith waited, her back to the stage, trembling with excitement, frightened that her brother would not agree to keep her with him in London, and knowing that now she could never return to her home in Stratford. O God. Arthur had returned, stood at her elbow, whispering.

"He says that he will keep you with him for a while, but that you must. . . ."

"Must what? What must I do?"

"And isn't this what I am trying to tell you even now? Judith love, you do discommode yourself by your impatience. You must learn discipline."

"Arthur, trouble me not with discipline. Nor patience. Say the words. Now. Am I to be a boy?"

"Your brother Will says he cannot condone such an action."

"Then tell him I am off this moment. I shall kill myself or. . .or something. Anyway, tell him I shall kill myself whether I do it or not, for I must be a boy."

"Ay God," said Arthur, and started back toward the stage.

Judith risked a quick look. And there stood Will, frowning and gesturing. In a moment more he jumped down from the stage and walked beside Arthur, they both talking, still frowning as they approached the place where Judith stood.

"Know you I am Richard," she said when they were within hearing. "It is Richard I am come and Richard I shall be."

And glared at Will and lifted her fist high over her head. Will stared, started to speak but could not. And then he broke into a merry laugh.

"Ay, God, then, Richard you shall be."

He opened his arms and Judith ran into them.

"O, Will, you must help me," she whispered into his ear. And hugged and clasped him as he held tight to her.

"We shall see," he said.

"Does that mean I can be a boy and stay with you in London forever?"

"We shall see."

Arthur Amboid bit his nether lip and sighed.

Meanwhile, outside in the field that surrounded the Theater, Sir Henry Wriothesley was lifting his noble foot into the stirrup when he remembered the sonnet concerning music which he had commissioned Will to write and which remained unwritten.

"I must go back," he announced.

"Undoubtedly," quoth the first gentleman usher.

The word was passed down the line of his retainers. And since the Earl was a high spirited youth, he chose to enter the Theater this time through the penny door and into the pit.

"The Honorable Sir Henry Wriothesley, Third Earl of Southampton and Baron of Titchfield," thundered the gentleman usher.

Will Shakespeare, still with Judith's head pillowed on his chest, looked about him for a place to hide her from Sir Henry's sight. For Judith, on closer inspection, looked no better than in his first glimpse from the stage. On the other hand, Judith, whose ears had been covered by Will's arms about her head, had not heard the gentleman usher, nor seen the approach of the company and was intent on exacting Will's promise that she might be a player.

"Judith. . .only for a moment. . ." Will began, yet was cut off by the speedy approach and jovial laughter of His Lordship himself.

"And who is this splendid lad you have here, Will Shakespeare?"

Sir Henry had stopped somewhat back from Judith's line of sight, and so she had to break away from Will and step around him for a full view. Ah, she sighed to herself. So it was the handsome player she had watched so boldly during the play.

"I am Richard Shakespeare," she said before Will could speak. "And I have come to London to be a player and to write plays."

His Lordship laughed heartily.

"Is it true, Will Shakespeare? Is this your brother?"

Will knew not which way the wind blew nor what to say, so that he hesitated, looked quizzically at Sir Henry, and in that moment Judith knew she would have her way.

"Go to," laughed His Lordship happily.

Sir Henry did not seem to be able to take his eyes off Judith. Will eyed him cautiously. And noticed that Arthur Amboid did the same.

"Richard," said Sir Henry. "By Our Lady, and such shoes. . .God's bodykins, surely you could set up house and live in those shoes. What monumental, gigantical shoes. . . Let me look at you, lad," Sir Henry said. "Turn. Turn."

Will expected Judith to refuse, but she smiled sweetly and turned herself about. Sir Henry tilted his head and brushed aside his flowing curls and squinted.

"I can see you are a Shakespeare." And he turned to Will. "Has this splendid brother of yours run off from home? It takes pluck to run off alone and come safely to London."

"I did not come entirely alone," Judith said. "My benefactor and friend Arthur Amboid here has eased my path along the way."

Arthur made a low bow before Sir Henry.

"At your service, sire," he said. "If you have need of poet, singer, lutenist, player, parson. . . ."

He broke off and looked intently at the ground before Sir Henry's feet.

"A man of many talents, I see."

After looking severely at Arthur for some moments, Sir Henry turned back to face Judith.

"First we must read Richard's poems," said His Lordship. "For I am planning an evening of poetry. It will be centered around Will's work, of course, but I think it would provide entertainment to hear the poems of a lad so young as Richard. And perhaps the songs of a wandering minstrel."

"Your Lordship honors us," said Will.

"Come to me tomorrow at eight," said Sir Henry. "Meanwhile Richard will require a proper doublet and hose, and. . ." Sir Henry smiled. "And do not forget to order shoes."

He bowed again and nodded to the gentleman usher who let fly with another silk purse into the hands of Will Shakespeare.

"Tomorrow at eight," said his Lordship. "And you, Will, must bring your sonnet on the subject of music."

"Who was that man?" Judith asked when the company had left them. "God's body, I thought he was a player."

"You thought Sir Henry Wriothesley was a player?"

"Who but a player would sit on the stage?"

"Where else should one of Sir Henry's breeding sit but on the stage? Would you have him seated in the third tier of the gallery beside a goldsmith's widow? Sir Henry is Earl of Southampton and Baron of Titchfield."

Judith gasped. To think that she had spoken so openly to an earl. To think that she had seen one. She looked up at Arthur who was in turn staring at her.

"What?" she asked him.

"I was about to ask the same of you, Judith love."

"Well, do not ask. And do not call me Judith. Nor you neither, Will. I am Richard Shakespeare."

"Whom some call Dick," said Arthur, smiling now.

"Yes," she said, then turned to Will. "I have longed these many days to meet Richard Burbage and his old father. Could we hurry and catch them before they leave the Theater?"

"If you will agree to behave yourself."

Will made off for the stage.

"Follow me," he said.

Richard Burbage had not tarried, but had left for home as soon as the dancing ended. His wife had sent for him to pacify a sick child. But his old father, along with the comic Will Kempe, were waiting in the tiring room behind the curtains, they both working among the barrels of costumes.

"And who is this, Will Shakespeare?" inquired the old man when they had parted the curtains and entered.

"James Burbage, Will Kempe, may I present my brother Richard, arrived this day from Stratford. And his companion, Arthur Amboid."

"It is easy to see the Shakespeare resemblance," said old James. "And I can see in the lad's face. . .you might say in the curve of the nose. . .or in truth, you might say in the dainty puckering of the lips. . .ah yes. . .Richard will break the hearts of the ladies. Am I right. . .or am I wrong there, Will Kempe?"

"Indeed, you are right," answered Will. And then he began a comic dance, whirling about Judith, crossing between her and Arthur, tweaking at her bare arm, at her jerkin. "Can you dance, boy? A boy must dance to get on with the ladies. Here, do you say your name is Arthur? Then take a turn with Richard and let me see how he lifts his knees."

Judith had never danced in her life. Had seldom touched a male unless to slap him. But when, at Will Kempe's insistence, she allowed Arthur to take her hands, careful of his bandage, and to lead her through the curtain and onto the stage, she found that she could follow his lead.

"Lightly, Judith love, lightly," said Arthur.

"Richard," Judith said, and missed a step.

"Ay God, Dick then, lift those toes. Turn. Turn."

Judith stumbled. Her foot slipped out of Launcelot Gobbo's shoe, and she fell hard against Arthur's shoulder. And when he put his arms about her to steady her, she could feel a tremor all through his body.

"Let me go," she said. "I am well enough."

But he did not. He held her tight against him until the two Wills and Old James Burbage joined them on the stage.

"Ay God, Will," said Will Kempe, "I think we have a comic here. I must look to my laurels lest he eclipse me before he becomes a licensed player."

"No," said Old James, "I say he shall be our heroine. Such lustrous, shining locks could go for a princess."

Judith smiled, could feel herself blushing at such complements.

"I thank you, sirs, and if you give me a chance, I know I can satisfy you. But first, if you please, I am much in need of shoes that fit my feet. I can not learn my dancing in such as this."

She reached down and gathered up the two gigantic shoes, shoes that had stepped daily into dung and dust, shoes that had rubbed Judith's toes and threatened her ankles all the way to London.

"Here, Arthur, give these to some poor lad," she said.

And then she accepted James Burbage's proffered hand and went with him to rummage through the costume barrels. Will Kempe jigged along behind them.

When the three of them were out of earshot, Arthur leant toward Will and whispered.

"Your sister is as imperious a female as I have yet seen. What do you propose to do with her?"

"Ay God, Arthur, I know not what to do. All her life she has been out of all rule. My father has whipped her. My mother has lectured her. But Judith is Judith, and cannot be changed." He paused and bit his lip. "And yet I love her. And I would not see her married against her wishes though God knows the versal world has done so."

"Yet if Judith were to love a man. . .And if the man were to love her. . .would you stand up to your father for him?"

"If, that is the question of it. Judith cares for nothing but writing poems. Likely it is my fault. Everyone says it is my fault, for I taught her to read, you see. And yet, it was hardly like teaching. It was almost as if she knew already and was waiting for me to reassure her."

"She is quick," said Arthur.

"Quick indeed. And so I think no man can look to marriage with Judith. I think she will have no man."

"Is that so?" said Arthur.

"Ay," said Will. "And so I suppose I am stuck with her. She cannot support herself, and yet I cannot send her home. Not now, in any case."

"Do not send her home, Will. I think her heart would break if you sent her home."

"And so I will keep her until this storm blows over. Perhaps when Henry Wilcome dies. . . But here, Arthur, I bore you with tales of my sister. Indeed, I am grateful for all you have done for her. If I can repay you. . . ."

Arthur lifted his hand, palm toward Will, and shook his head.

"But surely you will allow me to stand you a supper. Indeed, Arthur, you must get a room in the inn where I live. The host gives me a special rate for we are old friends, but I am sure you would find his rates within your means. And you can stable your horse there. Come, let us rouse out Judith and go."

"I thank you, Will Shakespeare, for your hospitality, and I will accept your offer to dine. But first, I have an errand. Give me the name of the inn and somewhat of direction, and I will see you there within the hour."

"Tis the Angel in Bishopsgate. We will look to see you there by seven."

When Judith made her appearance, with Old James nodding behind her and Will Kempe jigging behind him, she was wearing not only a pair of soft leather shoes, snug to her foot, but a whole new costume. Grey stocks and a bright blue doublet.

"By my life, Will Shakespeare," said Old James. "Richard here is the measure of poor Thomas Notbright. . .and I am sure the poor lad. . .not to say he is in any way deficient. . .but that he is. . .if it may be said. . .in certain difficulties. . .Well, in short, I have taken it upon myself to lend some several of the garments which he uses to present a page. Is your brother not a handsome lad?"

"Indeed, and it may be that the company would be willing to sell the clothes, for I am well supplied with money from Sir Henry. . . ."

"Then of course we will sell them," said Old James. "For if His Lordship has suggested. . . ."

"He has suggested," replied Will.

"Then it must be done," said Will Kempe. "I can see that this company has turned itself head over heels to do Sir Henry's bidding. If he wished it, I think you would all jig to Coventry and back."

Will Shakespeare frowned.

"It is much too late in the day to begin on this discussion. Suffice it to say that my brother and I are grateful for the clothing, and we must be off. Tomorrow will be soon enough to speak our minds on many things."

"Will," said Judith when they had crossed the field and come into Holywell Lane. "I must tell you that Old James told me, when we had gone off to look for shoes, that he would gladly give me a try at acting. An apprenticeship."

"No," said Will.

"No? And why not?" she replied.

"Because, Judith, it is utterly impossible."

"But, Will. . . ."

"Listen to me, and do not interrupt til I have finished. You may stay here in London. You may write all the poems your brain contains. But I cannot allow you to act with our company. For what if father returns? What if some merchant from Stratford should see you? It would fall out that you are a girl, and then we would have a steep fine to pay. And we would be disgraced. Do you understand me?"

Judith turned away from Will, too angry to speak. And at that moment could see in the distance two mounted figures. She ran forward, past two of the houses that lined the lane.

"Hurry, Will. I am sure I saw Arthur riding past the end of the lane."

"Likely you did, for he said he had an errand of great importance. But he will meet us at the Angel no later than seven."

Judith walked back to meet her brother, smiling now. She would wait. Calmly wait until her friend Arthur was at her side. And then she would tell Will that he was not to have the last word. She would surely be a player.

When Will and Judith reached the inn there was already a great company gathered in the public room. They paused momentarily at the door while Will looked about for the host, John Farley.

"You cannot dine below stairs, Judith. I will have a tray sent to you in my chamber."

"And why can Richard Shakespeare not dine with his brother and his friend Arthur Amboid anywhere he wishes?"

"But you. . . ."

"Listen, Will, we must start out as we will keep up. And I am your brother and can go wherever you go."

"But love, you do not know what sights you may see."

"And you do not know what sights I have already seen."

Without further word Judith strode into the chamber of drinkers and roisterers, and Will followed hard on her heels. He was greeted on every side with invitation to this table and that. Instead he made his way to the bar, now pushing Judith gently ahead of him.

"John Farley," he said. "My brother has come from Stratford.

Richard by name. He expects to be some time with me. Perhaps you can find a trundle for him. I prefer not to share my bed with him, for he is a most violent sleeper."

"And as handsome a lad as I have seen," said John. "Welcome, lad. Any brother of Will Shakespeare is my friend out of hand. What is your pleasure? Ale? Beer? Or do you care for a taste of French wine?"

At the mention of French wine, Judith shook her head.

"A taste of barley water, if you please," she said.

"And you will have the usual, Will? Then take your seat at table. Jennie will serve you momentarily."

There was one vacant table in the room. Will took his seat there, and bid Judith to sit beside him.

"We must save a seat for Arthur," she said.

"Indeed. Now Ju. . .Richard, let us use this time to settle many matters. John Farley and his wife, whom you are to call Mistress Farley, are as kind a couple as you would want. Therefore I do not hesitate to leave you during the day, in truth at any time, in their care. I am a busy man. But you may stay in our chamber, where I will provide you with writing materials. With food. With whatever you require. But I cannot look after you myself at every moment."

"Nor do I expect it. I can look after myself. And there is Arthur. He can show me about the city until I know it well."

"You cannot be on your own about the city even when you know it well. And I am sure that Arthur does not have the time for you either. I know not what his business in London is. . . ."

"He is a player."

"A player, you say? But I am sure he does not belong to any licensed company in the city. In any event players must work as hard as other men. You must realize. . . Ah, Jennie, you have come with our drink."

Judith looked up to see a lovely dark girl, somewhat younger than herself, with dancing curls all around the fringes of a white cap tied beneath her excellent chin. An apron hung none too tidily about her waist, her sleeves were rolled high up her arms, and her cheeks bore the blooming imprint of one who has lately been standing over a hot kitchen fire. She set a frothing tankard before Will and a piggin of barley water before Judith, then curtsied.

"Master Will," she said. "I hope the drink will suit you. And. . . ."

But here she stopped, mouth and eyes open wide, and staring straight at Judith.

"Jennie," said Will. "I hope nothing is amiss with you. Here, child, sit down. You look pale. What, can you not breathe? Shall I send for your father?"

Still gazing at Judith, she gasped, put her hand to her bosom, and sat flat down on Arthur Amboid's proffered chair.

"Jennie," said Will, "Are you having an attack of something? Did a morsel of food go in the wrong direction? What can be the matter with you?"

"O, Master Will," she said. "Who is this lovely boy you have brought with you?"

Will looked at Judith, scarcely able to contain his laughter. Now what, he seemed to be asking. Judith reached across the table and took the girl's hand.

"Jennie," she said. "I am Master Will's brother. I am Richard come all the way from Stratford. I hope I have not frightened you. I shall be staying with my brother here at the Angel, and I hope we may be friends."

"O, yes," she said. "We may be dear, dear friends."

And now her cheeks colored brighter even than the blush from the hot fire. She continued to stare intently into Judith's face.

"Jennie," said Will. "I am sorry to interrupt the introductions, but I am famished for food."

Jennie smiled.

"And my brother is hungry as well," said Will.

Instantly the girl stood and began to name off a list of puddings, and meats, and salads.

"And the breads is quite good tonight for I helped with the kneading myself. And I have nibbled the cheese for its flavor. And I could spear you a turnip or two. And provide you with peas shelled by these little hands."

"I leave it to your judgement, my girl," said Will. "I am sure you could choose for my brother and me better than we could choose for ourselves."

"Indeed, sir, I could. And I will. Never you fear, I shall be back in only seconds."

"I think we have our first problem, Richard," said Will when she was out of hearing.

"She is a foolish girl. Can I help that?"

"You can, you know. You would have only to put on a skirt to end it."

"But I shall not, so let us hear no more about it. Now, where is Arthur? I am anxious to hear how he has fared in London."

But they were not to see Arthur Amboid that night. His food sat waiting while Will gnawed at his breast of fowl and Judith toyed with her bread and cheese. When they had eaten their pudding, Will said he thought they had seen the last of Arthur and so should retire to their chamber.

"His whole aim in bringing me to London was to meet you, Will. I am sure he will turn up tomorrow."

"Perhaps," said Will. "Now, let us make our goodbyes. I have much to do tonight."

"Ay," said Judith. "But I think he will come tomorrow."

Judith pulled the curtain aside and stared into the darkness. To think that she was here. In London. With all these thousands of souls who had come to the capital to make their fortune. Will said Sir Henry lived in the Strand, which was not in London itself, but in nearby Westminster. She would go there too. Tomorrow night. And Will said she must not stand gape mouthed at all the wonders she would see. And that she must be mannerly. And that no matter what was said to her she must keep her temper. Judith pressed her forehead against the glass so that she could see further into the darkness.

And suddenly light spilled into the street as the door to the public room opened below her. She could see two figures, a man and a woman.

"Will, I thought you said no woman would walk the streets of London at night."

"I did."

"But there is one here. I can see her crossing the street."

"She is a whore," he said. "Now be quiet. I must have this poem ready by tomorrow night."

"A whore," Judith whispered. And knew she would sooner die than be a whore. To give her body to whatever man she met in the streets? Never. Yet what was the difference between whoring and a marriage without love? If she had stayed at home in Stratford and married Henry Wilcome, if he had come to her bed, she would have been a whore. Why could her father not see this?

Behind her in the room, she could hear the scratching of Will's pen. And then his breath let out in a great sigh. Then whispered words.

"Music to hear, why hear'st thou music sadly?
Sweets with sweets war not, joy delights in. . . . "

And then aloud.

"Holy Jesu, it will not come to me. I cannot write it."

Judith dropped the curtain and ran to the table where Will sat wiping his face and spearing at the paper with the feather end of his pen.

"Will. . .why not joy? Why not joy delights in joy?"

"Hold your peace, Judith. I have been working on this sonnet for a week. Do you think you can write it in an instant?"

"But listen, Will, this is good. . .
Sweets with sweets war not, joy delights in joy."

"And then what? What comes next? I cannot fathom it."

"So then. . .what is the matter of the piece? Music is joy. . .yet received sadly?"

"There is no matter. Sir Henry has asked me to write a sonnet on the subject of music. It could be anything. But I can think of nothing."

"Still, what you have already is quite good. Start over, Will, and read what you have on paper."

"Music to hear, why hear'st thou music sadly?
Sweets with sweets war not, joy delights in joy.
Now. . .Why?"

"Why. . ." Judith began. "Why lovest thou that. . .which thou receivest. . .not gladly. . .Or else receivest with pleasure. . .What should it rhyme to, Will?"

"To joy."

"Ah, then. . .receivest with pleasure thine annoy?"

"Ay, God, Judith. . . ."

Judith raised her eyebrows and frowned at her brother.

"Now who is this Judith you speak of? I know of no Judith who writes poetry, for surely you cannot have reached your exalted age and not have heard that a woman cannot write poetry."

"Very well then. Richard, if you would help me write this sonnet. . . ."

"Gladly," she said.

When Will had sighed again and stood up, Judith slipped quickly into his chair. She settled the ink pot to her comfort, smoothed the paper and began to write. And soon she had forgot London and all it contained. Her brother Will. His Lordship who would receive the sonnet. And Arthur Amboid who was lost somewhere, who, she understood, she might never see again.

CHAPTER VI

Will Shakespeare was in the habit of taking his morning meal in the inn kitchen. In winter he would seat himself on the settle close to the fire, and he would drink his ale and lounge about til he could see daylight through the back window. As it was summer now, he had for some days drawn a stool to this window, and he had cradled his warm ale mug in his fingers til the sun shone out amongst the plantings in the kitchen garden.

Old Nan the cook, who had one day come to the Theater to see the play of King Henry, would beg for a speech or a poem. And Will would oblige. And then Mistress Farley would stand idle beside the cupboard and John Farley would stick his head through the door. And Jennie would come running down the back stairs to hear him too. On this, Judith's first morning at the inn, all eyes were turned in her direction. Will took his ale unsmiling, watching to see if any one of them could see through Judith's disguise. Judith herself was at ease in her doublet and hose, was proud even of the slim line of her thighs. She bowed solemnly before Mistress Farley, nodded to Old Nan and the maids in turn. Saluted Master John. And came to Jennie.

The girl was paralyzed with shyness in the company of her parents. All to the good, thought Judith. She would endeavor to stay much in the company of Mistress Farley when she was at the inn. She drank her morning ale, chewed at her bread, watched Will as he entertained. And then it came to her. Since yesterday when she had first seen Will, he had not asked once about Anne nor about Susanna nor the twins. And when she came to herself enough to understand the conversation even then taking place between Will and Mistress Farley, she heard Will say plainly, "And if I should ever marry, Mistress Joan, you may be sure it would only be if Old John died and I could have you for a wife."

Ay God, Judith said to herself. His friends do not know he is married. And what of Old James Burbage? Did he know? Did

Richard Burbage know? And here he had told her she could not be a player for someone might discover she was a girl. What would happen if these same people discovered the presence of Anne back in Stratford? She would have a word with Will. As soon as they were alone in their chamber.

It did not work out that Judith would have Will alone that morning. As soon as he had broken his fast, he left Judith in Mistress Farley's care and was off, he would not say where. Judith was torn between going up to her chamber where Jennie might at any moment make entrance, and staying in the kitchen where the girl's eyes never left Judith's face and form.

"Will has told us of you, Richard, but he has spoken most of a sister. Judith I believe her name is," said Mistress Farley.

"Indeed, we do have a sister, but she is older than I am by a few years."

"And is not married?" asked the mistress.

"No, she is not married. I think no one would have her, for she has a sharp tongue. And my sister can read and write poems as fine as Will's."

"Do not say that, boy. There is no one in the kingdom who writes as fine as Will Shakespeare."

"My sister Judith does," Judith said somewhat defiantly.

"Ah then, it runs in the family, does it?"

"Indeed it does. Would you like to hear a poem of mine?"

Mistress Farley laughed, which set off Nan and all the maids. Only Jennie stared solemnly across at Judith from her place beside the window.

"Laugh then if you will, but you will change your tune when I have read before Sir Henry Wriothesley tonight."

"Now Richard, lad, I never meant to hurt your feelings. And I see that I have done so. Read to us. We are nothing but women here and so are unlearned, but we know a good rhyme when we hear it. And we will listen courteously."

Judith frowned down at the floor rushes. What would they say if she quoted them the sonnet about music? Still she could not do that. She could not harm Will even if he had lied about his own flesh and blood children.

"Very well," she said. "I shall speak a poem from memory since I have left my packet safely tucked away in our chamber.

I have not finished it yet, but I give you what I have."

"Do so," said Jennie dreamily.

"Shall I compare thee to a summer's day?
Thou art more lovely and more temperate:
Rough winds do shake the darling buds of May,
And summer's lease hath all too short a date:
Sometimes too hot the eye of heaven shines,
And often is his gold complexion dimm'd;
And every fair from fair sometime declines,
By chance or nature's changing course untrimm'ed."

"Ay God, Master Richard," spoke up Nan the cook. "It do sound as fine as when I heard Master Richard Burbage speak upon the stage. It do, Master Richard."

"It is fine, Richard," said Mistress Farley.

"Fine, o, fine," whispered Jennie.

When Will returned, he took Judith upstairs to their chamber where he felt safe to announce that he had gone to the fripperer without her, and had brought back a doublet of gold colored velvet with slashed sleeves with white silk showing through.

"You may wear the gray hose, I think," he said. "And I have placed an order for shoes which cannot be ready within the week, so those you have on must do. But I think Sir Henry will be pleased."

"And what about me, Will? Am I not to be pleased with my own clothing?"

"You have every reason to be," Will replied. "Unless you have decided to change to a bodice, in which case I will return to Robert Shaw's shop with great gladness."

"I did not mean that, Will. I only meant that I should liked to have gone to the fripperers myself and chosen."

"And have old Robert feel your knee? Robert likes boys, you see."

Will handed the clothes to Judith and started toward his desk.

"Then if he likes boys so well I could have made a better bargain."

"Judith, my God, you are innocence personified."

Judith ran to the desk, still holding the doublet knotted in her hands. She threw it down where it landed precariously close to the ink well. Will grabbed it up and thrust it back at her.

"Indeed I am not innocent," she replied as she took the velvet doublet.

"Judith, I hope I may say that you are innocent. I plead with you to tell me that you are innocent."

"What do you mean by that?"

"I mean you were on the road with Arthur Amboid, a handsome young man, for four days. I know nothing of Arthur's history. How did you sleep? Were you together? For from Sunday night on, I am given to believe he knew you were a girl."

"Well yes, but I had drunk all that French wine, and I. . . ."

Will took her by her hands and pulled her close where he could examine her expression.

"Judith, tell me, did you sleep with the man?"

"Sleep with him? Do you mean did I sleep in his presence, for I did, yes. On the stone floor of the church. And under the blackthorn hedge."

Will groaned.

"But I did not sleep in a bed with him. For when he knew I was a girl he insulted me and told me I had no breasts, and then he went to the kitchen wench."

"But Judith, what happened to you? Did Arthur Amboid lie with you?"

"As you did with Anne and got Susanna?"

Will blushed, and his face grew grim. He nodded.

"Then no. Of course not. Arthur is my friend. He would have no thought of country matters. But since the subject has come up, I noticed this morning in the kitchen that your landlords do not know you are married. And not once have you asked about Anne and the children."

"There was no need. I had word of them from father. He had seen them since you had."

"Yes, but is it true that your London friends think you are a single man?"

"Well. . .yes."

"Then you might have prompted me ahead of time. What if I had spoken of Susanna? Or of Hamnet?"

"Ay God, Judith, you are right. It is evil of me to renounce my children. But, and this will prove a shock to you but you must bear it, Judith; I have no love for my wife. She disgusts me. I can scarcely look at her when I am at home in Stratford."

"Indeed, I do not blame you. She disgusts me too. But your own children. . . ."

"Judith, say no more. It is my weakness. I do love a woman. Any woman. Even as Robert Shaw loves any boy."

"Ay God, Will."

"Judith, watch your language. What will our mother say when you return home speaking curses?"

"I shall not go home. And beside that, I knew many curses before I came. I suspect our mother will be glad to be rid of me. Then perfect Joan will find a husband to repair the family fortunes. In any event it will not be me."

"Judith, what can I say?"

"Say nothing, Will. Here, I will try on this doublet. Though I do not think it suits my coloring. Still, if it suffices to read my poem to Sir Henry. . . ."

"Ay, Judith, what a good lad."

While Judith sat on her trundle, still dressed in the gold colored doublet and poring over her papers of poems, Will slipped away to the Theater. He locked the door from the outside, but it remained unknown to Judith. She was thoroughly engrossed in her papers. So that when Will returned and announced they had little time to make ready and be off to the Strand, Judith scarcely knew he had been gone and said she was well prepared.

"I could read for an hour if asked," she said.

"I think you will not be," replied Will. "We read at Sir Henry's pleasure. No more and no less. If he has lost interest in you, you may not read at all."

"What do you mean not read at all? I have spent the entire afternoon practicing over my poems. I have fifteen of them by heart without the paper. And I shall speak them too, no matter what Sir Henry says."

"Judith, I do not think you have grasped the idea here. We are Sir Henry's servants. . . ."

"I am no man's servant. What do you think of me?"

"I think you have a lot to learn, Judith. And this evening may be a better teacher than I could ever be. Wait and see."

Judith gasped in spite of herself when she and Will were ushered into the great hall of Southampton House. Coming out of the darkness of the courtyard the light was too brilliant. The hundreds of candles were like stars on a summer night, glittering and dancing. There were gentlemen standing about, they too gleaming with jeweled doublets and gold chains about their necks. There were masked ladies with jeweled rings, and with diamonds sprinkled in their hair. There were tapestries hung on every wall, and a painted plaster frieze on the ceiling above her head. There was an abundance of tables covered in Turkey carpets; the stools and chairs had embroidered cushions. Liveried servants, all in red cloth, passed among the guests with glasses of wine and bowls of dainties.

"God's Mercy, Will," she said. "I am like to forget my name in all this finery. I think I shall speak no poem here tonight."

Will took her hand and held it tight. And Judith was glad again that she had such a brother.

Judith took no wine when the servant offered it. Yet she did reach out to touch the slim stem of the glass, to run her fingers across the silver pattern of vines around the bowl. She watched Will closely as he drank from his. Another footman passed with a silver salver heaped with small pasties.

"Try one," Will said to Judith. "The pastry is made by a French cook, I am told. It melts upon the tongue."

"I am well as I am," Judith said impatiently. "When do you think Sir Henry will come for us?"

"When he is ready, Judith."

"But he said it would be an entertainment of poems. Why else would we be here?"

"Why else indeed?"

Will looked suddenly across the room, somewhat startled in appearance. He drained his glass, set it on a passing tray, and then proceeded to straighten his doublet, to brush sideways at his hair.

"Is it Sir Henry?" Judith asked. "Do you see Sir Henry?"

"Yes," said Will."

Judith searched the room, twisting her neck and rising on her toes. There were so many people clustered about, so many servants passing with trays held high. So much chatter and laughter. She shook her head.

"I do not see him," she said.

"Here he comes," said Will then.

And Judith found him. Sir Henry, dressed in scarlet doublet and hose, with a masked lady on his arm. They walked in measured tread toward the spot where Will now cleared his throat nervously and smiled and gestured.

"Will Shakespeare," Sir Henry began when he was within hearing. The noise in the room was tremendous. "I say Will Shakespeare."

Sir Henry and the lady stopped a few feet away from them. Will bowed low.

"Your Lordship," said Will.

"Your Lordship," said Judith, trying hard to model herself after her brother.

The handsome pair walked through the crowd which parted at their approach, some bowing and others merely nodding as their own nobility called for. The lady herself seemed to float toward them, with only Sir Henry to hold her back.

"Will Shakespeare," Sir Henry said when they had bobbed and stopped. "I have here a lady who desires to meet you. She tells me you are the greatest poet in England, a theory which I myself hold. And which shall be demonstrated forthwith. Lady Clarise, this is the man. And this lady, Will, is my cousin, lady-in-waiting to our blessed queen. I present the Lady Clarise Brown." The lady gave her hand to Will to kiss, and he obliged. Judith was struck dumb. And then the lady lifted her mask well above her eyes and gave Will such a look. Ay God, it was a look Judith had not seen before, and she knew not if the lady were sick or, Holy mother of God, was she love sick? Of her brother Will?

"I have long waited for this moment, sir. On so many occasions I have sat silent at the Theater, my very breath shook from me at the sounds of your poetry. And my cousin tells me you will read tonight on the subject of music. Can it be true?"

"Indeed, my Lady, I am resolved to do that very thing."

Lady Clarise pushed her mask over her eyes, and suddenly turned toward Judith.

"And is this the lad Sir Henry has been telling of? You would think no lad but this one had ever made his way to London. What do you say to that, Richard Shakespeare?"

Judith knew nothing at all to say on such a matter. But her

mind was resolved on one thing. She would bear no love for Clarise Brown. And so she turned to Sir Henry, and found him gazing at her in much the same way that the Lady Clarise was looking at Will.

"Richard," he said. "Are we to be honored with a recitation tonight? I have taken your friend Arthur Amboid into my service, and he has spoken well for you. He says you spoke a poem to him which he took to be your brother's, but now suspects is of your composition."

"It was mine, Your Lordship. Truly. But tell me, is Arthur here? We have looked for him since yesterday, and he did not come to the inn as he promised."

"Arthur is indeed here in the very hall. And he will entertain us presently."

"In what way entertain us?" she asked.

"He will sing and play the lute."

"Arthur plays the lute?"

"Most brilliantly. And he has taught me my first lesson only this morning. He swears that I have great natural talent, and he will make the most of it."

"But where is he?" she asked.

"Look up to that small balcony beside the stair. He waits there for my signal."

Judith looked up. And there stood Arthur. He was dressed in motley, a clown's suit. Scarlet and green and silver. With a colored cap and bells upon his head. He held in his arms a glistening instrument. And at the moment Sir Henry clapped his hands, he began to play.

"O, mistress mine, where are you going?
O, mistress mine, where are you going?"

Judith sighed in wonderment. She had never heard human voice as magnificent. The liquid tone. The tumult of passion in these simple words. She was transfixed. She did not see her brother leave furtively, followed by Lady Clarise. She did not notice Sir Henry whose eyes never left her face.

It was late when Judith and Will returned to the inn. They went silently up the stairs to their chamber, both so involved in their own affairs they had nothing to say to each other. Judith removed her fine clothes carefully, hung them on the chair and slipped into her shirt with the one sleeve. But then she lay on her trundle hour after hour, unable to sleep, for her mind was in a turmoil.

Sir Henry had said her poems were brilliant. He had squeezed her hands, had smiled, had whispered words meant only for her ears. And all of this would be pleasure to her except that she knew he believed her to be a boy. Did this mean Sir Henry was akin to the fripperer? Did Sir Henry like boys? Her heart sank. What was she to do?

And then she would turn on her bed and before her eyes would come a vision of Arthur. His voice so beautiful, and yet he had become a nobleman's fool. And he had spoken no word to her, but had stood like a monument on the balcony all the while smiling like an idiot.

And Will. He was a fool too. For the Lady Clarise.

Judith stared across the room to where Will lay snoring on his elegant bed. And it came to her that being a boy was one thing, but being a man like any of these she knew was a fate she did not wish for herself.

Judith waked the next morning, assured that she heard a door slam. She looked at Will's bed and found it empty. Then she leapt up and went to the window. The sun was well up in the sky. She had slept much too late. Will had left for the Theater without her.

But when she looked down into the street, there stood Will. And a woman. The woman wore a long black cloak, but the cowl had fallen back to show her raven hair. Judith pressed her temple against the window pane for a better view, and saw that it was Lady Clarise.

"Go to, Will Shakespeare," she said. And rapped on the glass, only to have the two of them walk away, hurriedly, separately.

Judith dressed quickly. She would eat no food this morning. She would find her way to the Theater. And then what? What say? What do? Never mind, she would decide all that later.

But when she reached the door and pushed against it, she found that it was locked. And at that moment, all the fury she had suppressed since leaving Stratford rose up inside her. For days she had hidden her feelings so that she could win a point, get her ultimate way. But for now she could not think of politic response; she could only reason that no human woman should be so put upon.

"Will Shakespeare," she yelled first, knowing all the time that he was half the way to Holywell Lane. "Landlord. Mistress Farley. Somebody. Let me out of this chamber immediately."

Instantly she heard footsteps on the stairs, then running down the hallway. A bolt was drawn and the door flew open. Jennie appeared with a small tray. She curtsied, then ran through the door.

"Master Richard," she said. "I was set to listen for you. Master Will said I must open the door as soon as you waked. You see, he did not wish to leave you asleep and unattended. But I told him that so brave and strong a lad as you would need no protection."

"You are right, Jennie. I need nothing, neither breakfast nor listening after. I am off to join my brother at the Theater."

"Without your ale and bread? I think you must have your ale and bread."

Jennie put the tray quickly on the table and cut Judith off as she was sprinting for the door.

"Master Richard," she said, and leaned close to Judith's very face. "I think a mouth so handsome shaped should first be filled with drink. And then should find use in a kiss."

"Stand back," Judith said. "Away. I shall have none of this kissing."

"Say not so, Master Richard, for I do dearly love you. . . ."

Judith pushed past the girl and ran into the hallway.

"Master Richard," Jennie called after her. "Mother will be wroth with me that you have gone off without food. Come back."

Judith heard no more. She was off and running.

There was no one to hinder her at the penny entrance, so she slipped inside and stood against the wall so that she would not be noticed. Every man of the company was gathered on stage, twelve in all, and all shouting and gesturing. And in the midst of them stood the boy whose clothes she wore even now. Thomas Notbright. He was once more attired in the long white dress with sweeping train, and had woven into his hair some several twigs of summer flowering bushes. However, at this moment he was braying like a bull calf, and the white dress was in danger of falling into puckers from his flowing tears.

"Idiot," shouted Richard Burbage, and since he was the greatest actor in all London and could project his tones to Bishopsgate itself, he was heard above the rest. "God hath not seen fit to give him brains, I know not why."

The lad, Thomas, was clearly falling to pieces. His head lolled upon his neck. He sobbed most pitifully.

"Empty space," continued Richard Burbage, "and a load of cow's dung in his mouth for a tongue."

Thomas sank to his knees on the stage rushes.

"I should rather speak to air than this not-pate."

And so saying, Richard Burbage hurried from the stage.

The company grew quiet. All that could be heard was Thomas Notbright's blubbering.

"Well. . .it seems to me. . ." said Old James Burbage, "Since Richard takes the matter ill, we must peel the boy out of his costume and send him home by the next rider."

Thomas seemed to brighten at this, and rose to his feet at once. Off came the dress in one fell motion, and down he leapt through the trap door and into the regions below.

"What is to be done then about Corinthia?" asked Will Shakespeare.

"The other lads must double," said Thomas Pope.

"They are doubled already," said Will, "for the women in this play appear in droves."

"Then we must procure a lad," said Old James. "That is to say. . .Will Shakespeare, can you not reconsider? Your brother Richard is as apt a lad as I have seen. And when he spoke with me, he showed great interest in being a player."

"He changed his mind."

"But could you not talk to him, Will? If you could reason with him. . .if the lad once knew. . . .""

At this Judith stepped out of the shadow, and called up to the stage, walking as she spoke.

"I have on this instant changed my mind again, sir. Indeed, I will be more than happy to take on the role of Corinthia."

Old James went to the edge of the stage and put out his hand to pull her up.

"Ah lad, I knew you would. And is it possible you could learn such a role so quickly?"

"I can peruse any paper of words and come off with them instantly. And you know I am a very match to Thomas Notbright's size. I could wear this dress with no alteration. And I can act a girl better than one that is."

"Then you shall do it," James Burbage said. "Call my son. Take your places."

The play to be presented that day was an old one, greatly beloved in the provinces, but only occasionally played in the more sophisticated theaters of London. The "Saintly Sister" was the name of it, and many heart wrenching tears could be accounted for from any audience when the lad in the role of the sister, Corinthia, was possessed of wide inquisitive eyes, or pretty little clenched up fists, or if he could call up his tears to flow freely. All of which Judith found that she had at her disposal.

It was backstage in the tiring room that Judith came close to disaster. The other apprentices plainly disliked her. They eyed her suspiciously. They talked behind their hands about her. They made ugly faces in her direction. For they had been passed over, and now the adult players hung on her every word.

Beside this animosity from the apprentices, Judith had the problem of preserving her modesty. For since the whole company dressed together in the tiring room, struggling into hose and doublet, armor or bodice, beards and jewels, she was put to much leaping and hiding behind coffers to prevent her private parts from becoming public.

But since the old bumbling James Burbage attached himself to her at every turn, she made him her mask, her counterfeit. For he never ceased to talk, and prevented the speech of others. She held him as her shield.

At two o'clock, the hour when the action was to begin, the props were arranged, the costumes were hung in order, and every man made ready for whatever role or combination of roles he was to play. The prompter took his place. And Richard Burbage stood ready to make his entrance.

"Are you frightened then, Richard?" he asked and smiled grandly.

"A little," she said, sweeping forward in her train. "Yet, no. O, I do not know. I feel a flutter sometimes."

Old James hurried to her side and waved Richard onto the stage.

"Now then, Richard Shakespeare, have no fear. You have a certain way about you. . .a facility. Not to mention that your brother is a made man since these last two weeks. Anything touched of your brother. . .or connected to your brother. . .may be said to be a made man too. But there. . .go. . .For Richard speaks your cue."

Judith hurried down the stage to stand before the august presence of Richard Burbage, who played the part of the king. He had become, over the years, so kingly, that he could scarcely contain himself in the off hours when he was not playing, and now he seemed to glow in the reflection of some unseen light.

"Of virtue, beauty, love than she

Whose very soul shouldst cleave toward me," he was saying.

And there sat Sir Henry on the selfsame joint stool where she had first seen him. This day his doublet was of a watery green, stitched about with darker green stones and. . .of a certitude, a yellow ruff. It was with great difficulty that she removed her gaze from him. Yet for all this she did not miss her line.

"Your majesty, hast sent for me?"

And she bowed as Will Kempe had taught her, and spoke every line of the script with great perfection so that the audience sighed, and Sir Henry sighed louder.

And as the play proceeded, the story fell out that the king grew wroth at her chastity and imprisoned her brother (played by Will) who spoke piteously to her and begged her to give herself to the king to save his life. Which thing she forswore.

"Yet think'st thou then to save thy life
Shouldst my immortal soul in strife
Sink to the pit, the hole of hell?
Then, brother, think'st thou not well."

Applause broke out from the pit, and Judith, looking up suddenly, saw the face of Arthur Amboid, grinning broadly. And when he stepped forward she could see that he was dressed in a new doublet and round hose. He was a thing of beauty. Their eyes met and locked for a moment so that Judith lost her place.

Yet it was taken for grandeur of manner, this lengthy pause.

Sir Henry rose from his joint stool and waved his plumed hat. With this, the galleries rose, and fights broke out in the pit, and it was quite some time before the play could proceed.

Yet at the end a thing yet more wondrous was seen upon the stage. For when the company assembled for the dancing, His Lordship stepped forward and bowed low before Judith. Will was struck dumb, and watched in some discomfort, as things such as this should never happen. The world should not turn upside down.

Judith herself thought nothing of the world, but only of that space and moment. She was a player on the stage in London. Arthur Amboid was leading the groundlings in huzzas, and clamor claps, and whistling. The galleries resounded with applause. And on the stage, Sir Henry's own palms were set in hurried motion. Judith Shakespeare was as made a man as her brother.

CHAPTER VII

In less than two weeks, Judith had totally restructured her life. She was made aware of time, of its allotted sequence, of its true meaning and value. The succession of hours, the revolving of a day was no longer a fleeting whirl, a succession of picture, but separate points along a route.

For at two o'clock every afternoon, she proved yet again that she was a player. She had six roles by memory, and at every performance the crowds packed tight inside the Theater to see this wondrous boy.

Every morning at nine she arrived at the Theater. The company spent the hours rehearsing, assembling costumes, reading over plays. Judith herself listened endlessly as Richard Burbage taught her the intricacies of the player's craft. After this she gave her time to bouncing and jouncing through the patterns of a galliard, a jig, a courante with Will Kempe. For it was he who had taken her for a partner, and he was a worse taskmaster than even Richard Burbage.

Her brother took no hand in her theatrical training for he was still angry with her. "No good will come of this, Judith," he would mutter when they were alone together behind the closed door of their chamber. He would tell her almost daily about some Stratford man he had seen on London streets. And he would prophesy what day and hour they could expect their father to return to London.

But at eight o'clock on the nights they were summoned to Southampton House, time stood still and Judith proved to be. . .she knew not what. She and Will would arrive at the gates, dressed in velvet doublet and carrying an elegant parchment roll of poems, or of scenes selected from Will's plays. And each night as they entered the great arch of Southampton House and passed beside the screen into the Great Hall, Judith would feel her breath catch. She had not accustomed herself to the sight of the hanging tapestries, the painted plaster frieze high above her head, the carven overmantel. Nor of the furnishings, or the silver plate, the thin crystal glasses. Nor of the clothing of the courtiers, Sir Henry's friends, all cut from gold and black and crimson cloth, studded with jewels. Nor of Sir Henry himself.

With each passing two o'clock and eight o'clock, His Lordship's smile grew deeper and was directed longer in Judith's direction. At the Theater, he led the applause. He signaled daily that silk purses should be thrown in Will's direction. At Southampton House, standing beside the refreshment table, he selected with his own fingers an array of sugared nuts, and bits of orange, and flavored cakes for her to nibble over. He praised her poetry.

And on these occasions, as she was perhaps swallowing an orange section or sucking at a sugared almond, she would glance upward to the balcony where Arthur Amboid stood in his jester's motley. And always his eyes were following her, wherever she stood in the room. As they were each afternoon at the Theater. But still he did not come to the inn. He did not come near her or speak to her.

On the Friday of that second week, a messenger arrived as they sat at breakfast in the inn kitchen.

"A letter for William Shakespeare," the young lad said.

"Here, boy," Will called.

When the paper was delivered to him, he threw a sixpence in the general direction of the lad and blushed deeply.

"I require an answer," the boy said. "My mistress says I may not come within the confines of the palace without it."

Will blushed even higher, and mumbled that he must withdraw to his chamber to find pen and paper. Mistress Farley, who had been watching boldly all the time she was counting out spoons into a basket, now laughed aloud.

"What do you say, Master Richard? Has your brother been summoned to play before the queen?"

"I have no notion," Judith replied.

Though she did indeed have a notion. Only the night before the Lady Clarise Brown had arrived late at Southampton House, had sat behind a lattice to hear the reading. She had never removed her cape and hood, but for all that, Judith recognized her. She had seen that same cloak below her window the first morning she had been in London. Had seen it fall away to reveal the Lady's dark hair.

"I think it be the queen," Jennie said then, and ducked her head almost into the fowl she stood dressing at the table by the window.

"I am sure it be, Jennie, dear," replied Mistress Farley. "And I do not doubt that Master Richard will be included."

"Not I," said Judith.

Judith had lost all patience with both the Lady Clarise and Jennie Farley. She considered the Lady Clarise a whore. And Jennie was inordinately tiresome. The moment she set foot into the inn, there was Jennie. She lurked on the stairs if Judith mounted them. She was standing in wait in the kitchen if she went there. She would allow no one else to serve them at dinner. She picked the garden to its destruction if Judith wandered there. Even at this moment, Judith would run to join her brother except that Jennie would follow, dripping blood along the stair.

The messenger stuck his head in the door then and beckoned to Judith.

"Your brother asks you to hurry your repast and join him at the front door."

Judith jumped up immediately.

"Indeed I am finished. Good day, Mistress Farley. I shall see you tonight."

On the walk to the Theater, Will smiled at Judith.

"I have been thinking," he said. "Since you are going to be staying on in London at least a few weeks more, it will be better to give you your own room. I have spoken to John Farley, and he agrees to put you in a small, private room under the eaves on the third floor. Next to his family. In that way you will be as safe as if you were at home in Stratford."

"Safe? Safe in a room next to Jennie Farley?"

"How could Jennie possibly harm you? She is a child. I think you could overcome her if she made an attack on your honor."

"You know what I mean, Will. She drives me to distraction. Always hanging about me with those pitiful eyes."

"Judith, if you do not like the arrangements I make for you, you are perfectly free to return to Stratford on any pleasant day you choose."

"I will not return to Stratford. As long as I live I will not return to Stratford. But if you think I do not know who wrote that letter. If you think I do not see that she is after you."

"Hush, Judith."

Will paused and looked about at the people afoot in the street. He glanced shrewdly into the window of a mercer's shop set close to the walk.

"This is a serious matter. You must speak of this to no one. My whole career depends on it. The lady's reputation depends on it."

"Then why will you see her? If it were me, I would simply refuse her letter. I would spurn her when I encountered her in the street. Or at Southampton House."

"You have no understanding of these matters."

"What matters?"

"Matters of the heart, Judith. It is easy to see that you have no feelings when it comes to the heart. I think you will never write true poems since you will never know what it is to love."

For a moment, Judith could not reply. She walked quickly onward to the corner at Holywell. Her mind was so full of her anger that she could not find place for love or talk of love. It was only when the horror reached her, and despair that what Will said might be true, that her tongue was unleashed. She slowed her pace, then turned and walked back to him.

"O, Will," she said. "Is it true? O, mother of God, it cannot be true."

"What, Judith?"

"You know well what I mean. Do you believe I cannot write a true poem unless I love some man?"

"It is true, Judith, that a man cannot write of something he does not know. He cannot describe a thing he has not felt or seen. He cannot write of something he does not believe exists. You must answer the full question for yourself."

They walked on in silence. The brightness had gone from the summer morning. Judith despaired. How could she doubt her brother's words when he was the greatest poet in all England?

Sir Henry did not come to the Theater that afternoon. Nor did she see Arthur Amboid among the crowd. Judith did not feel the same affinity for her role, nor was the applause as deafening when she left the stage. And so she slipped outside to clear her head in the late summer sun, still dressed in the trailing white gown she wore to play Corinthia. Looking about she saw Jasmine standing some distance away, her head lowered to crop a blade of grass beside the ditch. Judith ran quickly to her side.

"Jasmine," she said. "I feared I would never see you again. How have you fared in London? I see you are eating better. Why you have taken on flesh."

And then a voice, a high lilting voice modeled on the whinny of a horse proceeded forth from Jasmine's open mouth.

"Master Richard, how pleasant to see you. But I fear you are as skinny as ever. Do Sir Henry's dainties not agree with you?"

Judith stared for a moment at the horse, then whirled about to face Arthur who stood laughing behind her.

"Ay God, Judith love, did you think Jasmine had been prompted to speech?"

"Of course not. What do you take me for?"

"What indeed? I am never sure. Still it is good to see that you have made your fortune here in London." He gestured toward her train which even then was trailing dangerously in the dust. "Between your brother and His Lordship, I see little opportunity for failure."

"And what do you mean by that, Arthur Amboid? I am a better player than my brother. And His Lordship admires my poems and favors me accordingly."

"Is that so? I have noted that Sir Henry is as entranced by the curve of your leg as by the line of your poems. You would do well to stick to poetry."

"And indeed I will. But it scarcely behooves you to talk of patronage. At least I am not Sir Henry's fool."

"I am an honest fool if I may say so. I do not dissemble. I do not make myself something other than my true nature."

Judith's eyes flashed, and she had her hand already moving to slap Arthur's very jowls when it occurred to her that he held her life in his hands. At any moment he could divulge her secret.

"Arthur," she moaned. "O, Arthur, you will not tell. O say you will not tell."

Arthur looked down at her solemnly. As if he were thinking over his position. Playing off gains and losses. It was an agony for Judith who despised the deceit she had been forced to. Who would like to look the world in the eye and say go hang.

"At present, Judith love, I will say nothing. We are friends, you and I. I have done much for you and I will expect much in return. But you must be careful. You must watch on all sides for there are those who would undo you."

"Ay God, Arthur, I am sure of that. At the inn where Will and I reside I am beloved by the daughter of the house. She is a sore trial to me."

Arthur laughed uproariously.

"To be the darling of both sexes," he said. "Ay God, Judith, you are in a thorn patch."

"And you must help me, Arthur. You must come to the inn and talk to the girl. In a moment you could win her affections for yourself. I well remember how Phoebe loved you."

"Me? Loved me? Why, Judith love, I am a very anchorite. No woman could love Arthur Amboid."

"Do not be foolish. A woman could love you."

Arthur grasped Judith lightly by the shoulders and pulled her closer to him.

"What woman could love me, Judith? What woman?"

Judith shook his fingers from her and stepped back. She was not sure what to say to him.

"I cannot answer this, Arthur," she began haltingly. "But I am sure you could help me with this girl, this Jennie Farley. Beyond that, I cannot say."

"You cannot say. Nor should you make answer to a fool. And I do not think James Burbage would take it kindly that you stand here in the dust in such a fine costume. Walk off before I mount."

"But will you not tell me whether you will come."

"Walk off, Judith love, for I must go to teach His Lordship how to strangle a lute and make it yowl."

"But will you come?"

"Ay, Judith love, you may count on it. In some several days you will find me on your doorstep. And I shall be ready to take on Mistress Jennie Farley. Or anyone of your choosing."

When Will and Judith arrived at the inn late that afternoon, John Farley had scarcely greeted them when he produced a dirty square of paper which he said had been left for them some two hours before. It proved to be a letter from Stratford, penned by the real Richard Shakespeare and dictated by John. Upstairs in Will's chamber, he read it out as Judith looked solemnly on.

Dear William,

I am told by one who has seen her that Judith has reached London. A bad word will travel fast. I do not know if she has come to you, but I expect she has. If you can find her a safe passage, by that I mean by one who is strong enough to beat her and hold onto her, then send her at once. Henry Wilcome bears her no ill will. He still wants her. But he will wait. So if you cannot find safe passage, keep her with you until you come home in August. All is quiet here.

As ever, your father,
John Shakespeare

"So you must keep me til August," said Judith.

"It is likely I shall be required to keep you til August," Will replied. "And so we must move your belongings to your new room. It will not be convenient to stay cramped up here for that long a time."

"Will, I do not wish to sleep in the next room to Jennie Farley."

"You have only to keep your latchstring pulled through to your side of the door. She is not a spirit. She cannot walk through wood."

"Sometimes I think she can."

"Come, sweet sister, cheer up. You are a great success at the Theater. And Sir Henry is quite taken with you. What more can you want?"

"Nothing, except to write great poems and plays. As great as yours, Will. I am sure I can. But tell me, was it true what you said this morning?"

"What did I say this morning?"

"That I must love a man in order to write well."

"Perhaps, Judith. I truly think so. Yet I am sure that one day you will love. Only do not force it as I tried to do when I married Anne. Forcing will not generate love. Be patient. And for now, gather your clothing and I will help you. Come."

Judith nodded. But still she thought of love. And the only face that came to her was the smiling countenance of Sir Henry Wriothesley, Third Earl of Southampton and Baron of Titchfield.

Judith's new room was a cubicle in the eaves, overlooking the street. There was a low bed, a rough table, and a stool. She hung her new finery on pegs along the wall. She arranged her papers on the table. Then she lay down on the bed. But she had not been prone for more than a few seconds when her brain began to tease.

"Two loves I have," she whispered. "But what does it mean? Ay God."

She sat up quickly and looked toward the table where sat the small ink pot Will had given her. Two quills lay sharpened beside it.

> *"Two loves I have of comfort and despair*
> *Which like two spirits do suggest me still:*
> *The better angel is a man right fair,*
> *The worser spirit a woman color'd ill."*

Judith ran to the table, dipped a pen and began to write. She grimaced. She sighed. But she did not look up until she had written the last word. Then she wiped the pen carefully and laid it on the table.

"What in the name of God does it mean?" she asked herself. "It requires something more. But there is no more. Ay God, it is like a spirit speaks inside my head, and not me at all. And when it chooses not to speak, I cannot tempt it."

She picked up the pen again and pressed its dry point onto the paper.

"More," she whispered. "There must be more."

But a loud knocking sounded at her door and Jennie's voice came through the latch.

"Master Richard, you must come at once. There is a gentleman asking for you. And for Master Will, but he is not in."

"What name did the gentleman give?"

"No name at all, Master Richard. He says you will know who it is. He says you are expecting him. He says he has come to dine with you."

"Ah," said Judith. "And Will is not in his chamber?"

"He went out some hour or so ago, but said he will be back. But he said you must not wait to dine with him. I have been expecting you below this long a time. The best of the little fowls is all gone, but I saved you a splendid piece of cheese for your bread."

"Thank you, Jennie. Now go below and tell the gentleman I will be down in a moment."

"I can wait and walk down with you."

"No. Go at once. If you do not, I shall surely slap you."

"O, Master Richard," Jennie said. "O, I shall surely enjoy a slap at your hands. I shall not budge a step til you open your door."

Judith emerged, and it was with great difficulty that she kept both hands at her sides and did not attack the simpering girl.

Indeed the gentleman waiting below was Arthur Amboid. He was dressed in a rust colored doublet with a peascod belly as pointed as an arrow and stuffed so full of bombast that it threatened to explode.

"Arthur," said Judith. "Where in the name of God did you find that doublet?"

"What, Dick old lad, no greeting? No expression of joy at my arrival? I think you have no excuse to insult my clothing upon first appearance. Why, I have only to walk outside the city walls, puncture myself with the tip of my dagger, and I could plant a field with beans."

"Is it true? Is your doublet stuffed with beans?"

"In very truth, Dick, it is."

"But where did you find such a monstrous thing?"

"Monstrous, do you call it ? I am dressed in the fashion of the hour. This doublet has graced the body of an Earl within the week. I was given to understand by the fripperer that he spent his entire patrimony on his back, and thus was forced to sell off a few items. So let us hear no more of monstrosity."

Arthur clapped his hands, and Jennie was instantly before them.

"Mistress Jennifer," he said. "We will require your finest seats, your most delicious viands, and a bottle of wine so new across the channel that it will bespeak us Bon Appetit."

Jennie giggled.

"Here, Master Richard, you walk close behind Jennie. She will not lead you wrong."

They made their way to a table beside the window. All heads were turned in their direction; chewing and quaffing ceased.

"This will do," said Arthur.

He gestured to Judith to be seated, then ensconced himself across the table from her.

"Jennie, fearing that you would not have glasses fine enough for my gentle lips, I have brought with me in my saddle bag, a brace of crystal glasses."

He leaned down, fumbled beneath the table for some seconds, then brought forth two stemmed glasses, decorated with silver birds and etched with the Wriothesley coat of arms.

"Arthur," said Judith, much shocked. "Surely you have not stolen Sir Henry's goblets."

"Borrowed, Dick old lad. Borrowed. How is it you can never tell a borrowed object from a stolen one? You have much to learn here in London."

"But what if Sir Henry were to find out?"

"Who would tell him? In any case, think what it would mean if I were an honest man. Think what would happen if I could not dissemble, if I spoke nothing but the truth about you."

"But that is different."

"How is it different? Explain your reasoning. But here, we haggle over straws. Jennie, quickly with the wine. My pipes are as dry as paper."

When Jennie had run off, Judith leaned across to Arthur.

"Do not play games with me, Arthur," she said. "Only today we received a letter from my father saying that Henry Wilcome still wants me, nay even will wait for me til August. I must hide my identity, now more than ever."

"And so daily you tread the boards in the bodice and skirts of a female. Your name is known throughout the city. There is not a pickpocket nor a street sweeper who has not heard of the great player, Richard Shakespeare. I think you have not gone a great way toward hiding yourself."

"But if I remain a boy. . . ."

"Or if your brother does not make his appearance. The real Richard Shakespeare could appear among us at any moment. Did you think of that? And if you continue to lead Sir Henry a merry chase, he will move to discover your sex, male or female, I know not which he prefers."

"What do you mean, Arthur?"

"I mean that Sir Henry is taken with you. And that means he either likes you as a boy, or that he senses you are a girl. Either way, you are lost, Judith love. There is nothing an Earl will not take for himself if he so desires."

"Arthur, you are upsetting me. I asked you to come here to

relieve me of the attentions of this. . .this. . . ."

Jennie materialized beside the table. She set down the wine bottle as if she were proffering the host of the presence.

"Father says this is the very best he has to offer. He hopes it will meet your taste."

Arthur took the bottle himself, poured a drink into the goblet, then tasted. His tongue worked forward and back, side to side. He closed his eyes. He breathed sharply. And then he swallowed.

"Nectar," he said.

He waved his hat in the general direction of John Farley.

"You like it then?" asked Jennie.

"Like it is no word, my girl. I am consumed by it. And I shall make short work of consuming it. And now, if you have already prepared in the kitchen a poached salmon or a stuffed peacock, bring it on. I leave the choice to you, Jennie love. But bring it quickly. I have not dined for some three days now, and I am famished."

Will came in about that time to join them. And throughout the evening, Jennie never ceased to run forward and back, bringing wine, bringing salad, bringing loaves, bringing joints and fishes and fowl. Her poor little feet must have ached with the effort. But the wonderment on her face left little doubt that her fickle heart had now settled on Arthur Amboid.

Before Judith could savor the comfort brought to her by Arthur's substitution in Jennie's heart, there came another evil to replace it. This new evil was the face of sudden death louring down upon the streets of London. The plague had come. Before many days, the sound of the death cart's wheels grinding through the street accompanied all pursuits. Judith ate to its rhythm, slept to it, or else lay awake and wondered at it. It was music to dance to at the Theater. A counter tune to Sir Henry's musicians at Southampton House.

Old James Burbage immediately began to mutter about starting the summer tours of the provinces early.

"The theaters will be closed soon. The city fathers will not allow of it when the death rate may be said to be rising most fluidly. Will you be off to Stratford, Will Shakespeare, or will you agree to travel with us this season?"

Will shook his head. The thought of returning to Stratford was never appealing to him. And this year, he was torn in two directions.

To return to Stratford and be rid of Judith would ease his burdens, but only two days before, Lady Clarise had begged him to find some way to travel to Titchfield with Sir Henry.

"I shall be visiting my old uncle no more than two miles further on," she had told him. "And surely if I can slip away from so shrewd a one as the queen, we could set up housekeeping in my blind uncle's rooms."

"I have come to no decision," Will told Old James.

Judith too was in a frenzy of worry over what would face her, perhaps within the week. She would not return to Stratford. And yet she feared the plague.

"I shall tour with the Burbages, Will, even if you do not," she told him.

"And how will you manage that?" Will replied. "Whose bed will you share? Whose horse will you ride? And chief of all, what would our mother say?"

On the following morning the issue came to a head. For as Judith opened the inn door to step into the street, her own eyes fixed instantly onto the eyes of a dead man. He lay flat of his back in the street, stretched stiff, with his hands over his head, and on every part of his body not covered by his pitiful clothing, there were the horrible black spots of the plague.

"Ay God," she shrieked.

Will had pushed past her into the street, then covered his nose and mouth with his cupped hand.

"Stand back," he said. "It is the plague. Ay God, it has come too close. We must leave London. Today."

So that when Sir Henry's messenger arrived on the instant with two letters, one for Will and one for Judith, there was little doubt that they would accept the invitation contained therein. His Lordship had invited Will and Judith to go with him to Titchfield Abbey, his home in Hampshire. It was agreed they would leave in three hours time. And then a silk purse was tossed. And caught.

Judith ran quickly to her chamber, panting slightly at the speed of her climb. She threw herself onto the bed, and with trembling fingers, broke the Wriothesley seal.

Richard,
Though I know your secret, fear not. I will be discreet. Yet

surely you must know my thoughts; you must sense my feelings even as I sensed your secret. My heart and my brain have many questions for you, but they will wait until we have arrived at Titchfield. Til then, still be my Richard.

As ever,
Sir Henry

Judith read the words through twice, then again for good measure. By this time she had memorized them, and they would ride with her through the countryside, playing over and over in her mind. For Judith too had many questions.

PART
II

CHAPTER VIII

The train of horsemen and equipages stretched for nearly a mile along the roadway. They had come south through Surrey and into Hampshire. Three wagons of His Lordship's private belongings. Two wagons of servants. A string of pike men. The gentleman ushers, their servants, their wagons of belongings. Baskets of food and drink packed in panniers each morning at whatever inn or house they had stayed overnight in. A vast, dusty chain moving slowly through the forest path.

It was a loud and merry company. They laughed often at some witticism provided by His Lordship, though for miles at a time they were content to listen as Arthur Amboid played the lute and sang. For Jasmine would amble on with the reins hanging loose on her neck, leaving Arthur's hands free to pluck the strings.

Sir Henry, on his splendid charger Chantene, rode at the head of the column. Judith, riding well back beside her brother, watched Sir Henry. His graceful shoulders. The straightness of his spine. The odd tilt of his head. Could this be love, she wondered, the thing Will had said she needed to feel in order to write true poetry? It must be. Her stomach churned; she had no appetite. She could think of nothing but Sir Henry, his eyes as he smiled at her over his wine glass. And of his letter which played in her mind, often superseding other conversation. He had said he knew her secret, but that she had nothing to fear; he would keep it. And if, in truth, she had nothing to fear from him, then she would love Sir Henry, silently, distantly, and she would write of this great love in plays and in poems.

There had been great excitement as they were leaving London. For as she and Arthur and Will had stood discussing whether she would ride with Will on his horse Dandee or with Arthur on Jasmine, up rode Ransley, Sir Henry's chief gentleman usher, he who was such a wielder of silk purses, and this time he was leading a horse. A beautiful grey gelding.

"Will Shakespeare," he called. "A mount for your brother

Richard. Sir Henry says he is to belong to the lad hereafter."

"Belong to Richard? Surely, sir, there is some mistake."

Will was obviously flustered, and Judith herself was somewhat shaken too. She had never owned a horse before, had only ridden her various brother's horses when they granted the favor or when she could sneak past them. And now this magnificent animal with flaring nostrils and nervous pawing of the right foot was to be hers?

"Surely, sir, there is some mistake," she agreed.

"No mistake," Ransley told them. "The animal's name is Mammet, and though he is spirited, he is well broken. The boy should have no trouble. Say no more and let us be off. It would not do to keep His Lordship waiting."

But this largesse was not Sir Henry's only gift. For when they had stopped that first night, it was discovered that he had also given her a box to carry her belongings, and that full to the top with four velvet doublets and seven pairs of hose and a pair of black shoes such as His Lordship wore. When Judith had solemnly thanked him, and said that he was much too kind to her, he had waved his hand and intimated there would be more, much more.

Judith looked sideways at Will who rode beside her. He was listening intently to Arthur's song, and whistling beneath his breath.

"When that I was and a little tiny boy,
With hey, ho, the wind and the rain,
A foolish thing was but a toy,
For the rain it raineth every day."

Judith's mind wandered back to Sir Henry so that she missed the rest of the song, and was startled at the general applause. Arthur bowed low in his saddle.

"If I may beg a rest, sire," Arthur called to Sir Henry, "I should be most obliged. My wind is cut off from so much singing."

Sir Henry turned in his saddle, waved and nodded. And when his eyes lit on Judith, he motioned again, this time in her direction.

"Come hither, boy," he said. "Since I have worn out my fool, you may entertain me with speaking poems."

Now Judith, who had little experience of spirited horses such as this grey gelding which His Lordship had chosen for her, in the excitement of the summons, squeezed her right leg against his hindquarters, and at the same time pulled on the right hand rein so that the horse did not know what direction to move, and so stood still. And when Sir Henry called again and this time impatiently, Judith grew impatient too and flapped both reins and dug both knees into Mammet's side. The horse reared on his hind legs and pawed the air for a full minute while Judith clung fighting to his back.

"Ay, God," she screamed.

"Look to her," called Sir Henry who even then had turned his horse and was riding back to them at full tilt. "Go to. Go to. Hold the horse."

But it was Judith who came to her senses and tugged at the reins until the pressure of the bit quieted the gelding. By the time Sir Henry reached her side, the animal was standing quietly.

"Are you hurt?" asked His Lordship.

"No," answered Judith. "No, I am not hurt, but I am not used to the ways of so fine a horse, Your Lordship. If I have done injury to him. . . ."

"Do not think for a moment of the horse. If you are not hurt. . . ."

"I am well," said Judith.

"Then come ride with me," said Sir Henry.

Sir Henry turned his mount and waited until Judith and Mammet started forward. And then he nudged his horse and they rode side by side across the forest floor.

Will watched Judith ride past him with something of the eye of a bearward minding his beast. Judith was a danger to herself and to him. Will had seen the horse rear, his heart in his throat, and not entirely for his sister's safety. For if she were thrown, it came to him, if she were injured, then her clothing would need to be loosened. . .Ay God, even her bare breasts might be revealed. Yet when she calmed her mount and was not thrown, a worse matter had come to light. Sir Henry had clearly said, "Look to her." So then His Lordship knew she was a girl. A woman. Whatever. And though no one else had noticed this gender change, Will knew it for what it was. Sir Henry was smitten of his sister. Even now His Lordship was leaning toward her in his saddle, bending to catch her every word, smiling at her every jest. Ay, God, it was assured that he was smitten. He had known all along this knotty problem of her sex could bring her downfall, yet what could he do about it? She would not listen to him. She was as innocent in the ways of the world as if she had never set out for London. As soon as they arrived at the Abbey, he would talk to her. Holy mother of God, he hoped he would be able to make her see the danger she was in. He hoped he was not already too late.

Yet after riding some miles and mulling over the speeches he would make to his sister, in truth his mind slipped from the matter to secrets of his own. There was a company riding straight behind them, keeping well back to escape their dust, and in this company rode his love, his raven-haired beauty. In these two weeks since he had met her, he had given over his wenches, his paid women, and he lived only for the beauteous Clarise. That she was soiled linen it was whispered, and though he knew it was true, it made no difference to him. To think that a lady-in-waiting to the queen should love him. For she swore she did.

The lady's family on her mother's side was of the old nobility though with reduced circumstances presently. She herself was as wily as a goat on the Welsh hills, as slippery as a long sided bacon pig. She could make her way out of the palace in the night, at morning, throughout the afternoon. She might come to him at any hour. And always her body was hot and prepared for the exquisite pleasure. In scarcely a moment her skirts were lifted up and her limbs parted, ready to receive him. Ay, God.

He looked backward into the distance. There was no sight of her company, but it was arranged between them that they should meet that night. For His Lordship had said they would be at Titchfield Abbey by nightfall. And the beauteous Clarise would be lodged at her uncle's house a few miles to the west, toward Southampton and the southern coast. If she could deceive the hawk-eyed queen, there was no doubt she could confound her doddering, ancient uncle.

The setting sun struck color to the plain, gray stone of Titchfield Abbey, once the property of the Roman Church, Old Sallie's church, given to Sir Thomas Wriothesley, First Earl of Southampton, by Henry VIII at the dissolution of the monasteries. Sir Thomas built a gatehouse into the center of the nave of the old church, and converted the remainder into chambers and suites for his guests. The cloister became the courtyard. On the floor above, he planned out the more important rooms, the suites and family apartments, the gallery, the great and small dining room. All this Sir Henry had explained to Judith as they rode through the lengthening shadows. He seemed unable to speak of anything else as they drew closer to the walls.

"My father added some several features, would have done more but for his untimely death. My mother. . . ."

But here he broke off, for ahead of them the trees parted to provide a view of the house.

"Do you see it?" he asked.

With no other word, he set spur to his horse, leaving Judith behind. Judith reined her horse and sat still until Will caught up to her.

"Look, Will," she said. "Tis a brave house to live in."

She shivered as she looked up to where the massive towers and chimneys ran skyward as far as birds flew. And the whole of it was as long athwart as a small city.

"We must bear ourselves as even as we can," she said.

"Yes," said Will. "And do not presume that his Lordship will prize you here as he has before, now that he is at home with his Lady mother."

"But I never presumed," said Judith. "He sent for me or I would not have come to ride beside him."

Yet still she shivered.

"Keep it in your mind he may never call again," said Will.

Judith started to protest, but Will hushed her. For as the company reached the gatehouse, out from the abbey came a thundering crowd of servants, swarms of men at arms with long pikes who stood at attention. And then a grouping of ladies, dressed all in splendid stuffs. And then the one lady who seemed to quiver alone in the space between the two tall towers as if her skirts were alive.

Sir Henry dismounted, strode forward with his sword tapping against his knee, and he knelt before this lady who touched her hands to his head in blessing.

"The Lady Southampton," Will whispered.

"Is it she then?" asked Judith.

Judith leaned forward in the saddle the better to see the Lady's face. Indeed, even from that distance there was a great resemblance between mother and son. Age had not dimmed the Lady's sparkling eyes nor splotched her skin, nor broadened her hips as it had Judith's own mother. Yet there was something about the Lady which gave Judith pause. Something which made her foolishly frightened.

Will began to laugh, quietly at first, then louder as he was joined by all the company. For Arthur had nosed Jasmine's head through the crowd until she stood side by side with Sir Henry's kneeling figure. Arthur had quickly dressed himself in the motley which he wore at Southampton House of an evening, and he sat forward in the saddle and began to pluck twanging, strident chords upon his lute. And when Lady Southampton had, after some degree of surprise broken into laughter herself, he began to sing.

> *"O mistress mine, where are you roaming?*
> *O mistress mine, where are you roaming?"*

The crowd grew quiet, and the lady stared silently up at him. Both lute and voice came together in consonance.

> *"O stay and hear your true love's coming,*
> *O stay and hear your true love's coming,*
> *That can sing both high and low.*
> *Trip no further, pretty sweeting;*
> *Journeys end in lovers meeting*
> *Every wise man's son doth know."*

When the applause ceased the lady's voice rang out in a strong treble, like a flute or an hautboy at the Theater.

"Welcome to Titchfield."

She waved her elegant hand and the company dismounted. Stable boys swarmed among them like bees, and every man began a rush of commands for the care of his horse. The gentlemen ushers gave up their horses first and proceeded toward the Lady Southampton, each bowing low before her.

And then Sir Henry called loudly for Will Shakespeare and for Master Richard. When they had come forward, he presented them courteously to the Lady mother.

"Lady," he said, "We have here the greatest poet in England, Will Shakespeare. And one that is like to be. His young brother, Richard."

The Lady mother smiled amiably, still holding tight to her son's wrist.

"Welcome to Titchfield," she said. "When we are settled and time permits, I shall expect to hear your poems. Or perhaps you would give us a scene from one of your plays."

Will bowed low.

"Nothing could make me prouder, Your Ladyship," he said.

Judith stood tongue tied. She could only bow profusely which she hoped would hide her blushes. But she was not to be let off easily.

"Sir Henry," said the Lady. "What name did you attach to this handsome lad?"

"Master Richard," said Sir Henry proudly.

"Ah," said Her Ladyship.

Judith's stomach churned yet more. For from that first moment, she was very sure that Lady Southampton knew the secret of her sex. Pray God she did not discover her attachment to Sir Henry.

It took some time to settle so large a company. Judith was given a small room next to her brother's chamber. It was neatly provided with all that Judith could need for her stay. There was a table set with papers and quills and ink pots, another table covered with a fine tapestry, a small bed with a beautifully woven cover. There was a carven cupboard where she could hang her clothing. And two chairs with embroidered cushions.

She was on her way to the window to see what sight might greet her there when she noticed the tapestry on the west wall. It pictured what seemed to be a baby boy with his hands filled with writhing snakes.

"It must be the young Hercules killing the serpents," she said. "And yet. . . ."

She took a step backward, away from the window, and when the light once more extended to the tapestry, she smiled at what she saw.

"Tis Sir Henry woven there," she said. "The very oval of his face. His eye. His lip. And he will be looking full at me all the while."

Judith had leaned forward to touch the face when a knock sounded at the door. She jumped back, and clasped both hands behind her.

"O," she said, "What if it is he?"

She ran her fingers through her hair and straightened her hose and pulled at her doublet.

"Enter," she said, as calmly as she could make herself.

The door opened and in strolled Arthur Amboid. He was strumming at the lute and humming softly.

"I am sent to entertain you," he said. "His Lordship is to be closeted with his Lady mother for some hours, and fears you will be despondent."

Arthur closed the door, and walked quickly to stand at her very nose.

"Judith love," he said in a loud whisper. "I feel it in my bones that the man knows your secret. I fear you will be undone."

"And why do you say that?" Judith replied.

"Ah," said Arthur, "A maiden blush. So then you know that he knows. It is to be wondered who else knows that he knows. Or does he perhaps know that he knows and yet knows not that he knows it?"

"Arthur, stop this foolishness. What business is it of yours what Sir Henry knows and does not know?"

"Ah, but, Judith love, we have put together quite a scene. I am sure it would play well to the stinkards. A great drama entitled, Does He Know That He Knows? I can see it now, Amboid and Shakespeare. Or would you insist on Shakespeare and Amboid?"

"The only thing I shall insist on is that you leave my chamber at once."

"But I am sent, Judith love. I cannot disobey my master."

"Then you can stop this foolish chatter. Speak sensibly or do not speak at all."

"Now what in all this vasty world and wild do I know that is sensible? I know that the nobility, mother and son, will dine alone in the mother's closet. I know that we, the upper servants are to pick daintily at a repast which shall be set forth in the gallery. And I know that your brother is even now standing at your chamber door ready to knock and enter."

The knock sounded.

"Did I not tell you, Judith love? I hope you will remember this in future and believe me when I pour my heart out to you."

Will was not pleased to see Arthur. He had prepared certain

sensible speeches to give to Judith on the subject of her relationship with Sir Henry. Will was in a precarious position. He had no desire to offend His Lordship. On the other hand he would not stand by and see his sister become a whore. For that would be the ending of it. Sir Henry would dally with her for a time, then put her away. After that, with no dowry, she would not be marriageable to anyone else. And so he looked stern, cleared his throat, and spoke his mind.

"Arthur, old friend, I must have private word with my sister."

"I hardly think that is possible, Will. Sir Henry has sent me to entertain, and to bring both of you to a small repast in the gallery. He will not be present, but we are to munch til we are full. Like the horses."

"We will be along anon. You go first and say we will be there."

"Ah, but can you find your way? I had a devil of a time finding my way to you, and I have spent most of my life in a castle."

"O come, Arthur," said Judith. "You have never spent a day in your life inside a castle like this."

"Judith love, you would be amazed where I have spent my days. But, since I am not one to tarry when my presence is unwanted, I shall go. And if you have not turned up in several days, I shall send Jasmine to find you."

He danced his way to the door, turned and bowed low.

"Anon," he said.

"Anon," said Will.

"What is this all about, Will? What do you have to say to me?" asked Judith.

"Judith, I scarcely know how to say this, and yet I feel I must. I have definite proof that Sir Henry knows you are a woman. No, do not speak now, but hear me out. This afternoon when Mammet came near to throwing you, I distinctly heard Sir Henry say, 'Look to her.' You, of course, heard nothing because of your predicament. Now I am sure he has said nothing to you, and perhaps he will not for a time. But. . .there will come an hour when he will. And you must prepare yourself for that hour. There is no need to antagonize him. You have only to be firm in your virtue. He is a good person at heart, and would not defile you against your will. But you must make him understand that you are a maiden and will remain so until God sees fit to send you a husband."

"Listen to me, Will Shakespeare, you are no man to talk to me about my maidenhead. With all that you have done. I am told that you and Anne were like animals under every hedge and ditch in Warwickshire. And now this Clarise. Don't think I did not understand why you sent me to sleep in a room on the third floor of the inn. She came to your room. You took her there in your very chamber."

"Judith, I forbid you to speak further. What I do is my business."

"And what I do is mine," Judith shouted back.

"Quiet. In heaven's name, do you wish to alarm the household? You have no idea of what you are saying. If you were to get yourself with child, I am sure Henry Wilcome would not have you. I am sure Father would not allow you to return home to Henley Street. And so it would be my responsibility. Do you see that? You are my responsibility."

"I can take care of myself."

"Judith, you try my patience sorely. If I did not love you, I would say to you, then do just that. But I do love you, and so I will say no more at this time. But watch for what I have told you. If you do see further evidence that Sir Henry knows your secret, let me know at once."

Judith nodded, hating the falsity. For she did love her brother. No matter that, she could not give up this new love which was to make her a true poet.

Will and Judith had no trouble finding their way to the gallery. However, Judith was somewhat awed at the passage. They went down corridors, up flights of stone steps. Past towers and chimneys. Arthur was pacing the floor when they arrived.

"The gentlemen ushers have come, eaten, and gone. I think they are more proud than Sir Henry. I think they do not enjoy the company of a fool and two players as he does."

"You may be right," said Will laughing. "The more for us without them."

But Judith had no more enjoyment in the company of Will and Arthur than the ushers did, and so she ate quickly, two wings from a fowl, a slice of fine bread and butter, and two sugary cakes. Then she interrupted them to say that she would retire to her chamber.

"Can you find the way?" Will asked. "We can call for a servant to lead you."

"I will be fine," she said.

And though Arthur launched into a tender love song, she went out immediately.

Judith was tired, and beside that, she was anxious for the morning when she hoped to see Sir Henry. And so, after taking a candle and standing close to Sir Henry's boyish face in the tapestry for some moments, she went to sleep.

She was awakened the next morning by a knock at the door. She sat up and called cheerfully that the caller should enter.

The door opened slowly, only part way, and then a serving maid appeared and slipped herself through the narrow opening. She was carrying a small tray of bread, butter, an apple, and a steaming mug of ale.

"I am sent with a tray for ye morning repast," the girl said. "Shall I serve ye, sir, or do ye be one to take matters in ye own hands?"

All out of breath from talking and from walking up flights of stairs, she went immediately to the covered table and set the tray down.

"Many thanks," said Judith. "I will serve myself later."

"Then I will go," said the girl. "But yet before I do, I have this question. I was told in the kitchen that you and your brother, and the fool too came to us from London. Is that true?"

"Yes," said Judith.

"Then in London, did ye ever see a half growed lad, likely the same age as you, of the name of Disby? I have reason to look out for that Disby, for he have run off from his word to me. Do ye know him?"

"No, I know none of that name."

"Yet if he be in London, it do seem to me ye would know Disby."

"Not at all, for there are too many people in London to know all of them."

"Yet ye knew Sir Henry. They say in the kitchen ye did."

"But that is different. All England knows The Earl of Southampton. Beside, Sir Henry made himself known to us at the Theater."

"Ay. They do say in the kitchen that in London he do naught but go to the plays. They say he do mingle amongst the players. And that do make him fantastical, and he do what he like no matter how the Lady mother do send message up to London. And they say he do not mean to marry the Lord Burghley's granddaughter that he is contracted by rights to have married this twelve month."

Judith swallowed hard.

"And why do they say Sir Henry will not marry her?" Judith asked wonderingly, for it was the first she had heard of the proposed contract.

"God knows," said the girl smoothing her dress down across a more than ample stomach, "but it is my careful thought he do like some other young lady."

"Do you think so?" Judith asked.

"Ay, but I know not which one. But if I hear, I will tell ye."

"Gentle thanks," Judith said, smiling.

"Well, I must be back to the kitchen," the girl said, "but if ye should ever see Disby, would ye tell him Nellie Quince back in Titchfield has need of him?"

"I will be sure to tell him if I see him, Nellie, but you must not count on that," said Judith.

"Then what am I to count on," asked the girl. "What am I to do?"

Nellie began to bawl loudly.

"Come now, Nellie," said Judith. "Stop this crying and tell me your problem."

"O Master Shakespeare, ye would not be wanting to hear of my problem."

"Of course I would. Now tell me. It might be that I can help you."

"There is no help but marriage, and that to Disby Warts. T'was his idea to go behind the buttery door and have at it. And no sooner than he finished, off he run to London. And now me belly is thrusting forth and it will surprise me much if it be not a baby. And what am I to do with a baby? I will be turned out to starve like many others before me."

"No, Nellie, I am sure if I have a word with Sir Henry. . . ."

"But the word need be spoke to the Lady mother, and she be a Christian that will have no traffic in sin. That is what she told Sallie Sly no more than two weeks ago."

"Still, I will do what I can. Now dry your eyes and go back to the kitchen."

"O thank ye, Master Shakespeare, and bless ye forever."

As soon as the girl had gone, Judith's brain began to whirl.

Marriage. What a hateful word was marriage. Human kind pressed to do what was abhorrent to them. And to think that Sir Henry was contracted to marry the granddaughter of Lord Burghley, the Queen's chiefest advisor. How could Sir Henry tell him no? For Sir Henry could not run off, change sex, nor find his heart's desire so easily as she had done.

Judith got up quickly, went to the table and took a piece of bread. It seemed that her confusion had made her hungry. She covered the fine slice in butter and chewed. And thought of poor Nellie whose belly was already protruding beneath her apron. How many weeks before the apron would no longer hide it?

"Damn that Disby, whoever he is," she whispered.

And once again, she vowed to die a virgin. She would love Sir Henry and write poems of her love. And she would write plays. And Sir Henry would be seated on the stage, his eyes following her about, for she would write longer roles for women and she would play them all. His ears would strain to hear her every speech. And she would smell the perfume of his scented gloves as she passed beside him. And sometimes their hands would touch. But that would be all. There would be no carnal traffic between them. But what if he were married to Lord Burghley's granddaughter? Od's Prittikins, she would not consider that such a thing was possible. No, they neither of them should marry.

She swallowed down the bread she had been chewing for this long time, and drank the ale. When she wiped her lips on the napkin provided, she could feel them puckered into a kiss. She smiled, still with her lips puckered in that kiss. And she walked shamelessly across the chamber to stand before the tapestry of the infant Hercules. Rising on tiptoe, she kissed his lips. Then she covered her face in her hands and sobbed.

When yet another knock sounded at the door, Judith flew to the bed and began to wipe at her tears with the coverlet.

"Enter," she called when she had felt her face and found it dry.

The door creaked open and in stepped the girl who had brought her to her chamber on the previous afternoon.

"Good day," she said, "and I do hope ye had a pleasant night of sleeping."

"Very well," said Judith.

"I am glad to hear that, Master Richard," replied the girl. "I have a message from the master. In simple it is that His Lordship do say that he will walk in the courtyard any time this several hour and would be pleased of ye company."

"Say that I shall be there shortly. But tell me, is my brother sent for?"

"He is sent for, but is not to be found."

"Not to be found? Did you go to his chamber?"

"To his chamber at first, but then I was told by one of the grooms that I might not bother to look. Your brother saddled his own horse in the middle of the night and rode out. To this hour he have not come back."

Judith shook her head wonderingly.

"You may tell Sir Henry I will be with him anon."

When Judith had dressed herself in the bright green doublet, and had combed her hair until it shone like gold, she retraced the previous day's steps to the gatehouse, motioned imperiously to the guard to stand aside and walked quickly to the back entrance and thus into the courtyard. As she walked, she had envisioned a greensward with a gravel path, and on that path, Sir Henry, alone, pacing slowly, thoughtfully, glancing often toward the arch where she would appear. What she found was a knot garden directly before her, shaped patterns of herbs and glowing flowers, with various hedges and a pleached allee of apple trees, and all of it filled with people. The twelve gentlemen ushers were playing a game of shuttlecock. The Lady mother and three of her women were seated halfway along the outer path on benches, one of them holding a shawl above the Lady mother's head to fend off the sun, the other two, as was the Lady mother, stitching at their embroidery frames.

Yet one part of her dream was true, for Sir Henry was there on the path amongst the flowers, walking and circling, so that when he saw her, he hastened his steps to meet her.

"Richard," he called. "For shame. You have slept away the day's best hours."

"I am sorry, Your Lordship. Yet here I am, ready to do you service."

"Come then, for my mother awaits you."

Judith bowed deeply before the Lady mother. Upon closer view, she still proved to be a great beauty, with that same oval face as her son. She was dressed in a simple morning gown and cap. And now, as she lifted her needle and paused in her work, she smiled a broad smile.

"Do not lecture the boy," she said to Sir Henry. "For a boy requires his sleep, does he not? How old would you be, Richard? My son had never thought to ask, he says, but I am full of questions."

"And I am full of answers," said Judith.

The company laughed and Judith had great hope this would suffice for the questioning. But it was not to be.

"What is your age?" the Lady Mother asked again.

"I am fifteen, Your Ladyship."

It was easily said, yet Judith was unnerved.

"Only fifteen?" the Lady continued. "Well, let it stand. But you must tell me where you were born and reared. What does your father do? Who was your mother? Have you other brothers and sisters? Have you been to school?"

"Mother," said Sir Henry. "You overencompass the lad. How should he remember what question to answer first?"

Yet memory was not the problem. Judith knew with exactitude the order and substance of all the Lady had asked. But she also knew that within these questions there lay a trap. She hesitated, and in that hesitation prayed for deliverance.

Will's smiling face was prayer's answer, he bowing low before the Lady mother, offering up some passages from his plays mixed into his speech, agreeing to read to her at any hour she chose, so that Judith appeared to be forgotten. She took this diversion to escape into a path which was hidden by a screen of apple trees. And soon she heard footsteps and turned to face Sir Henry.

"Dear one," he said, "I apologize for my mother's many questions. Yet I have many of my own. I would know your name above all. In my dreaming I have called you. . . ."

He broke off suddenly. And just as suddenly Arthur Amboid's head and shoulders appeared among the apples.

"Sir Henry," he said, "It is with great trepidation that I approach, yet I am sent. Tis true. Your Lady Mother is insistent that we begin our lesson on the lute. She is anxious to try it herself, and is insistent that you must begin and play what you have learned for her."

"In a moment," Sir Henry replied.

"She insists that you will come immediately."

"Very well. Then, Richard, what do you say to a ride through the countryside in the afternoon? There is much I would show you hereabout."

"You have only to send for me," she replied.

"Your Lordship," Arthur broke in. "I hear your Lady Mother calling you."

"I come," he said.

In spite of herself, Judith was entranced with the proceedings of the lesson. When Lady Southampton had tried to play for some moments and given it up because she said it hurt her fingers, Sir Henry said Richard must have a chance to learn.

"It will be useful in the theater," he said.

Arthur placed the lute in Judith's hands, and as he moved to show her how to hold it against her, he accidentally touched her breast. She frowned and pulled away.

"Master Richard," said Arthur, "You must learn to follow direction if you wish to play the lute. Now hold the instrument as I instructed."

And then he molded her fingers onto the strings, squeezing and rubbing them, even to her upturned palm. Judith squirmed and looked up at Sir Henry, thinking that he might intervene in her behalf. But he was overjoyed at the process, and was himself flexing his fingers and practicing the chords along with them.

In less than an hour, Judith was able to play a tune and accompany Arthur on several songs. And then Sir Henry, whose voice was not as fine as Arthur's but was nevertheless passable, insisted she should accompany him as well.

"We will have music between the scenes tonight. For my mother has asked that we hear something of your new play, Will. And Richard must read his best poems. Arthur, you can sing and accompany yourself. And you may play some several parts as well. You have told me of your skill at acting. Now you can show us."

"Excellent," said Lady Southampton. "And perhaps I may agree to favor the company with a song. Arthur, do you know Heart's Ease?"

"Indeed madonna," Arthur replied.

He began to play, his fingers moving quickly across the strings.

Yet in a moment he broke off.

"What am I thinking of? I am sure your Ladyship does not require rehearsal."

"And I am sure she does," the Lady replied. "Come to me in my closet at exactly four o'clock. Until then we will have a small repast, and then you and Richard and Will Shakespeare must spend your time in rehearsing."

"But Sir Henry and I were going to ride," Judith began.

Lady Southampton turned quickly to Judith. She frowned, then shook her head.

"Sir Henry has duties connected with the household. He has been long in London leaving me to manage on my own. I shall insist the afternoon be spent as I have suggested for each of you. Tomorrow is another day."

Judith looked once in Sir Henry's direction, but could not catch his eye. She glanced back toward his mother who was smiling now. But that smile, Judith thought was conditional on having her own way. If Judith should resist her, the frown would return. The anger would spill over. Judith was in too precarious a position to chance it.

"Tomorrow," Judith murmured, and allowed Will to lead her out of the warm sunlight of the courtyard and into the outer passage of the Abbey.

Will Shakespeare was in a mood to forgive the world, and so he did not lecture Judith on her outburst to the Lady mother.

Instead, he smiled absentmindedly, for his thoughts were too full of the Lady Clarise to consider anything else with any degree of attention. He could close his eyes and see her, naked on scented sheets, a smile playing on her lips. For hours they had lain together, he speaking often of leaving and she begging him to stay. At last, they had both slept, and when they woke, the sun was high in the sky and the household was awake. Will had climbed from her window, along the branch of a tall elm, and finally passing from limb to limb til he was close enough, had dropped to the ground. But he would do it again. Indeed, he planned it for that very night.

"Will," said Judith. "You have not heard a word I said."

"No, love, I have not. But speak again and I will attend you."

"I asked you why you rode out at midnight and where you have been so long."

"How did you know I rode out at midnight?"

"I had it of one of the maids. She had it of the stable boy. Or one of the grooms. Some such."

"It is a secret, my dear sister. A deep, dark secret."

Will laughed.

"Are you laughing at me? Indeed I think you are. But all the same, if you will not tell me where you went, I will discover it for myself."

"Very well. But I think you will have a hard task to discover it."

They walked in silence until they came to the door of Judith's chamber.

"Make ready now, for as soon as we have dined, we must begin our rehearsal," Will said.

"It is too lovely a day to be inside rehearsing," Judith replied. "I should sooner be riding across the downs to the seaside."

"Can my ears be hearing such words?" Will said and laughed aloud. "For a lad who desires above all the world to be a player, these are strange sounds indeed. Have you given up our noble profession?"

"No, Will, of course not."

"Then if you would be a player, you must be one at all seasons and hours. Let us not hear another word about riding across the downs to the seaside."

Will watched his sister until she had entered her chamber and closed the door. There was no doubt in his mind that this watching would need to be continued as long as they remained at Titchfield Abbey.

CHAPTER IX

Judith had no more than made her way across the room to the tapestry when she heard a clatter of footsteps and a small soft knocking at her chamber door.

"I pray it may not be Arthur again," she said, and ran to answer.

But before she had the door half open, she smelled the distinctly acrid odor of manure and stable straw. And when she saw the figure poised there, she slammed the door closed, full on the foot of the personage before her.

"If ye please, your playership, me shin is somewhat broke, and I would beg ye to let up to some small extent on me boot so that I may withdraw from the doorway."

She opened the door and in scarce an instant the lad, whose filthy boot had been pinned against the door jamb, leapt inside the room and stood quivering beside the trundle bed. A full view of him did not quiet her fears. He was a hefty, half grown boy with what looked like straw for hair and large, luminous eyes, a crooked nose and cheeks as pock marked as clabbered milk.

"What are you doing here?" Judith asked him. "Who gave you permission to wander the halls and enter chambers and who knows what else?"

"If ye would shut the door, ye playership, it would be pleasing to all, and I will make meself known to ye, for I have a somewhat delivery to make to ye."

"There is nothing in the versal world you could have which I want. Now remove yourself from this chamber or I shall call my brother who is in the next room."

"Do not do so, I beg ye. For I am sworn to secrecy, and if any should know I have come here. . .or what I have brought ye. . . ."

"I have told you plainly I can want nothing you might have about your stinking personage. . . ."

Judith broke off, for Snark had taken from his jerkin a white paper which he wafted about before his face.

"What is it?" she asked. "Where did you get it?"

She went to him, grabbed it from his hand and carried it to the window. A folded paper with a waxen seal. A tall W laced about with vines and flowers. A twin to the letter she had received from Sir Henry in London.

"You may go then," she said. "At once. My brother will later provide you a coin. I have none about me."

"No matter. I have been provided with more than coin. This very day I have been chosen to be personal groom to Sir Henry's horse as long as he is at Titchfield."

"That is all very well, but still you should not have thrust yourself upon me as you did. How could I know you were not some mad man sent to do me harm?"

"There be no mad men at Titchfield, Master Richard. And ye may be sure ye will see more of me beside, for Sir Henry says I have been chosen to carry letters and messages of importance for him."

"Very well," Judith said, still breathing heavily. "But for this time you may go. I will be pleased to see you whenever you come with letters in the future."

"I thank ye for that, ye playership. And I shall go at once."

Judith scarcely looked to see if the boy had closed the door. She went to her bed, settled herself against a cushion, then snapped the seal, tore open the letter and read quickly.

My Dearest unnamed one,

My heart flies toward your chamber though my dull steps are prevented by accounts and business. There is so much that I would ask you, so much that I do not know about you. And there is that which I would tell you beside. I will work diligently to settle the present business, and then I will come to you. Til then I keep you in my heart as I will soon hold you in my arms.

Yours,
Sir Henry Wriothesley

Judith hid the letter quickly inside her doublet. Her hands were trembling so that she could scarcely rebutton herself. She did not know what to make of this heart which flew toward her chamber. She had never considered that Sir Henry's heart should fly in her direction. She was prepared to love him, to gaze at him longingly, to talk to him, to entertain him, and in turn to smell the wafting scent of his gloves. But what would she do if he came to her, and in truth desired to hold her in his arms? Then Will was right. And Arthur. O Holy Mother of God, what was she to do?

The long gallery had been chosen for the night's performance, and so all through that afternoon as the shadows lengthened along the gray stone walls, Judith and Arthur and Will toiled to polish the selected scenes. Will had chosen to perform Sir Henry's favorite's from KING HENRY, VI, plus portions of scenes from his new play, KING RICHARD, III. Arthur was proving to be a well trained player. As good as Richard Burbage, Will thought. It was Judith who had spent the time haranguing Arthur and insulting him at every hand. And so Will had told Judith in simple words that he would bear no more. She must go behind the arras and await her entrance in Scene II. Arthur should have the stage to himself for the great opening scene in which King Richard declares his villainy.

"Now is the winter of our discontent
Made glorious summer by this sun of York," spoke Arthur.

Will had settled himself on a joint stool and was reveling in the sound of his own words on the tongue of this man who had so lately become his friend. Perfect intonation, Will told himself. A sense of true nobility. Will smiled and relaxed still further. But at this moment, Judith stepped forward from her place behind the arras and stood squarely before Arthur, spoiling Will's line of sight.

"You are much too fine and handsome to be King Richard," she told Arthur.

Will half rose to his feet.

"I thank you for the complement," Arthur replied.

"It was no complement," said Judith quickly. "I am right, am I not, Will? King Richard is to have a hump on his back, and is to be scowling and awesome. Arthur plays him as if he were a lover and not a great sinner and murderer."

"Judith," Will began, but Arthur cut him off.

"And who says that a great sinner and murderer cannot be handsome beside? How else am I to woo the Lady Anne in Scene II, and win her heart in scarcely a hundred words? Tell me that."

"You have a point there."

She turned to face Will.

"You know I have often told you, Will, that the lady allows herself to be won too easily. I know that I should never give my heart in such a sudden manner."

"Be sure you do not," said Arthur.

They stood glaring at each other while Will sighed with his head in his hands.

"Judith," he said. "Arthur. How can we present a program of scenes in three hours time when you stand about arguing? I have never before seen two such prima donnas. Yes, Arthur, I call you prima donna too."

"If I am to be allowed to proceed, I think I can make my performance speak for itself. It is my true judgement that Richard cannot have been so vilely deformed as you make him out to be. He is a soldier. A leader of men. I shall play him with only a suggestion of a hump which I need no bag of feathers to create. Retire, Judith, this moment. Watch and you shall see."

"Very well," she said. "I shall retire, but I am sure I will see nothing to my liking. And I will thank you both in future to remember that my name is Richard. Like the king."

The arras closed behind Judith and Will took his seat on the joint stool.

"Proceed, Arthur," said Will.

Arthur continued with his speech, and showed himself to be rudely stamped, curtailed of this fair proportion even as Will's words proclaimed him. The trace of a hump was there beneath Arthur's doublet. A hint of lameness. Will nodded his approval.

And Judith herself had no more to say about Arthur's imperfections. Indeed, in the second scene, when she played the role of Anne, widow of the murdered King Henry, she spit her poisoned words toward Arthur as she would have toward the devil himself. They thrust and parried with their charmed words until the time when Richard bared his breast and offered Anne his sword to kill him.

"Nay, do not pause: for I did kill King Henry-
But t'was thy beauty that provoked me.
Nay, now dispatch: t'was I that stabbed young Edward-
But twas thy heavenly face that set me on."

Judith let the sword fall from her hand. And knew within her heart that Arthur Amboid was the finest actor in all England. It was perhaps his lying soul that eased him so completely into whatever role he was asked to play.

"Take up the sword again or take up me," he continued.

Arthur bowed his head before her, then lifted his chin until he could see her face. His eyes glistened. His lips trembled.

Judith paused, and in that pause Will thought he saw. . .but no, twas only a play, and Judith was a player. When she spoke there was no venom in the venomous words.

"Arise, dissembler, though I wish thy death, I will not be thy executioner."

The performance was perfection. All that Will could ever have hoped for. And in a moment Judith spoke the words, "I would I knew thy heart," which was as much of the scene as any player could possibly memorize in one sitting. Even Judith.

"Bravo," said Will. "I would be glad to have the two of you play it on the stage in London. We will surely please Sir Henry and his Lady mother this night."

"But not too much," said Arthur, staring down at Judith. "I would not have Sir Henry know too great a pleasure on this night."

Judith blushed and could not speak.

Lady Southampton had graciously supplied Judith with costumes for the performance. She sent Nellie Quince with a parcel and a note in the Lady's own handwriting. For Master Richard Shakespeare was inscribed in large flowing letters. Beneath it, in letters so small that they required careful study were these words.

"I am sending several gowns which were left behind by a young girl who aspired to be one of my ladies. She was such a scrawny little thing that I have never seen another who could wear them. Perhaps you, Master Richard, could use one of them in the performance. And you may keep the rest. Something tells me you will have need of them very soon."

Judith shivered. She read the note over, then folded it and tore it, folded it and tore it until it was impossible that anyone could make out a single word.

The performance was a great success. All of Sir Henry's gentlemen ushers and all of Lady Southampton's ladies were there.

Some few trusted servants were allowed to peep through doorways, and many more disobeyed orders and watched from a tower window. There was applause after each scene, and when the performance was done, the assembly continued to clamor clap for some five minutes before Lady Southampton held up her hand to end it. She rose from her chair, and, when there was quiet, declared that she had never seen better on the London stage or in the performances at court.

"And now," she said, "Let us have refreshment. I am sure our players are in need of wine to comfort their most excellent throats and voices."

Tables were brought in and filled with wines and cakes and fruits and nuts. Judith took only a glass of wine. She was too weary to think of eating. And when Arthur brought a stool, she sat down gratefully and smoothed her skirts and rested her back against the stone wall.

Sir Henry waited upon his Lady mother, bringing her a glass and some several cracked nuts and a sliver of cake. She sat too, and looked around until she discovered Judith across the room. She frowned for a moment, then looked up smiling. When she was sure she had the attention of the group, she laughed aloud then spoke in a loud voice.

"One would almost believe," she said, "that Master Richard is, in truth, a young lady. I scarcely see how a lad could hold himself so, or how he would know the emotions he has so clearly expressed."

Sir Henry looked stunned for a moment, then rushed to speak.

"Years of training, mother," he said. "It takes years of training to equip these lads."

"But I was given to believe that Richard had arrived in London no more than a month ago. What say you to that?"

"I say he is a genius. Even as his brother is a genius with the pen," Sir Henry replied.

"And what do you say, Arthur Amboid?" asked Lady Southampton. "You have had great experience on the stage, or so you have said. And I can well believe it since I have watched your performance. What do you think accounts for the womanly qualities which Richard shows?"

Arthur swallowed down a glass of wine, chewed frantically at a mouthful of cake, then replied.

"Womanly qualities, Your Ladyship? I see no womanly qualities. Master Richard is a scrawny, pasty faced boy. I am sure that no male would see in him any womanly qualities to be desired. No, Lady Southampton, it is your natural goodness and sympathetic nature that draws you to see womanly qualities."

Arthur set down his glass and began to dance a jig, all the time playing a fast tune on the lute until the whole company began to laugh and to clap in time with the rhythm. And in the upheaval that followed, he jounced past Judith and whispered into her very ear.

"Write it down, my sweeting. I have saved your hide again. And I shall expect thanks in future."

"Thanks?" Judith whispered. "Thanks for an insult?"

"But all the same an insult which might, and only might save you. Judith, I tell you, you must. . . ."

Arthur broke off and began to sing once more. A bawdy tune which should have brought a blush to Lady Southampton's cheeks, but instead brought laughter to her lips. He was joined in song by all the company except Judith and Sir Henry who stood staring toward one another wonderingly. And in the melee Sir Henry slipped a letter into Judith's hand. She clenched her fist around it and felt the seal break inside her fingers.

"You were wonderful tonight," Sir Henry said. "I could feel the Lady Anne's very presence in your enactment. And I could feel her confusion even as I see it now in your eyes. Do not be afraid of me, little one."

"I am not afraid."

"Then be not confused neither. But I may not speak more at this moment. Later. I will come to you. Or I will send for you. In any case, do not disappoint me."

"No, Your Lordship," Judith said. "I will never do that."

It was not long before the Lady mother announced that she would retire and that she thought it best that all the company should disperse to their separate chambers. Will was glad to go because he was anxious to be on his way to visit Clarise. Judith went with him quickly, she tired to the bone on the one hand, and on the other anxious to see what message Sir Henry had sent her.

Yet she was scarcely inside her chamber with the door fast closed when there came a knock.

"You may enter," she called, atremble that it might be Sir Henry.

But it was Arthur, dressed still in the kingly robes he had worn to play Richard.

"Ah, Judith love," he said when he had closed the door behind him. "I was fearful that you would not sleep well this night unless I had come to tuck you in. Quickly. Out of your dress. Hop into bed."

"And that I shall not. Arthur Amboid, what has got the matter with you? You have been acting strangely these last days, even for you. I am perfectly able to undress myself and get to bed. But not as long as you stand about gawking."

"You were wont to sleep most soundly in my presence."

"But that was before you discovered I was a. . .a woman."

"Do not women sleep?"

"Not with men. That is, they do sleep with men, those that are married do. O, Arthur, you know what I mean. I am so tired from all this rehearsing and performing, I scarce know what I am saying."

"Then go to bed."

"I have every intention of doing just that when I am finally rid of you."

"But you will read your letter first I take it?"

"What letter?"

"The letter you presently crush inside your dainty little hand. Judith, do not think that you may keep secrets from me. I am your friend. You seem to forget it from time to time."

"And you seem to forget it also. After what you said about me tonight. I am not pasty faced."

"Did I say that? Ay God, Judith love, I am sure I never did. But let that pass for now. Off with your dress."

"Arthur Amboid, I have had enough of this foolishness. Leave my chamber at once. Out, I say."

"Ah, but, Judith love, if you had only said this before, I would have known your mind on the subject. How can I know your mind if you do not speak it to me? Of course I shall go."

Arthur threw back his shoulders and proceeded toward the door, striding like the king he had portrayed. When he had opened it and was half outside in the corridor, he turned his head over his shoulder and looked stern.

"Judith, I beseech you, and now I am playing no part, speaking no foolish lines. For the rest of this night, say that you will not leave this chamber. And say that you will allow no one to enter. Say it, Judith."

"I shall do as I like," she told him. "It is no business of yours."

Arthur groaned.

"Judith love, if only you knew my true business."

It was well past midnight when Judith heard a second knock on the door. And all this time she had sat waiting, still dressed in the fine silk gown in which she had played the Lady Anne. In spite of herself she had felt a certain pride in the way she knew she must look. The rise of her breasts which were made prominent by a small pocket of bombast. The narrowness of her waist above the widening of the farthingale. Yet for all this she trembled at the sound of the knocking. Sir Henry's letter had said that he would send for her this night. That he would receive her in such a chamber that there would be no interruptions as had been in the past. Her mind was all in six directions concerning the answer she must make.

The knocking sounded again, insistently.

"Come in," Judith said.

A maidservant she had not seen before stepped into the room.

"Master Shakespeare," she called out briskly. "Master Richard Shakespeare."

"Yes?" answered Judith.

There was but one candle lighted in the room besides the one the maidservant brought with her. They could not see each other clearly. Yet when the girl pinched her face into a frown, Judith looked down into her silken lap and smiled.

"I am Richard Shakespeare," she said. "It is only that I have not changed out of my player's clothing. But you may give me your message."

"I am sent from the master," the girl said, still frowning. "I am to bring ye to him in the library."

"Very well. I am ready."

Judith reached for the candle beside her on the table.

"No," said the girl. "Ye must take no candle. Mine is to be the only light. And ye must stick close to me too, else ye shall be lost about in the darkness."

"I see no reason that I cannot provide myself with a candle," Judith said.

"Nor do I. But that is all as nothing. The master says ye shall have no candle and so ye shall have none."

The girl led Judith through winding ways, up many stairs she had not known before for she had ventured through the house no further than the gallery.

"This way," whispered the girl. "And ye must be more quiet now as we pass beside the mistress' chamber."

They walked on, Judith slightly behind. Until they came to another tower, another stair, and here the girl stopped.

"Tis at the top of this stair," she whispered. "A lovely room the master uses for his books and pictures and such. Go on, lad."

"But I have no candle. How am I to make my way?"

"I am to light ye up the first steps. After that ye will see an abundance of light pouring down from the room above. Go on. Ye shall see it is as I told ye. I hope ye be not a fearful sort."

"Indeed I am not a fearful sort. Do not worry about me."

And so Judith was forced to pull her skirts up around her knees and begin the climb into the darkness. She had not gone far, however, when, true to the maidservant's words, light flooded the stairs and she moved quickly to a landing and into a glowing chamber.

When Judith's eyes had become accustomed to the brightness of the room, she saw Sir Henry, his figure gleaming as bright as candle flame in gold velvet breeches and doublet. His sword flashed as he took a step toward her.

"Come hither, boy," he said. And smiled a knowing smile.

Judith could not move. She felt in some ways as if she were made of lead and so her body would obey no impulse. In other ways she felt as if she were made of air, and was already floating invisibly around the ceiling.

"Are you afraid then?"

Sir Henry laughed aloud.

"Surely you cannot fear me. What hours we have spent together, you and I. And I have thought I knew your mind from the content of your poetry. And from certain looks I have noted in your eye."

Judith nodded. She could not speak. She could not smile for she did not know her mind. It seemed to her that no man should be as handsome as he now appeared to her.

"Here," said Sir Henry as he took her hand and led her to a kind of daybed on the far side of the tower room. "Sit down and we will talk. I have as many questions as my Lady mother had of you this morning."

Judith was glad to sit, for now her legs were trembling so that she could scarcely stand.

"First of all, you must tell me your name. I have dreamed of many names for you. And it is to be. . . ."

"Judith," she said.

"Judith. Of course. What else could it be but Judith? Of all the names it best becomes you. And what is your age?"

"I am eighteen," she said.

"And how did you come to read and write? I am given to understand that women of the lower orders do not generally read. Does your mother read and write?"

"No, she does not. But still she is an Arden, and is not so low as you might think."

"O, Judith, have I offended you? I did not mean to do so. It is just that I want to know everything about you and I have no idea of how to ask. I cannot imagine what your experience could be."

"I am not offended. Indeed, you cannot know. But my brother taught me to read when I was but five years old, and I have loved reading more than life itself. I have never owned a book, but there were those in Stratford who would lend me what they had. And Will has let me read his few books. And I have read his plays and sonnets since I can remember."

She seemed not to be able to stop talking once she had started. Sir Henry stood beside her, enthralled.

"I had not been able to read very long when I wrote a poem too. And Will praised me and told the schoolmaster about it. And then the word got out and all of Stratford knew that I had written a poem, and in a few days many could quote it from memory. Which made my father angry and he said I must write no more poems. But I never desisted for a moment. From time to time he would discover that I still wrote and would lock me in my room, or set Old Sallie to watch me."

"And who is Old Sallie?"

"Old Sallie is our cook who came with my mother from Asbyes which was the name of my mother's home in the country. But

Old Sallie never stopped me. In truth, she hid my poems for me beneath the settle in the kitchen. And when I was locked inside the cupboard. . . ."

"Locked in a cupboard? Why should you ever be locked inside a cupboard?"

"Because. . . ."

"Why, dear Judith? You must tell me."

"Because I would not marry a rich old man so to repair my father's fortune."

"I am very glad that you did not," Sir Henry said.

He leant down to her and took her hands in his. She was instantly on her feet, the two of them now quite close together.

"I shall not hurt you, Judith," he said.

"No, Your Lordship," she said at last. "I never thought so."

And lifted her face up toward him as tall as she could make herself.

"You are as fair in looks as your pen can write."

"My thanks, Your Lordship."

"What present would you have from me?"

"No present, Your Lordship."

"No money, jewel, no velvet cloak?"

"No, Your Lordship. I have no need of such as that. I have no desire except to write poems and plays as fine as my brother does."

"Perhaps you may do that, Judith, if you will let me help you."

Judith had no answer to this. She could think of nothing except Sir Henry's palm laid tight against hers, and the cinnamon smell of his breath as he leant close to her.

"First I shall present you with a gift I am sure you do want. Close your eyes, Judith. And stand very still. It will take only a moment to retrieve it."

Judith closed her eyes and waited, and while he was gone she somewhat recovered herself and began to be sorry she had allowed herself to be led here. Why had she not told the maidservant that she was too tired? Why had she not undressed and gone to bed as Arthur said she should? She opened her eyes even as Sir Henry approached.

"I said that you must close your eyes," Sir Henry teased. "There, that is better. Now. Hold out your hands. Very good."

She could feel a soft weight resting on her hands.

"Now you may open your eyes," he said.

When Judith looked down at her hands, she gasped.

"Ay God," she said.

Sir Henry laughed aloud.

"Do you like it?"

"O, I have never seen such a thing. Is it a book? Truly? And bound in velvet? And what? A clasp of gold?"

"Yes, Judith, it is all this. And do you not want to know the title of the book?"

"I do indeed, but I am too consumed with the binding at present to think of the contents."

"But it is an English translation of Ovid's *METAMORPHOSIS*. Have you heard your brother speak of it?"

"O, yes. Will talks of it and uses it for his stories all the time. O, Sir Henry, how can I thank you?"

"You have no need to thank me, Judith. You shall never need to thank me. I want to do so much for you," he said.

He smiled gently down at her, then touched his hand to her hair.

"It shines like gold itself," he said.

And then he touched her cheek. Her eyes. Her lips. All with the points of his fingers so that fire raced through her body and she thought she would lose her breath.

"O, Judith," he said. "Your tender lips."

And then he matched his own lips to hers. And forced her mouth open so that his tongue played at her teeth. And entered them.

And then her own hands raised without her knowing and clasped his body against hers. And she thought no more, but pressed herself ever harder against him, and gasped as he did as she felt his hand touch her throat and begin to rub in tiny circles toward her breasts.

"Dearest one," he moaned.

And then he straightened himself and stepped back. And brushed at his doublet and pulled his sword belt flush to his side.

"Who is it?" he called. "I say who is it on the stairs?"

"Only me," came a voice from below. "Do I have permission to attend you, sire? I come with an important message."

"Important?" asked Sir Henry. "At this time of night?"

Sir Henry walked to the stairs and looked down.

"O, tis you, Arthur. You look a fright. Has something untoward happened?"

"May I approach?"

Judith recognized the voice of the faltering old man, the voice she had heard so many weeks before when they were begging for food on the road to London.

"Tis late, sire, but a terrible act has been committed here at Titchfield, and I felt you should know immediately."

"Come up, Arthur, and tell me. Tis only Richard here with me. We neither could sleep and so I asked him to recite me his poems."

Arthur bounded up the stairs. Judith could hear his feet click on every step. He flew into the room like a madman, staring about him, tearing at his hair. When he had seen her, looked her over from top to toe, he smiled.

"Master Richard," he said. "I am glad it is only you. For I have a terrible tale to tell. Some conspiracy, I am sure. I feel it in my bones."

"What, Arthur, what? Speak, man," said Sir Henry impatiently.

"I fear some heads may roll for this, Your Lordship. For when the servants get out of hand. . . ."

He paused as if he could not get his breath.

"Arthur, for God's sake," Judith hissed.

"In short, Your Lordship, a messenger has come to you from the queen, arrived a little after midnight. And, here is where your temper will flare, Sir Henry, the stable grooms took it upon themselves to circumvent the message until you should arise in the morning. But here it is. I have brought it."

Arthur bowed low and presented the letter. When Sir Henry had it in his hand, he shook his head and frowned.

"This is not from the queen," he said impatiently. "Tis from Lord Burghley."

"How was I to know," Arthur said. "I am an ignorant fool. Forgive me, sire."

"Very well," said Sir Henry. "But it could well have waited til morning. He asks me to attend him at Theobalds. He says the queen is there and would have words with me."

"Then you must go, sire. Immediately," said Arthur.

"Indeed, I must, first thing in the morning."

"And it is morning, sire. The servants are up. Fires rage on the kitchen hearth. Here, go quickly, sire, to your chamber, and catch a brief nap. I will see Richard to his own chamber. Think of nothing further. Tis in my hands."

"Many thanks then. I am off. But you must come to me when I have slept, for I shall require your attendance on the journey."

Sir Henry pushed past Arthur and was out of sight. He had not looked once in Judith's direction.

CHAPTER X

Judith stood at her chamber window and watched them ride out. Sir Henry on Chantene, the twelve gentlemen ushers, a number of servants on horseback, a small wagon of Sir Henry's belongings, and bringing up the rear, Arthur Amboid and Jasmine.

Judith had not slept at all. She had stood at the window, watching for daylight, had then watched on until the riders came in sight. She could think of nothing except Sir Henry. What did it all mean? She had brought the bound velvet book with her when she and Arthur had crept down the tower steps in fear of their lives. For Arthur had insisted on snuffing all the candles, not remembering to leave the one he had brought with him burning. And so they had clung to each other and felt their way along the walls, stepping cautiously, counting steps. For Arthur swore he knew how many steps led to the tower. And he had not after all. They had fallen in a heap down the last two.

At least she could take comfort in the fact that Arthur was to be seen riding off to Theobalds. Pray God he would never return. Pray God she would never see him again. As for Sir Henry, she could come to no decision. She rubbed the velvet book cover and remembered his honied words. His kiss that had left her with a soreness in her upper lip. Another way that she could know the meeting was real, that she had not dreamt it, nor constructed it in her mind to be a play. Yet how could he leave her without a word? Without a glance in her direction?

She heard a sound, more like scratching than like a knock at the door. She walked slowly, turning her head, then faster and smiling for she had begun to smell a familiar odor. It had to be Snark, sent from the stables with a message. She threw open the door.

"Master Richard," Snark whispered. "If I might come in for just the moment, I would give ye. . . ."

"Come in. Quickly. Give me the letter, and then you may go just as quickly."

"But I have none. There were no time for a second letter, which, if I may tell ye, Arthur Amboid made away with the first one. It were not my fault, and I pray ye may tell Sir Henry when ye see him."

"What are you telling me? Do you mean to say that Arthur Amboid has stolen my letter?"

"Not stolen so much as that his horse, Jasmine ye know, was said to have eat it. Twas a natural mistake. Arthur said so. But for all that, I think His Lordship was in some ways angry with him."

"In what ways?"

"In the ways that he told Arthur to ride at the back of the company and not to come in his eyesight til they arrived at Theobalds."

"Od's Prittikins. Still, you do have a message by memory, do you not?"

"That I do, Master Richard, though it do not in all ways make sense to me."

"No matter. Recite it to me."

Snark cleared his throat, and stared straight ahead, his eyes unblinking.

"There was no time to write, and no. . .no. . .Lord, I have lost the word but I think Sir Henry said that he had no privy to write it in. Could that be it?"

"Privacy, yes, but go on."

He cleared his throat again and once more stared off into space, his brows tight together.

"Ye must remain at Titchfield til I send further word. Do not lose faith in me."

"Go on."

"I think that were all. He did say that he had more he needed to tell ye, but doubted me wit to remember it. But that be all he left directly to my speaking."

"And for this I thank you. If you should receive another message. . . ."

"Now that be the very thing, Master Richard. His Lordship did say that he would send further message, but he did not say that I should tell you that directly. I am a man for following orders, and I would say no more, no less than I was told."

"Thank you, Snark. You may go now. But if there is further

message, could you bring it to me privately? I would not wish my brother to know."

"And isn't it your brother who asked me not to tell you nor no man that he rides out every night at midnight and comes in by dawn? So I have promised him that I will tell not a soul."

"Yet I am grateful that you have told me."

"I will tell no other, I can promise ye."

"Very good, Snark."

"Now I will be off, ye playership. But I have no doubt I will be returning soon with news."

"I pray you may be."

Will Shakespeare had slept no more than Judith, beside which, he had greatly exerted himself in his lovemaking with the Lady Clarise. When he had reached his chamber, late again, he had thrown himself across the bed, fully clothed, and was nearing sleep when he heard a knock at the door. A firm, loud knock which he knew would persist until answered.

And it was no ordinary maidservant either. It was Lady Southampton's young cousin, just come to her from Beaulieu.

"Master Shakespeare," she said severely. "Lady Southampton would have a word with you. I am to bring you directly to her closet."

Will bowed.

"If I might make myself presentable. . . ."

"You are presentable as you are. Her Ladyship has much business this morning, and says she must relieve herself of this first."

"I am Her Ladyship's most humble servant," Will replied.

He followed her in silence through the corridors and up the stairs. When the girl stopped and knocked, Will quickly brushed at his doublet, his hair. And thought to sniff to see if Clarise's perfume still lingered about him.

"Enter," came Lady Southampton's voice.

Lady Southampton was seated at a small table. She was reading over numbers in an account book, and did not pause till she had finished out the line. She closed the book, pushed it from her and turned toward Will and the girl.

"You may go, Emillee," she said. "I have words for Will Shakespeare's ears alone.'

When the girl had gone out, Will stepped closer, and bowed deeply.

"You may stand as you are," the Lady said.

Will straightened himself and smiled.

"I suppose you have heard that my son has been summoned to Theobalds by Lord Burghley."

"No, Your Ladyship, I had not. I hope there is no cause for concern."

"None whatever. The queen wishes to see him. And Lord Burghley too. And I hope I may count on your service concerning this same matter, Will Shakespeare."

"In all things, I am your servant," Will replied. "You have only to speak the word."

"Very good. Now. I have noted since your arrival at Titchfield that you have great influence over my son. He seems to think that if a thing is written in your poems, it is then truth eternal."

"You do me too much honor," Will said.

"I do you no honor at all. I speak what is there to see. And there is another matter which is there to see if one but looks. You do not have a young brother named Richard."

"But, Your Ladyship, I swear I do."

"Then if you do, he is not here at Titchfield. That person who calls herself Richard Shakespeare is in truth a woman. I am not blind though my son thinks I am. Now what is her name?"

"But, Your Ladyship. . . ."

"What is her name?"

"Her name is Judith. But I beg you not to divulge her secret. It would go hard with her if you did."

"I am not a cruel person. I have no wish to harm the girl. I only wish to set the record straight for here and now. When she has left Titchfield, she may be anyone she chooses. But for as long as she remains here, she is to be Judith Shakespeare. And she is to wear the clothing I gave her for costumes. Is that clear?"

"It is clear to me, Your Ladyship, but I am not sure about my sister. My sister is not easily managed. She has a mind of her own."

"And so have I. She will do as I say. And so shall you. And I say that you must remain here at Titchfield for some weeks. And while you are here, you must write poems to the effect that my son must marry, and that he must marry no other than the Lady Elizabeth Vere, Lord Burghley's granddaughter. Do you understand?"

"I shall endeavor to do all that you ask me. But, I think there is no assurance that Sir Henry will heed my words."

"That is a chance I take. Something must be done to get the boy in hand. He is young and frivolous. He does not consider his own good. I will provide all the writing materials you could possibly need for yourself, and for your sister. But you must remain here until I decide you may leave. Are we agreed?"

"In truth, Your Ladyship, I would be glad to remain until the summer is over and the plague subsides. After that, I must return to London. It is my living. I have no choice but to be there."

"Much can happen before the summer's end. I think we are agreed."

Will bowed deeply, then waited to be dismissed.

"There is one other matter. I will not try to stop you from riding out at midnight. But you must be careful that no one besides me knows where you go."

Will blushed deeply.

"Leave me now. But I will expect regular deliveries of your poetry. We must have a volume of them written before my son returns."

Judith was remarkably quiet when Will told her of Lady Southampton's commands.

"Very well," she said. "I will change to a dress as soon as I finish my writing."

Yet Will thought Judith had scarcely heard him so deeply was she involved in her composition.

"What are you writing, Judith?" he asked.

"I am working over my play, the one I told you about. The one about the lovers whose families were dread enemies."

"O yes. The one you took from Brooke's poem. *ROMEO AND JULIET.*"

"Yes, and if you would leave me now, I would be most grateful. My brain is full of poetry this morning, and I must unload it before I drop to sleep. I slept not a moment last night, Will."

"Nor I."

"Then were you with the Lady Clarise?"

"What do you think?"

"I think you were. And wait. Before you go. I must ask you this. When a man is making love to a woman, what does she do?"

"What do you mean?"

"I mean does she always wait until he kisses her? And does she never touch his body as he touches hers?"

"Judith. What questions. I am sure you have no need to know such matters."

"And I am sure I do. How can I write of lovers if I do not know how they make love?"

"On the stage, Judith, as you well know, there is no touching. There is no kissing. Loving is done through spoken words. That is all you need to know. Concentrate on your words, Judith."

"I think there is no fault to be found in my words. I was only wondering how it is to love someone."

Will looked at her curiously.

"In good time," he told her.

If he had not been asleep on his feet, he would have questioned her further. As it was he left her with her head bent low over the paper and her hand racing the letters across the page.

When Judith had written all that her brain contained for that day, she put away her writing materials and rose from the table. She removed her doublet and breeches, and folded them away carefully in the carven cabinet. She took out a blue silk bodice with frog closings. And a matching skirt. She put on the skirt, let it slide noisily down her hips to the floor. She closed the frogs together. And looked down at herself. "You are as lovely as your pen can write," Sir Henry had said. Could it be possible? "A pasty faced lad," said Arthur.

There was a small framed mirror on the chest. She ran to it, took it down, and gazed at portions of herself, one after the other as she moved the mirror up and down her body. She ended at her face.

"Ay God," she said. "I am white as a snowflake. And my eyes are bloodshot. My forehead wrinkled. My cheeks sagging. Then Arthur is right. Pasty faced."

She moved the mirror to show her narrow waist, then up to her breasts made firm and high with bombast. And shook her head.

"Words," she said. "Words."

She went back to the table and picked up her manuscript. She flipped the pages til she came to the passage she sought.

"Love is a smoke raised with the fume of sighs;
Being purged, a fire sparkling in lovers' eyes;
Being vexed, a sea nourished with lovers' tears.
What is it else? A madness most discreet,
A choking gall, and a preserving sweet."

Judith put the manuscript on the table, and stood for some time staring intently at Sir Henry's face in the tapestry.

"When I have slept," she said, "I will know my mind."

Judith was wrong. Neither sleeping nor the passing days lessened the turmoil in her thoughts. She worked constantly at her play of *ROMEO AND JULIET*; she read her velvet bound book. The world, she came to think, was filled with lovers. Lovers who would die for each other. Lovers who pined away when parted. Lovers who scarcely breathed air. And she, if truth be told, was content to sit day after day at a table filled with fresh paper and sharp quills and a charming small pot which always was filled with ink. But was it enough? Was there true greatness here? She redoubled her efforts.

In time Romeo came to have Sir Henry's face, to speak with his elegant inflections. Judith tried valiantly to turn herself into Juliet, or else Juliet into herself. What did Juliet feel for Romeo? What did Judith feel? Relentlessly she asked herself that question, what did she feel? How could she not love a man so handsome, so noble? Ah then, so she must. She did. She surely must love Sir Henry.

She would take up the pen and try again to rework the words she had written so long ago in Stratford.

"Give me my Romeo; and when he shall die,
Take him and cut him out in little stars,
And he will make the face of heaven so fine
That all the world will be in love with night."

These were the very words she had spoken to Arthur Amboid to convince him that Will Shakespeare was her brother. He had said, "None other. None other than Will Shakespeare could have written such." Judith smiled, remembering Arthur's voice. "What woman could love me, Judith?" he had asked her. "What woman?"

Judith stood up abruptly, upsetting the ink pot.

"Ay God," she said. "What a mess I have made."

She ran quickly to call for a maidservant to clean the ink spots. Then off she ran to the stable. She would have Snark saddle Mammet. She would ride across the fields until she was so tired that she would hear no more voices, til she had ceased to consider what manifestations love could make.

One evening at sunset a messenger rode in. Judith had seen the lone rider from her chamber window, and so she had run with all speed toward the stable there to intercept him. But the message was for Will. James Burbage had written from London to say there had been no new cases of plague in several weeks, and that Will and Judith were needed for the new season. Will was pleased with the idea because only the night before, Clarise had told him she would be leaving in two days time to return to the court at Nonesuch.

"The danger of plague is past, Will," she had said, "and I would fear to lose my place at court. But you must come too. It is time you were at work on plays of love and heart's ease."

Will had gone straight to Lady Southampton with a sheaf of poems, all proclaiming the joys of marriage and the duty to procreate.

"Excellent," the Lady mother had told him. "And in truth, I think you must go. I will be returning to London myself by the end of the week."

She shook the sheaf of papers at him.

"I will present you a purse on the day of your departure. You have done well. Now, all I ask is that you take your sister in hand, and keep her as far from Sir Henry as possible."

"We are agreed in that, Your Ladyship. I am hoping to be able to send her on to Stratford as soon as we get to London."

"Be sure you do."

Lady Southampton spread the poems across the table, counting as she worked.

"A round dozen," she said. "I am grateful to you. Now, go and make ready for your journey."

"With all my heart," Will replied.

Judith made no protests about the return to London. On the

contrary, she seemed glad to go. She packed away her dresses, dressed herself in doublet and hose, and insisted that, once again, Will should call her Richard.

"What should I do about this book?" she asked him. "Sir Henry gave it to me, but I cannot help thinking it is too fanciful to belong to me."

Will took it in his hand.

"Sir Henry gave you this? Why did you never tell me?"

"Because you were too busy with the Lady Clarise. I have read it through four times, and I do love the words of it, but I think I would prefer a plainer binding. It makes me think that the binding is prized above the content."

Will handed the book back to her. He studied her face carefully. What was in her heart? She had not so much as spoken Sir Henry's name to him for several weeks until she told him of the book. Should she perhaps leave the book, leave remembering him? Still it was a splendid book. It was worth twenty pounds at the least.

"You say he gave it to you?"

Judith nodded.

"When?"

Judith blushed, and Will's heart sank.

"Judith, what was the occasion? Pray God it was not in payment for favors."

"Will, you have a lascivious mind. Can you think of nothing but lovemaking? I am a virgin still, and shall remain so. Sir Henry told me he wanted to help me to write my plays and poems. He said he wanted to do many things for me. And so he gave me the book. And now that I think of it, I shall keep it. You may say no more on the subject. And from this moment, I am Richard again. I am an apprentice with James Burbage's company, and if you do not like it, you may have no more to do with me."

"Judith, dear sister, I shall most certainly have more to do with you. Calm yourself. Take the book if you like. Be Richard if you like. For a time. But there must be an end to all this one of these days. You know that."

"I know many things, Will Shakespeare, but that is not one of them. Now. I have packed my box, so let us be off."

"I follow you, my general."

Judith rode out from Titchfield Abbey with the same confusion of mind she had been afflicted with for the past weeks. She was glad to return to London and the Theater. Yet now that she was actually leaving, there was part of her which desired to remain until a message came from Sir Henry.

"Snark," she had said to the boy as they were leaving the stables. "You must promise to send me word in London if a message comes to me from His Lordship."

"Ye can count on that. I am one to deliver messages as I follows orders. In sooth, I have devoted me life to following orders and delivering messages. Still there is one thing which I do find troublesome, ye playership."

"And what is that?"

"How some-ever ye turns yeself from a boy to a girl and back, I know not," said the lad. "Still I wish ye good luck as either or both."

"Thank you, Snark. And I do thank you for all that you have done in my behalf. I hope I may see you again."

One further thing Judith had done before they rode out. She had left Will in conference with Lady Southampton and gone in search of Nellie Quince.

"Nellie," she had said. "I am off to London. Now stop whimpering. What I am telling you is that I will ask for your friend among all my acquaintances. And if I find him, I shall surely tell him where his duty lies."

Judith marveled that Nellie's stomach had grown to such proportions in these several weeks since she had seen her.

"O, Master Richard, take me with you. I know I shall be turned away to starve within the week. I have swore that I am swole with gas from eating green apples, but I think Her ladyship do not believe me."

"There is no way I can take you with me, but I have a friend who can do anything he chooses, find out anything, and I am sure find anybody."

"Do ye mean the fool Arthur Amboid?"

"Well. . .yes. I do."

"Lord, Master Richard, what a pretty gentleman. I am sure some lucky woman may hope to secure him to herself some day."

"I know nothing about that," Judith said. "But when I see him, for I am sure he will be in attendance to His Lordship, I will broach the subject of Disby Warts."

"Bless ye, Master Richard. And if Arthur do not find him but do find some other willing lad, send him. I am after a husband any way I can. Do ye see? Do ye see that I need one?"

"I do see, indeed, I do, and I shall do my utmost to find your baby's father. And now I must be off. My brother awaits me."

Will and Judith arrived in London in three days time, late on a Monday afternoon. The streets looked much as they had left them except there were no death carts, no bells tolling constantly for the dead. They were welcomed warmly at the inn. Mistress Farley came out from the kitchen to hug them both. John Farley presented them with a bottle of his best wine. And Jennie ran eagerly to help Judith with her box, insisted that she should help with carrying it to the third floor to Judith's room.

When they were out of hearing of the others, she leaned close to Judith's ear and whispered.

"O, Master Richard, have you seen aught of Arthur Amboid?"

"No," said Judith, out of breath from the weight of the box. "No. I have seen nothing of him since he rode out from Titchfield some four weeks ago. And pray God I do not."

"O, Master Richard, why would you say such a thing? I pray daily at the church that he may return to. . .us."

"Then may he return to you. I could live my life without ever again encountering him. Still, I am sure he will return when Sir Henry does. I will be sure to tell you when I see him."

"O, thank you, Master Richard. Now, here we are at your door. Set the box down that I may open it."

"I can open the door, I thank you."

"Lord, how masterful you are. Were it not for Arthur Amboid. . . ."

Judith frowned. Yet admitted to herself that she would be glad if he would appear to relieve her of this Jennie.

"Jennie, tell my brother that I am too tired to dine with him below. But if you could bring me a cup of milk and some bread and butter, I would eternally thank you. And I would promise to speak for you to Arthur when he returns."

"How can I ever repay you for that? O, never think you must come below stairs. I will surely bring you a fine repast. And then I shall be sure there is no noise on the stairs, nor no loud singing from below. You must have your rest."

Judith did drop off to sleep when she had eaten, but was wakened shortly after when Will came barging in with a candle and a sheaf of letters.

"This is for you," he said, and handed her a wrinkled dirty mass.

"What? What do you say?"

"I say you have received a letter from your lover."

"My lover?"

Judith sat up quickly and grabbed the letter from his hand.

"I mean," said Will, laughing gently, "I mean it is from Henry Wilcome. He begs you to return to him."

"And how do you know that? Have you read my letter?"

"No, I have not read your letter. But there were two others, both from father, and he says that Old Henry is writing to beg you to return. But more to the point, father says we may expect him at any day. He says that if he does not Old Henry is threatening to come on his own. Father does not think he would live to make the trip and does not care to have his death on his conscience."

"But he does not mind that he would have my death on his conscience."

"Do not be so dramatic. It would not kill you to marry the old man."

"Perhaps not. But I would kill myself before I would do it."

"Foolish talk," Will replied.

"It is not foolish talk, Will. I will die before I marry him. I have vowed to die a virgin even as our blessed queen, and I shall not break my vow."

"You think that now, Judith, but when some young man comes along. . . ."

"No. There will be no young man to come along, Will. So you may write my father that he need not make the trip to London. And you may tell him to advise Henry Wilcome of the same. And further, if you tell James Burbage of my true sex, and if he will no longer allow me to be a player, I shall indeed kill myself. It is your choice, Will Shakespeare."

"Judith, you do not know what you are saying."

"Then tell him and find out if I know what I am saying. It is easy to find a knife and easy to cut through skin. Or I could leap from London Bridge. You know the place where even a skilled boatman will not ply his boat. There would be no help for me in that whirlpool."

Will stood looking at his sister for some moments. Then he handed her the letter and turned to leave. Judith tore the letter in half and threw it in the floor beside the bed. They continued to stare at each other.

"Yet when father comes, Judith, it will not be my decision," he said.

Judith smiled.

"Til then, Will, you will do nothing on your own? Am I to believe that?"

"Ay God, Judith, I suppose so. When we are at the Theater tomorrow, we will see how it goes."

"Thank you, Will. I will make you proud of me."

At the Theater, Judith was greeted warmly by all save the other apprentices. They had not changed feelings nor actions toward her. If possible, they were more spiteful. And so, when there was a break, a space where she would not appear on stage for some twenty minutes, she sneaked across the pit and out into the open sunshine.

It was a bright autumn day with a hint of coolness in the air. A turning of the seasons. She took a deep breath and held it, closed her eyes, let it out slowly. And heard a soft moaning sound, a kind of grunting, followed by deep and audible sighs. She turned quickly toward the direction of the sound, and there, by the stage door, she saw a wretched figure, a man, who teetered back and forth, supported by his cane alone, whose doublet flapped, whose hose puddled, whose nose glinted like a full red sun.

"Henry Wilcome," she whispered. "He has come to fetch me."

She turned to run back inside the Theater, but was overpowered by a trembling voice, calling out her name.

"Judith Shakespeare, I have come for you. You are to be my wife. Mine, and no man else's."

There was no mistaking that doublet, those knobs of knees within those discolored hose.

"I have a pretty for you, Judith. Come and see."

"No," she said. "I want nothing you could bring me. And beside that, I am not Judith Shakespeare, nor have I heard of such a one as she. My name is Richard Shakespeare and I have no notion of who you might be."

"You say you do not know me?" the voice quavered. "You have no inkling of who I might be?"

The old man raised himself to a height two feet taller, and broke into a merry laugh.

"O, Arthur," said Judith. "Then it is you. Yet for all that, how did you know the exact manner and clothing of Old Henry Wilcome? You could have been his twin."

"Judith love, I have had many adventures since I last saw you at Titchfield. I have been journeying, seeking knowledge and understanding. I think it may be truly said that I know the whole of Warwickshire since I have made it my business to.

"But what of Sir Henry? Where is he?"

"Now that information, Judith love, I am not privy to. His Lordship has turned me out of his service. I was not fool enough for him."

"What do you mean?"

"I mean that I meddled into his affairs. He told me so. And told me beside that he wished never to see my face again. Said even, that if he did, he would call the watch and have me put in prison."

"But why, Arthur?"

"It seems, Judith love, that Sir Henry and you have one great flaw in common. Neither of you can see the difference between what is stolen and what is borrowed. There is a matter of some letters. And the matter of some several crystal goblets which were crushed into powder while being transported in my saddle bag."

"Mother of God, Arthur, then you are a thief."

"Judith love, I would not have expected this from you. My companion on the road. My dearest friend. Fellow player."

"I think, Arthur, you do not have the friendship for me that you pretend. I think you have always wanted one thing."

"And what is that, my love?"

"Access to my brother. I think you have wanted his help in finding a position as a player. I think you have never had any feelings of kindness nor amity toward me."

"Amity? What a word, Judith love. Where did you learn that one? I think you were better spoken before you met with the nobility. Indeed I think Old Sallie and Nancy and Launcelot would be most perturbed to hear such a word as amity."

"You know all these? O, what of Old Sallie? Is she well? Did she send messages?"

"She was scarcely able to. Indeed, when I first saw her she

was starving to death. Your father turned her out of house, you know, because she helped you run away to London."

"O Arthur, is that true? Then I must send something to her. Could you go? You are free to roam wherever you choose."

"And it is all to Old Sallie's benefit that I am. I have provided for her temporarily. We must think further for the future."

"Arthur, did you? Then I am most grateful to you, and I shall assuredly consider that our friendship has been resumed. But if ever I find that you have made off with another of my letters. . ."

"Me? Me? Am I to be crucified for the actions of my horse? You should know better than anyone that Jasmine is her own master. I can make suggestions to Jasmine, but I am powerless to control her."

"Then let that pass. Still, I am grateful to you for helping Old Sallie. And, I would love to hear more of her, and of my family, but I must go back. I shall miss my cue in the next scene. Come to us tonight, Arthur. Come to us for dinner at the inn."

"Ah, Judith love, I will do my best to talk Jasmine into that very thing."

Arthur did not come to dine with them that night. Nor on the next, nor the next. Nor was there any word of Sir Henry. Judith did not know if she were glad or sorry. Each afternoon when the play was ended and the audience clapped and called her name, and she stepped forward to bow to them, she thought life could bring nothing finer. In her quiet room at the inn at night as she sat at her desk tinkering endlessly with certain passages of poetry, she knew her life was complete. Yet there was something lodged at the back of her brain which threatened her. Calamity. And who would bring it? Her father? Sir Henry? Henry Wilcome? Or Arthur?

On the fifth day, due to a clamor of requests, James Burbage decided that the company must perform "The Saint's Sister," though it was not a great favorite with Richard Burbage nor the other players. The Theater was filled to overflowing. Old James came to Judith backstage, smiling and gesturing.

"There is a gentleman," he told Judith, "of your acquaintance and of mine who has purchased a seat upon the stage. I think you will be amazed at his doublet which is slashed and cut and shewing forth such silks. . .and I might add colored silks. . .great fiery colors, yet not withal unpleasing to the eye. . . ."

The old man talked on, resisting questions until Judith was forced to make her entrance without knowing the name of this peacock gentleman. And found him sitting on the joint stool where she had first seen Sir Henry and thought him a player. Which took her breath for a slight moment though she saw nothing but his shoulders and the back of his head. As she stepped forward she could see from the corner of an eye, his graceful gloved hand, and his shapely knee. Indeed, the doublet was jeweled like Sir Henry's. The gloves were embroidered like Sir Henry's. The plumed hat was as wide as Sir Henry's.

Then he had returned. For better or for worse, he was there upon the stage. She would meet his eye in only a moment, and she must keep her wits about her. She must speak her line clearly, must follow Richard Burbage's speeches, must manage the train of her white dress, must have breath left within her body to speak again. She turned to face Richard Burbage directly, and there behind his left shoulder she could see the eyes. Ay God, it was Arthur. How could he have gathered up money to buy himself such clothes and yet pay to sit on the stage? Then he had been into further thievery. For surely such clothing as this must have been stolen from Sir Henry.

She forced herself to speak, to think of her lines, to recite them to the end of the scene. But when she had left the stage, she went immediately to find Will.

"Will," she said. "Did you see Arthur on the stage? Did you see what doublet he is wearing? I fear the watch will soon be summoned to bear him off to prison, for he cannot have obtained such by any honest means."

"I am sure that Arthur is no thief. Think no more on that score."

"But Will, you do not know him as I do. I know that his dice are heavy, and I know that he borrows things, at least that is what he calls it. And what I have never told you in these last few days is that Sir Henry has turned him off for thievery and has threatened to set the watch on him."

"Then so be it. We can have no hand in that. Yet I am called to make an entrance and must go. But my advise is to think no more on the subject."

Throughout the play, Judith could feel Arthur's eyes wherever she turned. By the play's end, she had come to a final decision. She would have no more of Arthur Amboid. No matter that he had saved Old Sallie's life.

Judith had hidden herself behind a clothes barrel, and was just beginning to unfasten the ribbons of her train when she heard a loud voice calling out the name of Judith Shakespeare. She stooped to hide herself still further. And waited, scarcely breathing.

"I am sure you cannot mean the name of Judith," mumbled Old James Burbage. "There is no female amongst us. Though in truth, our company is honored by two of the surname of Shakespeare. You could perhaps mean William, the elder brother. Or you could be seeking our Richard."

"I am seeking Judith," replied the first voice. "If any man here knows the said Judith Shakespeare or the whereabouts of the said Judith Shakespeare and tells it not, it will go hard with him."

Old James had begun his roundabout oration on the genealogy of the entire Shakespeare family when he was suddenly shocked into silence.

"I cannot lie," said Arthur in a quavering voice. "I have tried since boyhood to utter falsehood, but have never yet been able to bring it off. Falsehood does not lie within my soul."

Judith rose up on tiptoe so that she could see above the barrel. Arthur was shaking hands with a strange gentleman who was dressed in rich black robes with a long gold chain about his neck. From the confidence with which they viewed each other, Judith could see that it was not their first meeting.

"Arthur Amboid," said the man in black. "I was sure you would be true to your word. Now if you will be good enough to lead me to the said gentlewoman."

"My Lord, the said gentlewoman stands even now behind yon barrel. I hope she is still clothed. For indeed, she is fetching in her white gown."

"I still cannot for my life see why a gentlewoman would be hiding in the tiring room of a Theater, but if you say she is there, Arthur, then I believe you," said the man. "Let her come forth."

"Come forth, Judith love," Arthur called.

And Will, who had instantly recognized the old man as Sir Thomas Grevel, chief magistrate of Warwickshire, added his voice.

"You may as well come out, Judith."

For a further moment, Judith hid herself behind the barrel, quickly retying the train and sleeve of her dress. Then, when she had run her fingers through her hair to neaten it, she stepped out. She lifted her chin, and she stared boldly at the man in the long black robes.

CHAPTER XI

"I am Judith Shakespeare," she said softly.

Judith nodded toward her brother, then turned to face the other players.

"It is quite true that I am a woman. And I am sorry, Master James, if I have brought ruin on your company. You must not blame my brother. If you remember, he was greatly opposed to my apprenticeship. Yet because of the difficulty of my situation, I enforced him to the lie."

"What is this?" Old James blubbered. "Can this be true? Can Richard indeed be a woman?"

"It seems so, father," replied Richard Burbage. "And yet I scarcely see how we can be blamed for something we did not know."

A great hubbub of noise broke out with every man accusing the other, each eager to save his own hide.

"If I might have a modicum of quiet and decorum," said the magistrate, "I would clear up the matter instantly."

He looked down at Judith sternly.

"Now," he said. "Am I truly to believe that you are the said Judith Shakespeare?"

"I am," said Judith, even as Old James had to be supported by his son Richard til one of the laughing apprentices had brought a stool.

"Your Honor," Will broke in. "You will probably not recognize me, but I am well cognizant of your august name and presence. May I present to you, my friends, Sir Thomas Grevel of the magistracy of Warwickshire. We are honored with your presence, sire, and will do all we can to clear up any difficulties which may have risen."

Will bowed low before the old man.

"First in order, I would like to know what charges you bring against my sister. She can be guilty of no fault for she has scarcely left my company in the weeks she has been in London, and surely before she left Stratford, my father. . . ."

"Silence," thundered the magistrate. "Silence. I have not come with any charge against your sister. I have come as friend and nearest neighbor of Henry Wilcome."

"Then you might as well have stayed at home," Judith said. "I will not marry him."

"Indeed you will not," replied Sir Thomas. "Henry Wilcome died some seven days ago. I am come with news of an inheritance, a substantial inheritance, I might add."

"But how can this be?" Will asked.

Sir Thomas stared hard at Will.

"You must be the eldest son who ran off and left his wife and children back in Stratford."

Another murmur ran through the company.

"Wife?" whispered Old James. "Ran off and left his wife? And can there be children beside?"

"Quiet," said Sir Thomas. "Quiet. I am worn out with travel. I demand that I be allowed to read this document and return to my inn."

The murmur subsided, even as Sir Thomas reached into his bosom, and pulled forth a voluminous paper. He broke the seal and it unrolled itself and dangled from his hand.

"Are you ready to hear this paper, Judith Shakespeare?"

"I suppose so, though I cannot think what it could mean to me now."

"It will mean great riches to you for one thing, young lady. And if great riches means nothing to you, then I am at a loss to compass your thinking in any respect. So tell me, are you ready?"

"Go on," Judith said softly.

The magistrate straightened the paper and began to read the Last Will and Testament of Henry Wilcome of Wilcome Place. Old Henry had revised his will three days before his marriage to Judith was to have taken place, and he had never changed it again. His entire estate was devised to her sole and free, and could be used for her benefit as she desired.

"But I cannot accept it," Judith said when he had finished. "I do not deserve it."

"Few people deserve what they are given," said Sir Thomas. "You must accept it anyway."

"Indeed, you must accept it anyway," said Arthur and Will together.

"But I did not love the old man. I would have killed myself before I would have married him. No, I tell you I do not deserve it."

Sir Thomas smiled for the first time.

"Such honesty is a virtue indeed, Mistress Judith, and seldom seen," said Sir Thomas. "But I am afraid that you have no choice in the matter. The law is the law. You must accept the inheritance."

"Then I shall give it away the instant I receive it."

"Judith," said Will, "I think you do not mean that. May I talk with you privately?"

"In God's name, talk to her, Will," said Arthur.

"There is no need to talk privately," Judith said. "These are our friends. And in any course, Sir Thomas must know our minds."

"Very well," said Will. "If you do not wish to go home to live in Henley Street with our parents, you must keep this inheritance. I have not the wherewithal to support you. And you must surely see that you will no longer be able to act upon the stage."

"That is true, Will." Judith said sadly.

James Burbage wept. He could not look in Judith's direction without breaking out in loud sobs. And so Richard Burbage came forward and took Judith's hand.

"We will miss you, Judith, all of us. And we do not wish to be harsh with you nor with Will. But you have used us ill in lying about your sex. We could be fined so heavily that we could never play again if it were known a woman acted on our stage. I beseech Sir Thomas that he will not speak to the authorities. We were guiltless, my father and I. You see, sir, we truly believed that she was Will's brother."

"Richard, I am sorry," Will began.

"Say no more, Will. Your plays have made our fortune. We will seek to protect you even as we protect ourselves. But your sister must leave London as soon as possible. When she has been in the country some months, her name will be forgotten. But we must ask now, for our sakes, that she go."

Judith walked to the curtain and pulled it aside. She looked longingly down into the pit. She peered upward at the empty balcony. She stared along the boards of the stage for some moments. Then she turned back to her brother.

"Will?" she asked, "Is this to be the end of everything?"

"By no means, dear sister. Why, it is even as it should be. You will be mistress of a fine place. You can direct your servants and fuss and stitch and potter. And at last you may be as fine a lady as our mother."

"I will not. I can not," said Judith.

She looked wildly about her, searching out a kindly face. At last she lit on Arthur Amboid.

"I shall not go to the country. I shall not accept this place. . . ."

"You must," said Old James Burbage. "You must do it for me, Judith."

"It will not be so bad, Judith love," said Arthur. "In the country you will have time to write many poems and stories.

"Indeed you will be free to write any amount of plays and poems," said Will.

"Belike some day we may act one of your plays, dear child," said Old James. "I think there is no law against that."

"Truly? You would do that?"

"We will look into it, and if there is no law. . . ."

But Will and Arthur and Richard Burbage together jumped in with assurance that the company could indeed present Judith's plays.

And so she turned to the magistrate to sign the paper, to accept the riches into her two hands.

When all was signed and settled, when Old James and Richard Burbage and all the adult players had made her a fond goodbye and Arthur had ushered the magistrate to the door, when she had started once again to change out of her costume, she heard a familiar voice which caused her to stop, to turn and to smile broadly.

"I must come into this house," said the voice, "I have paid ye the penny, and I be coming in."

Will Kempe, the last of the company to leave, was pushing and shoving against a stout lad, seeking to keep him from entering the Theater.

"Keep your money," said Will Kempe. "There is no play. You are too late."

"And it is no play I come to see, Ye Playership. I have business with one of ye company by the name of Richard, who yet I know is Judith Shakespeare but I have sworn to tell no man. And I may tell ye that I have upon me person such as if she should know of it, ye would see her jump to, and claw eye to get it."

"Will Kempe," called Judith. "Let him in. I know the boy."

Snark, somewhat dustier than usual from his long travel, thinner perhaps since he was not well provided for the trip, came grinning through the door.

"What are you doing in London?" Judith asked him as he approached the stage. "Come along. No one will harm you."

"I thank Ye Playership for ye kind words." he said.

"You are mightily welcome, though I must tell you that I am no longer a player. You must speak no more on that score. But surely you have not come all this way to London without news."

"I do have news, both good and bad account, Ye Ladyship. Which would ye have first?"

"I would have the good," she said. "But you must not call me Your Ladyship neither."

"Then what am I to call ye? I can make no head nor tail of one who can be boy and woman, and yet can receive letters from His Lordship as either."

"Call me nothing at all, yet give me the letter. I can tell you that you shall be rewarded for your efforts as I have just become a rich woman."

"Which is well, and ye will know it when I tell ye the bad news."

Arthur returned from ushering out the magistrate, and lounged at the edge of the stage, smiling broadly.

"So you have bad news, do you, Snark?" he asked.

"Ay, I do. For I am turnt away and beat withal by my mistress, the Lady mother. She did shake me up, down, and sideways to find the letter. Yet I had hid it where I would blush to tell ye, Master Arthur."

Arthur laughed aloud.

"So what say ye, Judith Shakespeare," Snark went on, he laughing now too. "Can ye be my mistress? I would serve ye for all of my life, if ye please."

"I do not know how I may use a servant," she said.

"Judith, how can you say so?" said Arthur.

He jumped nimbly to the stage and bowed before her.

"We shall need grooms more than one when we have removed to the country."

"We?" she asked.

"Ay, we. We are shuffled together, we three." he said. "Heaven has ordained it. Eh, Snark?"

"If ye say so, Master Arthur."

"Indeed, I do say so. Now, Judith love, you must go to your lodgings at once and rest for the morrow. Snark and I can be trusted to arrange everything. Have no fear. We three will go to the country in style."

Arthur was walking to the door with Snark at his heels when Judith called his name. The sound of it reverberated through the galleries of the Theater, up through the opening of the pit, and out into Holywell Lane.

"What do you think you are doing?" she said. "Snark is my servant, carrying somewhere about him in some inner place my letter. And furthermore, I do not need you to accompany me to the country. I have half a mind to believe it was you who fingered me to Sir Thomas."

"I? You think it was I? And if I did was it not to your good fortune? Still, I am not saying that I did so. But whether I did or no, tell me this. If I do not make arrangements, how are you to get to Wilcome Place?"

"I shall mount my horse and ride," she said.

"And shall poor Snark run all the way at Mammet's heels? And shall you both eat air along the way?"

"I shall buy a horse for Snark to ride. And I will lodge where I like along the way. And buy whatever food strikes our fancy. After all, it is my money. . . ."

"Your money? I notice not a conducement of golden angels and silver half crowns running forth from your pocket. Nor yet a groat nor a hammered sixpence neither. To put a fine point on it, I see not a penny piece. Your fortune awaits you in Warwickshire, and if you can not find a way to get there. . . ."

"I can get there. Never fear for that."

"Methinks I can remember a certain starving lad that would have died had he not met a certain companion in the road."

"I am sure I would not have died," said Judith. "I am sure. . . ."

She broke off, and stood listening as Arthur held up his hand and inclined his head toward the door.

"Come, Judith love, we must walk thither on tiptoe and see

what greets us behind yon portal. I have heard some small scratchings all the way through your charming conversation."

Judith allowed Arthur to take her hand and lead her through the curtain, through the tiring room and across to the side door. Snark followed behind, he too tiptoeing. When they had reached the door, Arthur grasped the bolt and threw it open, where it met resistance, crashed against a shadowy figure and slammed shut.

"What or who was that, Arthur?" said Judith.

"I do not know, but neither do I like it," Arthur replied. "Stand back, love. There is no telling what fiends may set upon a rich woman. I have heard tales that would make you shiver with the telling."

Arthur drew his dagger, and slowly pushed against the door. This time it opened wide. When it was at its fullest arc, Judith could see a head, then shoulders, then the whole body of a ragged man. She leaned forward and sniffed.

"Launcelot," said Judith. "Launcelot Gobbo, is it you or your ghost that has come to London?"

Instantly Launcelot began to bawl and cry.

"I want me breeches, Judith Shakespeare," he said. "Ye lied to me and stole me very clothes. And when me old mother died, I could not so much as go to her very funeral for lack of good breeches and doublet. Nor shoes neither." And he held up first one foot and then the other, one cut severely, one bruised, and both unbelievably dirty.

"O, Launcelot, I never thought your old mother would die. Launcelot, forgive me and cry no more. Can we not reenact the funeral? For I would buy you fine clothing to make it up. I am rich now, Launcelot."

"So I have heard ye say before and twas all a lie."

"But this time it is true. Old Henry Wilcome that I was to marry has died and left me all his money. Tell him it is true, Arthur."

Launcelot looked up and blinked.

"Go to. Are ye Arthur that was in Stratford not long since and gave such alms to the poor, and saved the life of Old Sallie that was John Shakespeare's cook?"

Arthur looked stern.

"Say no more, Launcelot Gobbo, for alms must be done in secret to be seen by heaven."

"Tis nevertheless true that ye done so. And if ye could see ye way clear to provide a fraction more, I would be obliged as I am starving and can remain on me feet no longer."

So saying, Launcelot fell to his knees, then lay prostrate on the floor, groaning most piteously.

"Arthur," said Judith. "Could you see to these boy's food and comfort for this night? I think they cannot come to the Angel as dirty as they are. I have no idea what to do with them."

"Nor should you, Judith love. A rich woman has no time for such as this. But if I am taken into your service, perhaps in the position of steward. . . ."

"Very well then, Arthur. As long as you understand that you are to do as you are told. And only what you are told. I will have none of your borrowings and other tricks."

"Judith love. . . ."

"Do you understand me, Arthur Amboid?"

"In every aspect, Judith love, I understand you."

"Then be about your business."

"Without doubt. Here, Snark. Help Launcelot to the outer air. I am off to call Jasmine. We will find bread and ale to stave off certain death. And then to a fripperer to buy a proper livery for the three of us."

"What shall you use as money, Arthur?" Judith called after him.

"I shall empty my coffers in your service, mistress."

Arthur removed the large ring he wore at all times on his middle finger. He kissed it and held it high over his head.

"You would pawn your ring, Arthur? How can I let you do this?"

"Ah, but you must not think of me. It is you, Judith love, who must be provided for. Can you somehow extract yourself from that train which even now trails so fetchingly through the dust. It would not do for you to borrow costumery from Old James Burbage. I would not like to be chased by the watch throughout London on the morrow. Now, shall I buy you proper women's clothes at the fripperer while I am there?"

"There is no need for that. I was given several kirtles and bodices by the Lady Southampton while at Titchfield. There is no need for you to spend yet more of your money on me."

"I shall be repaid," said Arthur. "Never fear for that. And now, lads, let us be off."

"One moment before you go. Snark, did you have a letter for me?"

"That I did, mistress, and still do, but I must have a moment to meself to extract it from me person."

"Where, upon your person?" Judith asked severely.

"That I cannot tell a woman. Yet if you will give me a few moments to meself."

"Ay God, step behind the barrel and secure it. Then for God's sake fan it about in the air a bit before you hand it to me."

"Yes, mistress."

Which service being done, Arthur and the boys left Judith to remove her costume. For the last time.

Judith ran through the streets in the darkness of early evening, dressed again in doublet and hose. A boy would be safe alone, she told herself, though in fact she had never been alone on the streets of London after dark. She longed to see her brother come rounding a corner, calling out for her. Or, Arthur. Yes, even Arthur to see her to the Angel and safe inside. And then he could go about his duties. For she dearly longed to be alone in her chamber, so that she could read Sir Henry's letter.

She reached into her doublet to feel the waxen seal. The tall W with flowers woven in a circle around it. What would he say to her? And where was he? The court had returned to Nonesuch. Will said so. Was this letter to say that he would be in London soon? Was he telling her that he would be at the Theater tomorrow? And, O God, she would not. Never again would she leap and jump about the tiring room to hide her nakedness. Never would she make entrance, speak lines, take her bow.

But, and here her heart grew exultant, James Burbage had told her the company would present her plays. She would write of all the stories contained in her precious velvet book of Ovid. Night and day she would write. And her servants would do her bidding. Arthur would see that they did, and that they did not disturb her unless she called. They would leave tomorrow. And in three days time she would be the mistress of her own house. The mistress of herself. Let any man try to make her less, and it would be at his own peril.

Judith entered the inn quietly, slipped up the stairs and into her chamber. Not until she was inside with the door closed did she light a candle. And only then did she take the letter from her doublet, break the seal, and hold it out to read.

Dearest Judith,
What a time has passed since our last meeting at the Abbey.
Each day I longed to be allowed to leave Theobalds. When at
last permission was granted, it contained the provision that I leave
for France with all speed. I rode like the wind to Titchfield, hoping
you would be there, only to find you were in London. I will not
be long in France, and when I return, know, my Judith, that
wherever you are, I will find you. I cannot bear to lose you. Since
tasting the sweetness of your two lips, my heart and blood cries
out for more. Keep me ever in your thoughts as you are in mine.
And in my heart.
                              Yours,
                              Sir Henry Wriothesley

Judith read the letter three times over before she hid it carefully away with the others in her box. And then she took out a fine blue bodice with slashed sleeves and a small white ruff. She took off her doublet and her hose. She dressed herself to go below to the kitchen where she would eat her bread and butter and make her explanations and her farewells.

By the next morning the Farley's and their servants had quite got used to the idea of Judith as a woman.

"I always knew there was something strange afoot," Mistress Farley told her. "I could not put my finger on it, but yet I knew. Eh, Jennie? Didn't I tell you?"

Jennie was tongue tied. She shook her head and would not speak.

"And surely," said John Farley, "In future, when you have business in London, I pray you may stay with us. Our finest chamber will be yours. Indeed, I would turn out the queen to make room for you."

"I thank you both. And I thank you for all past favors. I shall be in London often after I have put my estate to rights."

"And may that be done right quickly. With Arthur as your steward, you will have no worries."

"Arthur Amboid is to be your steward?" said Jennie, coming to life.

"It seems that he has taken that position onto himself," said Judith.

"We expect him within the hour," said Will, pleased now that matters were turning out so well. "Arthur is a man to make arrangements. He sent a message last night to say that he had bought two horses for the two lads, and proper clothing for all three of them. And sent a list of provisions he would need for the journey."

"He has? Then why was I not told of this?" asked Judith.

"Lord, Mistress Judith, it is not the rich woman's place to know of such trifles," said Mistress Farley. "I have packed a basket myself, and so has John Farley with all the best wines he has in hand."

"I think," said Will, "We will not need worry when Arthur is in charge."

Within moments, they all were aware of loud shouts mixed with tinkling bells coming from the stable yard behind the inn. Judith drank her ale down in a gulp and ran to the door, followed closely by Jennie.

Arthur Amboid trotted into view, bells tinkling from Jasmine's neck, and on his saddle. Behind him came Snark on a fine grey mare and Launcelot on one as closely matched as it was possible for horseflesh to be. They too had bells attached at every possible point the saddler's art could devise.

"Ah, Judith love," Arthur said as he came abreast of her, he being no longer dressed in the fine doublets he used for London's streets, but changed to a dark green fustian doublet and breeches. "I trust you have slept well, for we must be off betimes. Snark, speak to the hostler about the mistress's horse. Launcelot, go inside and fetch the mistress's box. Master Will can direct you to it."

Judith watched them scurry off, too amazed to speak. She felt a pull at her elbow, looked around, and there was Jennie, pressed close beside her.

"Mistress Judith, now that you are a woman, you will not forget your promise to me, will you?"

"What promise?"

"You forgot already? Twas not long ago I asked it."

"What then? Ask me again."

"I asked that you will speak for me to Arthur Amboid. Can you give a good word for me?"

"O, Jennie, surely you do not ask me to. Arthur is not the man for you. You should be able to see that."

"And who is he the man for? I hope you have not gone against our friendship and taken him for yourself."

"Do not be a fool, Jennie. I have taken neither him nor any other man for myself."

Yet Judith could not help blushing when she thought of Sir Henry's letter. My heart and blood cries out for you. What a vile phrase.

"O Lord," said Jennie, peering now into Judith's face. "O Lord, I see it. I see you do love Arthur Amboid, and now my heart is broke, for surely he will choose a rich woman over me."

"Jennie, be quiet. He will hear you. And I do assure you I love no man. If Arthur loves you or does not love you, it will have nothing to do with me."

"O yes it will. I see it all. I see the two of you. O, my heart, my poor heart."

Jennie ran back through the kitchen door, leaving Judith to stare after her. She had taken two steps to follow when Arthur called her and Will came running.

"Come, Judith," he said. "I am not anxious to be rid of your glorious company, but since you must go, and since the journey is long, let me help you to your horse."

He embraced her, then took her arm.

"There," he said. "You are well mounted. You can thank Sir Henry for that. Wrap your cloak tighter about you. You must not catch a sickness on the way. Give my love to father and mother. And to Anne and the children when you see them."

"If I see them," Judith replied. "But I do thank you, Will, for all that you have done for me. And I am sorry your marriage came to light because of me."

Will put his finger to his lips.

"You mean you have not told the Farley's?"

"That would have been too many shocks for one day," Will said. "Now, be off before you tell more tales."

"Come, mistress," said Arthur. "Snark. Launcelot. Off we go. Good bye, Will. Do not fail to visit us when you come to the country."

And they were off.

Many an eye was turned to watch Judith Shakespeare and her company of servants as they passed through Newgate and into

Holborn, jingling and prancing. Mammet was feeling frisky; he nipped at Jasmine's rump and rolled his eyes toward the two gray mares. Launcelot sat his horse uneasily. He had never been allowed to ride any man's horse before that morning, and his eyes never left his own hands. Snark had given him the reins, told him how to hold them, how to make commands. Launcelot watched himself, lest he give the wrong impression to the horse.

"I would not have the horse running," he said again and again.

"Twill not run unless ye tell her to," Snark would reply patiently.

"But still these bells," Launcelot said. "I could wish we had not so many bells."

"And I too," said Judith. "Though I do not think twill make the horses run. I think it turns us into a procession. I could have wished we might go more quietly."

"Judith love, how can you say so? This is, in a sense, your coronation. At last you will take your rightful place in Warwickshire society. I am sure your mother will be pleased, for I had it from her very breath that she is an Arden, that Will is an Arden, that you, Judith are an Arden. At last the world will know."

"And did you have it from her very breath that my grandfather Shakespeare was a tenant farmer on her father's lands? You may be sure I will take no place in Warwickshire society."

"You may have to eat your words there, Judith love."

"In any case, when did you see my mother? I do not believe you ever have."

"What do you think of me? Would I be so gross as to visit Stratford and fail to call on the family of my dearest friends, Will and Judith Shakespeare?"

"Did you so? And what did they say about me? Did they ask you about my situation in London?"

"I gave them no opportunity to ask anything. I talked without ceasing. Even while eating and digesting a sugar cake, I bombarded their ears with the honors you have received."

"What honors?"

"Honors, Judith love, such as you have never dreamt of. You would be amazed."

"Arthur, I hope you have not made matters worse than they were."

"That would hardly have been possible. But let that pass. Come, my dear, we loiter. Let us ride on."

At St. Giles in the Fields, they came upon a company of travelers waiting for companionship to ride together those next dangerous miles where footpads, bandits and every degree of robber lay in wait. Among these was Sir Thomas Grevel and his servants. Arthur greeted him warmly, and Sir Thomas in turn greeted Judith still more warmly and they fell in line together. Sir Thomas and Judith in front, Arthur just behind them, and Snark and Launcelot joining in with the Grevel servants.

"Mistress Judith," said Sir Thomas. "I intend that we will become great friends, you and I. Your lands adjoin mine and it seems only proper that we should pass our time in pleasant conversation."

"I will have no time for frivolities," Judith replied. "I plan to spend my time in study and in writing. And I must look to my estate."

"Surely you may leave such matters to your steward."

"What, leave it to Arthur? Arthur has no more idea of how to manage an estate than Jasmine his horse would."

"Then you must allow me to give him the benefit of my expertise. I assure you I would have your best interests at heart. I hope you will trust me in all things."

"I would not want to be a bother to you, Sir Thomas."

"Mistress Judith, you could never be a bother to me. It will be great joy to introduce you to the neighborhood, and to see your every need is met."

"But you must have your hands full with your own affairs."

"Say no more, my dear. I have time and to spare. If you have questions on any subject, I am your servant to answer."

Throughout the remainder of the trip, Sir Thomas was Judith's constant companion. Arthur watched them, his eyes moving from one to the other. He spoke little, and was sharp with the serving maids who hovered around him. At night, in each inn where they stayed, he sat long after the others had gone to bed. And he drank sherris sack which he himself heated over the dying fires in each public room. And he mumbled and murmured and paced the floor til he had worn himself out. He slept no more than an hour before the crowing cock and the stirring of the households wakened him. Each day his eyes grew redder and his skin more pallid.

"Ay, God," he sighed. "Ay, God.

Judith slept little more than Arthur did. Her mind played constantly among the words of Sir Henry's letter. And then a poem would leap, full grown, into her head. She would light the candle, sit up from her downy bed, and write it out on the back sides of her packet of poems.

When she lay down again, she would hear Sir Henry's voice. In the darkness he would read to her. I cannot bear to lose you. Since tasting the sweetness of your two lips. . .And she would run the tip of her tongue along her bottom lip, up the side and underneath the top one. . .And taste nothing. My heart and blood cries out. . .And she would place her hand on her chest, for she had read that a woman's heart beat close beside her breast. . .Nothing. The blood which came each month. . .a spilt drop when she had pricked her finger on Mammet's bridle no longer ago than yesterday. . .They sang no song to her.

But she did keep Sir Henry ever in her thoughts as he had asked her to. She could not put him out of her mind. He sat staring at her poems as they unfolded in her brain. And so she decided that Will had spoken truly when he told her that only those who loved could understand life and write truly. Then she would love Sir Henry. She would force herself to it.

Late on the third day, just as the sun was setting, they spied a timbered house with three chimneys and a wide expanse, a stone wall with vines growing on it, a wooden gate. Sir Thomas, who rode close beside Judith, turned in his saddle and took her left hand from the reins.

"I suppose you remember, Mistress Judith, that this is Wilcome Place."

"No. I seldom walked in this direction though I have walked many miles more than four when I was a growing girl."

Judith took her hand back on the pretext of shading her eyes with it. As they drew nearer, she could see flowers growing even now beside the front door and in the yard at back. There were an abundance of barns and low sheds. And more gates and walls. And trees and bushes.

"Judith love, you are home," said Arthur, the first words he had spoken that day.

"Truly?" Judith asked. Her voice quivered and her throat closed and choked her. "Mine?"

"Yours," said Sir Thomas warmly.

"Then let us go forward," Judith said. "For your kindness, Sir Thomas, if there is food prepared, you must dine with us. But then I do not know what conditions we may find within. I do not know. . . ."

Judith hesitated. For in the instant she had spoken this invitation, she knew her words had the ring, the very intonation of her mother's. She knew that her brain was summoning up feasts of meat and salads and small cakes. And then she knew she would be trapped if she set foot within those walls. She pulled on Mammet's reins. She stopped in the dead center of the high road. She could not go on.

But then the front door of the house was thrown open and a familiar figure ran out and down the two steps and onto the path.

"Old Sallie," Judith called out joyously.

CHAPTER XII

Judith dismounted quickly and ran toward the gate. Old Sallie met her there, and threw her arms around Judith even as Judith opened her arms to receive her.

"Thanks to the Holy Virgin that I have lived so long as to see ye again," Old Sallie said.

"Hush, Old Sallie, for you would not like a magistrate of Warwickshire to hear you speak of the old faith. He sits his horse at our very gate. But tell me, how did you happen to be here? How did you know I was coming?"

"Why Master Arthur sent a messenger all the way from London, who rode night and day, and arrived yesterday morning. We have not ceased to cook since we got the message."

"But how did you come to be here at Wilcome Place at all?"

"O, wasn't it Master Arthur who arranged that too."

Old Sallie rose on tiptoe and waved to Arthur.

"Master Arthur. Heaven bless ye."

She took Judith's hands and squeezed them, laughing and crying at once.

"Lud, mistress, yet I had been dead long before was it not for Master Arthur. When I was turned out for helping ye off to London, I was near starvation when Master Arthur came. He gave me money and food, and found me a lodging. And it was not many days before he brought me to Wilcome Place, me riding up on Jasmine's poor back and Master Arthur alongside leading us. And since that day I have been head cook here."

"You say you are head cook? By which you mean there is more than one?"

"In a manner of speaking. I think before I came there was precious little cooked that human palate could abide. Still there is a flock of scullery maids and house maids and stable grooms and such like. You will not lack for service here."

"And I have brought two more servants. You remember

Launcelot Gobbo."

"I do indeed, and here he stands behind ye. Without smell nor odor. Ye have been washed then, have ye, Launcelot Gobbo?" asked Old Sallie.

"Perilous washed. Master Arthur here laid out half a crown to me washing and dressing."

"Ay, mistress cook. And half a crown to my washing too."

Snark stepped up and bowed slightly to the old woman.

"I be Snark who come up from the south to be a stable groom. But horse is horse, I say, and if there be horse, I will be groom to it."

"Ye be both good lads," said Old Sallie. "And if ye have stomachs to eat, there be nothing to hinder ye. Come into the house, all of ye. But mind ye, Launcelot and Snark is to go round to the kitchen door. And Launcelot, there be a surprise for ye in the scullery. Hurry and see."

Judith turned back to where Sir Thomas and Arthur still sat their horses, talking and laughing.

"You go in, Old Sallie," she said. "I will be along as soon as I have invited our companion, Sir Thomas Grevel, to dine with us."

Sir Thomas dismounted, bowed deeply, but said he was too close home not to proceed.

"But I shall be back soon and often," he said. "Never fear for that. And Arthur, I will be available from this hour forward to advise you on Mistress Judith's affairs. I will make an accounting to you of her property and all other assets. But that will not be an end of it. I will remain deeply interested in all that concerns her."

"I am sure of that," Arthur replied. "I am sure that every jingle of coin will echo across the fields to you, sir. We will be much in your debt."

Sir Thomas rode off, his servants in single file behind him. Judith watched them out of sight, then started for the house door with no further word to Arthur.

"Mistress," said Arthur solemnly. "Have you no orders for me to execute? No particular instructions?"

"Of course not, Arthur. Have the boys stable the horses and come inside. I am anxious to see within my house. And we shall eat our dinner shortly."

"And then?"

"What do you mean?"

"I mean that I am trying to search out my place here. What is my place, Judith love?"

"Arthur, I am too tired for such talk as this. Come inside. We will make the decisions needed as time proceeds."

"As you wish," Arthur said, and rode jingling off to the stable yard.

The parlor was a fine chamber, with windows along the back side for light, and a fine wainscot beneath them. With a broad fireplace at the east end, a mantel board over it, set with a number of valuable objects which no doubt had been the dower of Mistress Wilcome. There was a chest with seven keys. A broad table where meals could be served. A settle with a great tall back, several stools and one carven chair.

"A very magnificence," said Old Sallie.

Judith looked about her house with interest, and yet with the eyes of one who has seen greater splendor. What would Sir Henry think of it if he were to come here? And what else could he mean by his protestations except that he would come here to find her when he returned from France?

"Mistress? Are ye all right? Ye do look somewhat distressed. And pale too. Do ye need to sit down, or shall we proceed?"

"Proceed, by all means."

Above stairs Old Sallie pointed out four large chambers.

"I have given ye the large one, Mistress Judith," Old Sallie said. "It fronts the road so ye can see the comings and goings, what little there be. But I fear for ye to be all alone above stairs and me and the maids in the kitchen. Still there is naught to be done at present. Not until Master John have found ye a husband."

"I shall have no husband if my father must do the choosing, Judith said. "In any case, I am well enough without one."

Yet in her mind she pictured Sir Henry asleep upon the big, carven bed across the room. He would lie abed late in the morning, like a leaf which had floated down on her feather mattress.

"In time, Mistress Judith, I would ye could find a husband to ye liking. Now if I was to pick for ye. . . ."

"But you are not to pick for me, so say no more. Show me the other chambers. We must choose one for Master Arthur."

"Master Arthur is to sleep above stairs? And not another soul in the house? O, Mistress Judith, what will ye mother say? And Master John?"

"It matters nothing to me what they say. I am a rich woman now, and I shall do as I please."

"Yes, mistress, but. . . ."

"Old Sallie, I will hear no more. I am tired to the bone. I am hungry. Let us choose a chamber for Master Arthur and say no more about it."

Old Sallie followed Judith from the room, her face pinched into a scowl.

The back chamber was given to Arthur.

"You shall not sleep on the floor like a servant," Judith told him. "A player, even a player with no licensed company, must not be treated so."

"As you will, Judith love," he had said. "Though I can as easily sleep in the stables with the grooms. Or beside the hearth in the parlor."

"No," said Judith. "I will not have such foolishness. There are three empty chambers here. You shall not sleep on the floor."

As night came on a sudden rain sprang up, and Judith felt a chill around the parlor windows where she sat reading. She looked at the small silver bell Old Sallie had placed by her chair, contemplated the ringing of it, the scurrying that would follow hard upon the sound, and knew she could do no such thing. She placed her book carefully on the table, then bounded out to the kitchen.

The fire burned brightly on the hearth. Old Sallie was leaning over a gigantic kettle, stirring and sniffing at the aroma of the wafting steam. Three serving girls with their backs to her were talking all at once as they cut and chopped and stole snippets of this and that. They stuck meat and bread and salad in their open mouths, licked their greasy fingers and continued to cut.

"Well," she said. "This is a jolly company indeed. What have we here?"

"Mistress," Old Sallie began, "what mean ye to be here amongst the servants at this time of day? We will be serving dinner to ye presently."

"It is cold in the parlor. Besides, I am lonely. I would much sooner eat here."

Arthur, who had the moment before come in out of the rain and was drying himself beside the hearth, looked at Judith sternly.

"Mistress Judith, you must consider your position. How are we to have order among the servantry if you vacate your authority?"

Arthur clapped his hands.

"Here, Launcelot, go to the wood pile and get logs to make up a fire in the parlor. You, Maryanne, prepare a hot drink for the mistress. Old Sallie, we must choose a plate of dainties for her delicate palate. Quickly, all of you."

Arthur took Judith's elbow and led her past the stewpots and the loaves of bread and the platters of baked meats, into the hallway, past the second chamber and into the parlor itself.

"Judith love, you must give no thought to the management of your household. You must spend all your hours in study and in composition. What poems have you written since we arrived at Wilcome Place?"

"We have been here no more than two hours," Judith replied.

"And you have wasted two whole hours? What would Old James Burbage say? He waits breathlessly in London for your first play. I have saddled Jasmine and she awaits me in the barn. I am ready to ride with it as soon as the ink is dry."

"Arthur, stop this foolishness. I am tired. I am hungry. And I would have conversation with something other than a madman."

"Then shall I send for Sir Thomas Grevel? You seemed to enjoy your conversations with him well enough on our journey from London."

"Indeed, he was most kind. But I do not care to see him more tonight. It only seems to me, Arthur, that you could order your senses, sit yourself down, and speak to me as we were wont to do in the past."

"Judith love, in the past we have more often spoken as madmen than otherwise. Nevertheless, if your heart desires it, I will speak gently and sensibly. You have only to choose a subject."

Judith took her seat in the chair by the window, and motioned for Arthur to pull a joint stool close beside her.

"I have no specific subject to speak on. It may be that you could begin to tell me the story of your life. Where were you born? Who were your parents? That sort of thing."

"Ay, God, Judith love, if only I knew. I have no memory before my sixteenth year when I was discovered roaming about the streets of London, spouting Greek poems. I was dressed in cloth of gold and had pinned to my elbow a riddle which all London tried for six months to solve and could not. Besides which I had about my person a cloth bag filled with gold coin and several ancient bones. All this led the general public to think that I was a prince, but I denied this so fiercely that no man has dared to speak those words to me since."

"Arthur, say not another word or I shall turn you out of the house immediately. I cannot bear such prattle. If you will not tell me truthfully about yourself, let us turn to other matters."

"As you wish, mistress."

Launcelot Gobbo sprang through the doorway bearing an arm of logs.

"Mistress Judith," he said, beaming. "I can never thank ye til my dying day for all ye have done to provide for my happiness."

"What do you mean?"

"Did ye not see in the kitchen? Did ye not see Jane Bigsby? That were my surprise. She says she were sent for to be a scullery maid at Wilcome Place, and says that since she is here, she would just as soon marry me. Particularly since I have been washed and am no longer stinking. Do we have your blessing?"

"As long as you hurry with the fire, I care not who you marry. But who does she say sent for her?"

"She says it were a messenger from Master Arthur."

Arthur rose and bowed, then sat down again on the joint stool.

"I go about doing good; that is from henceforth my vocation."

"And I should say, mistress, that it will make up for the stealing of me clothes so that I could not go to me poor mother's burying. I should say, mistress, that I hold nothing against ye now, and me and Jane Bigsby will serve ye faithfully til we die. If ye go not before us."

"Then I am glad matters are settled, Launcelot. Still, if you could see your way to making the fire, I would be entirely grateful. My teeth are chattering with the cold."

Arthur was on his feet at once.

"Then Launcelot, take what logs you have and go instantly to the mistress' bedchamber. Judith love, you must be put to bed at once. I see that you do look pale. And you are shivering. I will call one of the maids to help you. And Old Sallie will bring you warm milk. And you shall eat your repast propped high on your bolster. I will hear no argument, Judith love. Can you go on your own or should I carry you?"

"Arthur, for heaven's sake. I can walk upstairs well enough."

Yet she did not argue when Arthur took her arm, and she did somewhat lean her weight on him. And when Jane Bigsby came up to turn down the coverlet and plump up the pillows, Judith was pleased to climb into the tall bed and lay her head on the pillows.

"I fear my wanderings are catching up with me, Jane Bigsby," she said. "Yet I can rest here while you put away my clothes and belongings. And you may give me news of Stratford."

"Tis little news in Stratford, mistress. Still I must thank ye for me position. I will be a worker, wait and see."

Judith nodded.

"But surely you can tell me when you last saw my family. Is my mother well? And my father?"

"I have not seen ye mother these last days, but ye father is often seen about as he is in the midst of a civil suit as they call it."

"Without doubt," Judith replied. "My father would sue the Holy Virgin were she to appear."

"Lord, mistress, do ye think she will? For I have seen that Old Sallie wears a cross about her neck. And so it may be that she knows of it. I never had a cross meself, but me old mother died in her bed with a woven cross held tight in her hands, and if I thought the virgin would appear to us. . . ."

"Jane, I am too tired for this. Say no more, but do your work and leave me. I hope you will not prove a great talker."

Jane smoothed her apron and looked blankly down at her mistress.

"I was only thrusting about in me mind for entertainment. Tis not me usual way. But I wanted to get on with ye, and so I. . . ."

"Yes, Jane. Thank you. Now go below and tell Old Sallie I can only drink a little warm milk and a crust of her good bread."

"Yes, mistress."

Jane Bigsby ducked her head and started for the door.

"And, Jane, see that you tell no one about Old Sallie's cross."

"Yes, mistress. I thank ye."

When the girl had gone out and closed the door, Judith closed her eyes again. And only opened them long enough to drink down the milk and chew the bread. Then Judith knew no more.

By morning, Judith was restored to herself and was up early. But the wind and rain did not stop for a moment throughout the next day and night. Judith paced her chamber, or stared through the high window into the highroad where she could see no traveler, no stray beast, nothing. She would go down to the parlor and pace there. And press her face against the window to watch Arthur and Snark and Launcelot dash in and out of the barn, laughing and calling to each other. She would walk to the door of the kitchen where Old Sallie and the maids were cooking soups and breads and heating ale and brewing beer.

She had read Sir Henry's letters until they lost all meaning to her. And though she took pen in hand and longed to compose some tender lines, some sonnet to say her love, she could only copy over her embroideries to his three composed letters. When she had made a stack of them, she gave it up. And paced again.

"Ay God, why did Henry Wilcome have to leave me all this? I could be in London. This very afternoon, if the sun is out, I could be on the stage."

She went back to the window and watched the raindrops sliding noisily down the panes.

In London, the sun indeed was out. And though the pit was deep with mud, James Burbage decided they should give a performance that afternoon. The boy players were sent through the streets bearing signs, and little sheets were published in all the taverns. There was a sea of blue-clothed apprentices waiting at the door by one o'clock. It was beside rumored that a raft of plumed courtiers were making up over in the Strand.

Will had been late to the Theater that day because, just as he was leaving the inn, the Lady Clarise had met him at the door, grasped his hand and whispered that she must have a moment with him in his chamber. The moment had lengthened into an hour with Clarise naked on his bed rug moaning, and panting, and squealing.

"More," she would cry out. "Surely once more."

His mind was filled with Clarise as he hooked himself into his armor and pasted on his orange tawny beard. He scarcely heard Old James' excited chatter, so that when he came on the stage to take his part, he was not prepared for what awaited him. Sir Henry Wriothesley was seated on the stage, smiling behind a scented handkerchief.

When the play was over and the dancing done, Sir Henry asked Will to walk apart with him.

"Your servant," Will had replied.

"Will Shakespeare," Sir Henry said in soft tones, not to be heard even by one of his gentlemen. "I have only just returned from what I must tell you was a worthless errand, and I find the world turned upside down."

"What can you mean by that, Your Lordship?"

"I mean that my favorite player made no entrance today. And, upon further inquiry, I am told that my favorite player has retired from the theater. Can that be true?"

"Yes, Your Lordship, it is true. Richard. . . ."

"Do not speak to me of Richard. You know well that I am aware of your sister's gender."

"Then, yes, my sister has retired to the country. She has inherited a fine place, by Warwickshire standards, though Your Lordship would hardly value it, but. . . ."

"Will Shakespeare, I would know the whereabouts of your sister. Do not play games with me."

"Your Lordship, it were better that you did not see her again. Your Lady mother thinks as much, and I. . .I think it better too that you forget her entirely."

"Say not so, Will Shakespeare. It were better I should find her."

"But what can it profit you? Or, and I blush to speak, what can it profit her?"

"Do you dare to speak so to me? Think who I am and what I have done for you. I say I shall see your sister."

"But your Lordship. . . ."

Sir Henry put his hand to his rapier and pulled it some little distance from its sheath. Will watched his fingers, watched the blade shine in the light, yet said nothing.

"Will Shakespeare, what will it profit you to defy me?"

Sir Henry slid the rapier back, then smiled suddenly.

"For I can devise profit to you, Will. And I ask no great thing.

Simply, tell me where she is. Or if you prefer not to tell me where she is, send her this letter. She will come to me. I know she will."

"Sir Henry, belike. . . ."

"No, Will Shakespeare, I will not hear more. Take the letter, and this purse."

Sir Henry drew the silken bag from his own doublet, a larger purse than Will had received before. And then the folded paper, engraved with the Wriothesley seal.

"Speak only the one word, Will Shakespeare. Say you will send her the letter."

"But, Sir Henry. . . ."

"Will you do it? Say no more than that."

"Yes."

Later that same afternoon, at Wilcome Place, the rains slowed to a drizzle. Judith had gone to her bed chamber to get her cloak when, happening to look out the window, she saw a horse and rider in the highroad and stopped short.

"Ay God, it is my father," she said.

She ran to find her comb, all the while calling for Jane Bigsby or for Maryanne. When neither came, she herself began to tear at her hair until the tangles brought her to curses. She ran back to the window, and saw her father below, saw Snark run forward to take the reins of his horse, saw Arthur saunter around the house, smiling and gesturing.

"Ay God," she said. "Yet my father need not think I shall do as he tells me. Nor will I allow him to take Launcelot Gobbo. Nor Old Sallie."

Back at the mirror, she threw down the comb, called once more for Maryanne, pinched at her pale cheeks, licked her lips and her teeth, then flounced down the stairs. She had made herself quite breathless from the wasted effort. So that she could scarcely gasp out, "Father," when the door opened and Arthur ushered him inside.

"Judith love, your father has come," said Arthur. "We must kill something fatted to greet him."

"Not at all," said John, "though a good glass of beer would cheer me. There was never human woman could brew beer like Old Sallie though that is one of the things I have come here to say. You must turn her away, Judith. The old woman is a bad influence on you."

"Old Sallie?" Judith said indignantly. "Turn away Old Sallie?"

"That is exactly what I said. But let that pass. I am here on more important business."

Arthur stepped quickly between Judith and her father.

"But here sir, I forget my manners. Let me take your cloak. And you must come into the parlor. Rest yourself upon this carven chair. You will find it comfortable. My mistress and I can sit ourselves both together on the settle."

John frowned at Arthur and shook his head.

"I have business for my daughter's ears alone," he said.

"But I am your daughter's steward, and I serve her in every detail. She is, as you know, of a timid nature. And truth to say, she has no more idea of business than a swaddled baby."

"Arthur," said Judith.

"Yet here, I forget my service. I go to prepare your beer. But when I return, we may discuss whatever proposition you have in mind."

"Arthur, forget the beer and leave us," Judith said.

"John Shakespeare, you have raised up a great lady. As sweet tempered as I have seen. It is pure pleasure to be in her employ. I live for her gentle words. And I employ myself daily to supply her every need."

"Go, Arthur. And if it is possible in all this versal world, do not say another word."

Arthur placed both hands across his mouth, one atop the other. He turned, and with great dignity, left the room.

"Now, father, what business do you have with me?"

"If I might sit down, Judith. . . ."

"Certainly. You may sit upon the settle. I have already grown accustomed to the chair. I shall sit there."

John Shakespeare looked strangely at his daughter, but did not correct her. He went to the settle and lowered himself onto the end closest to the fire.

"My business," he said, "is twofold. I am here first to assess your wealth, and to take charge and possession of. . . ."

"Stop there, father. You shall not take charge and possession of anything. I have hired a steward. He will manage my affairs, and I will keep close check on him."

"Judith, how can you say so? The man was a wandering player."

"And so is your son a player. And so was I until four days ago when it was revealed to the company that I was a girl."

"Judith do not say so. Do you mean that your brother allowed you to play scenes upon a stage? Pray God it does not come to the ears of the Stratford council."

"I care not whose ears it may come to. They were the happiest days of my life. And even now I will have some part in the theater for I am writing a play. . . ."

"Judith, I have told you on many occasions that you are overstepping yourself. . . ."

"And is Will overstepping himself to write plays? I notice you are very willing to take the money he sends home to you. Will acts in the plays too. Do you forget that?"

"Judith, I will not hear another word of plays and playing. I have come on yet more urgent business, and you will sit where you are and listen to me."

Judith stood up and started for the door.

"Judith, I beg you, please sit yourself down and listen. You have only to listen."

"Very well. I will listen. But that is not to say that I will do what you ask me."

John waited until she had sat down. He whistled beneath his breath for a few moments before he could begin.

"Judith, you must know that you cannot live at Wilcome Place alone as long as you are unmarried."

"I am not alone, but if I were, I would see nothing wrong in that."

"You are alone. You have nothing about you except servants. We had hoped your sister Joan would come to stay with you. She says she cannot leave her mother, and I do not argue with such loyalty. Therefore, to stop the mouths of the gossips, I propose an early marriage."

"Another marriage proposal?"

"You said you would listen, Judith."

"Go on."

"I have talked with several eligible younger men hoping that would satisfy you. In the past you had seemed to dwell on our chosen suitor's age. I am pleased to tell you that I have found a willing husband. He has some wealth, though not as great as yours. He is a man of presentable parts, hard working, intelligent.

In short, I propose you marry Timothy Whateley."

"Timothy Whateley? Why he hasn't the brain of a newt. I should sooner be married to the slop boy."

"Judith, you would do well to marry Timothy Whateley. I order you to marry Timothy Whateley. He is expecting it, and you shall do it. The banns will be read in the church this Sunday."

"The banns may be read in Westminster Abbey for all I care, but I will not marry him. You cannot make me do it. I shall speak to Sir Thomas Grevel on the subject. I am sure he will be on my side."

"You know Sir Thomas Grevel?"

"Quite well as it happens. He is a kindly soul once you get to know him. We rode in his company on the return from London. It was he who brought word to London of my inheritance."

"I know of that, but I did not know. . . Now, this may perhaps put a different outlook on matters. This bears some looking into. Very well, Judith, we will wait for a week or two before we proceed. But you must live very circumspectly here at Wilcome Place. I suppose one of the servant girls sleeps on your hearth."

"I suppose she does not. I am awake a great deal at night. My poems have a way of stealing into my brain at strange hours. I need to be alone."

"Then outside your door. She can prop herself against the very door and sleep."

"I could hear her breathing, and I could not bear it."

"Judith, I swear you are the most troublous burden a man has ever had."

"But you no longer have me, father. I am not your burden. And you have only yourself to blame that I am mistress of Wilcome Place. It is what you planned and wanted."

"But not this way. My plan was for you to be married."

"What difference would that make? If I am to live in sin, I might as well be single as a widow."

"If you are to live in sin? What is this, Judith? Do you tell me you are no longer a maiden?"

Judith hesitated. She toyed with the idea of telling him all manner of lies. It would serve him right.

"Judith, is it Arthur Amboid? Ay God, I did not trust the man from the first. Nor did your mother."

"It is not Arthur Amboid. Nor is it any other man, father. I am a maiden. And I am liable to stay that way. That is, if I choose to."

"If you choose to," John Shakespeare said wearily, then rose from the settle and started for the door.

"Where is that Arthur?" he said. "I shall need some lad to bring my horse around."

"You do not have to go, father, without refreshment. If you will agree to say no more of marriage, we could have a pleasant chat."

"I am too busy a man for chatting, Judith. But you have not heard the last from me."

"I should be most pleased to have you and mother visit me on any day. Joan and my brothers too. As long as there is no mention of marriage."

"We shall see," John Shakespeare said. "Meanwhile, I myself shall have a talk with Sir Thomas."

"I am sure you will find him most willing to speak in my behalf."

"Pray God I do."

Judith did not rise to go with him. But she heard Arthur at the front door. The two men laughed heartily, and spoke rapidly for some moments together.

"Liars," she whispered. "Liars all."

Though Judith felt no greater joy than she had before her father's coming, she was somehow released from inaction. She sat all that day and most of the next two at a table in her bedchamber, words pouring onto the pages, scarce knowing them in her mind before she saw them appear. The play of *ROMEO AND JULIET* was complete and she was revising some of the scenes.

Late in the morning, while she was deep in study of the lines she had revised, she had looked up and caught a glimpse of a solitary rider who came into the yard and disappeared around the house corner. She thought no more of it as she was busy with the scene of Mercutio's death, and she was considering the rapiers they must use and what terms from fencing she should know.

"It may be that Arthur has knowledge of swordplay. I must ask him," she told herself.

Perhaps she would never have thought more of the rider had

Snark not come scratching at her door and begged admittance.

"Mistress Judith," said Snark when he was within. "I hope ye will not be angry toward me. I mean no harm to Master Arthur. But once I made promise to Sir Henry to carry his letters to ye and to tell no man about them."

"And so you did, Snark. And made a good job of it. But you can have no opportunity for further service to Sir Henry."

Judith pushed back her chair and came to stand by the boy.

"But that, mistress, is where ye be wrong, if ye please to hear me say so. And yet I do not wish to speak against Master Arthur neither. Master Arthur is my true friend as well as my master, and so I. . . ."

"Snark, come to the point. What do you mean by all this gibberish?"

"What I mean is that a letter was brought this day. . . ."

"A letter for me? Then where is it?'

"I am coming to that, mistress, but it is not an easy matter to speak of. There was a letter brought today, this morning to be exact, by a certain messenger from London."

"And this messenger was from Sir Henry? Do you mean to say that Sir Henry has returned so soon from France?"

"I know not where Sir Henry is. And it was not his messenger. The messenger was sent from Master Will Shakespeare."

"Then why did you make me believe the letter was from Sir Henry?"

"Because it was from Sir Henry. I know not his hand for that I know not reading, but I know his seal."

"Then where is it, you idiot?"

"So we are to the kernel of it, mistress. This is what is very hard to tell ye."

"Nevertheless, you must tell me."

"Then, the kernel of it is that Master Arthur is not to be trusted where letters is concerned. Mistress, I must tell ye that I had the very letter in me hand and was on me way to bring it to this same chamber where we both stand, when I met Master Arthur on the stairs. He said he was on his way to see ye and could take it straight."

"Arthur Amboid told you that? Then Arthur Amboid is a liar."

"It would seem so, for not ten minutes ago, I saw Master Arthur standing over a small fire he had built behind the stables. And I would have thought nothing of that except that close beside it I saw a bit of sealing wax. And even then I would have thought nothing of it except that it was Sir Henry's seal. I would know that sign anywhere. And at once I was given to suspect Master Arthur. And though it pains me to speak against him, I suspect he has burnt Sir Henry's letter."

"Arthur Amboid has burnt Sir Henry's letter?"

"It seems to me that he has. Now I cannot tell ye. . . ."

Judith grabbed Snark by both shoulders and shook him, she could not have said why. The boy cried out and she let him go. Then pushed him toward the door.

"Go find Arthur Amboid. Tell him to come to me in the parlor. Tell him I. . .No, tell him nothing. Leave that to me."

CHAPTER XIII

Judith had settled herself on the carven chair, and had to some extent regained her composure before Arthur appeared at the parlor door.

"You require my attendance, mistress?" he asked.

"Arthur Amboid," said Judith.

And once again her anger flared.

"I have borne with you. I have suffered your insults and your bungling. And now I have had enough."

"Judith love, how can you say such things to me? I have done nothing which was not for your own good. I have worked for you. I have spent my entire patrimony even to selling my father's ring."

"For which I shall pay you. But after that, I do not wish to hear another word about what you have done for me. I only want to discover why you have done this particular monstrous act today."

"What particular monstrous act?"

"You know very well. You have burnt my letter from Sir Henry."

Arthur rushed into the room then, and bowed on one knee before Judith's chair.

"I do confess as much, Judith love," he said.

"And why did you do it?" she cried. "What business is it of yours?"

Arthur looked up at her, reached for her hand.

"You are my business, Judith Shakespeare," he said solemnly. "And it is not meet that nobility should direct itself to commoners."

Judith stared intently into Arthur's eyes, her face as stern as a judge.

"Arthur Amboid, did you read my letter?" she asked.

"I did."

"Then tell me what he says. That much you can surely do for me."

"Judith love, I dare not tell you. . . ."

"Arthur, I beg you."

"No, Judith love, I cannot."

"Is it that you cannot remember it or that you choose not to tell me."

"I choose not to tell you. At point of death, I would not tell you."

Arthur grasped her hands then though she resisted, and he pulled them to his lips and covered them with kisses. Judith gasped and started and trembled, pulled back from him.

"Let me go," she said.

But he would not. She pulled yet more but he held tighter.

"Let me go, you idiot."

He released her hands, and she jumped up and stepped around him and started to the door.

"Arthur Amboid, I shall struggle to control myself. I shall not stoop to your low place to strike you as I would like to do. But you must leave my house at once. And you must never come into my door again. Not under any circumstances."

"Judith love. . . ."

"Go."

And would say no more. Yet walked behind him up the stairs, and stood over him as he packed his leathern bag with his intricate belongings. Followed him down again and out to the stables, stood not two feet away as he saddled Jasmine, walked with him as he led her from the barn and as he mounted.

"Judith love, can you not reconsider?"

He smiled down at her and winked.

"Arthur Amboid, if you do not take yourself from my sight. . . ."

"I must tell you, Judith," he said. "That I fear the effect this action may have on poor Jasmine. She is sensitive, and does love you so distractedly."

"Go, Arthur Amboid."

"Do you not see the tears amassing on Jasmine's cheek? Coursing along her proud Arabian nose? Do you not hear her choking sobs?"

"Arthur Amboid, tis pity that so gentle an animal should have so vile an owner. Yet there is no help for it. She must go to bear you on your way."

"Yet if you should need me, Judith love, ever in your lifetime. . . ."

"I shall not need you. Now go."

Judith ran forward and gave Jasmine such a whack on the rump that she started out in a dead run. In seconds they were lost to Judith's sight. She brushed her hands together lightly and looked long into the distance til there was only a speck to see.

"Pray God this be the last of him," she said.

And never once did she remember the money she did, in truth, owe to Arthur Amboid.

Judith could think of no other course than to leave for London as soon as possible. She would go to Will. Since the messenger had come from him, he would know something of the letter and the circumstances. But no matter what the letter contained, and no matter what the circumstances she would not allow Arthur Amboid to take control of her life. For when she came to think of it, that was exactly what he had been doing. Arthur was taking the place of her father, keeping things from her, leading her about. He had no right to think for her, to tell her what was best for her.

And so she called for Old Sallie to bring up her box, and together they packed two of the velvet doublets, the clocked hose, the small leather boots, all made for her at Sir Henry's direction.

"Then ye will be a boy again?" asked Old Sallie.

"Only for the journey, Old Sallie. It is safer for a boy along the highroad. But we must pack two skirts and bodices beside, for when I am in London, I will appear as myself. "

"But why are ye going, mistress? Ye have not been here long enough to settle yeself."

"I have business in London."

"But could ye not call Master Arthur back and have him settle ye business for ye?"

"Under no circumstances will I ever take Arthur Amboid back into my service," Judith said.

"O, ye must not say that, Mistress Judith. I shall fear for ye in this life without Master Arthur. I shall fear for ye on the highroad without him."

"Nonsense. I shall have Snark to ride with me."

"And ye must take Launcelot too, for there be more danger on the highroad than in the furthest pits of hell. O, mistress, do not go."

"I must. Say no more about it."

Judith would not hear another word. Neither from Old Sallie, nor from Launcelot, nor from Snark. The next morning at daybreak, the three of them set off. But not before Judith had wrapped and tied her play of *ROMEO AND JULIET* and hidden it inside her doublet beside her heart.

Some four days later, Judith and her two servants rode through Newgate and into the city of London. They had passed through many trials. The first of being lost because Judith had dozed a few moments in the saddle and trusted the way to Snark. The second of being hungry because Launcelot ate all the prepared lunch, and the third of being set on by a robber who, for an unknown reason, took to his heels just as Judith was ordering Launcelot to hand out what few shillings she had brought with her.

They did not linger along the crowded streets, but rode at once to the Angel to find Will.

Will was not surprised to see Judith. He had little hope that she would not come to London when she had read Sir Henry's letter. Yet when she walked through the inn door in her doublet and hose, his heart sank all the same.

"Will," she said. "I must speak to you. Privately. Let us go up to your chamber at once."

Will did not argue. He had words for her as private as those she had for him. He walked behind her up the stair, tired from the afternoon's performance, but in some ways energized by the thought that he could have this out with her once and for all. But when they were inside with the door closed, Judith began before he could open his mouth.

"Will, you cannot imagine what has happened. The messenger you sent, the letter, twas to no avail. Now I know that the letter was from Sir Henry. But what it contained, I can only imagine. And where it came from or where Sir Henry is, I have yet to discover. For," and here her voice rose sharply, "That dim witted rascal Arthur Amboid has burnt it. So, tell me what you know. Where is Sir Henry?"

"At this moment?" Will asked.

"Not at this very moment. I care not if he is washing his face nor yet combing his hair, I want to know where he is situated. Has he returned from France? Is he yet there?"

"He has not returned from France in that he was not there at all."

"But he sent me a letter to say he was going."

"And indeed he thought he would go. He was sent by Lord Burghley, but, before he could embark, a messenger came from the queen that he should repair to London."

"So then he is in London?"

"Yes. He was at the Theater this very afternoon for the performance."

"Then I shall see him there tomorrow."

"I think, Judith, that you may not go to the Theater."

"And why may I not go to the Theater? I have money to sit on the very stage if I should choose to."

"But I hope you will not. There are rumors circulating about London concerning your tenure on the stage. James Burbage would not be pleased to see you. And you did promise that you would stay out of London until the scandal blew over."

"Then I would go in a disguise."

"I think not, Judith. I think you would not be well received."

"But surely. . . ."

"No, Judith."

"But I must see Old James. He has promised to read my play, and it is now complete. I am sure he would want to play it."

"And I am sure he would not."

"Will, I can scarcely believe it of you, but you are jealous. You know my play is better than yours, and so you want no one to see it."

"Judith, I would be glad for the world to see it, but I know what I know. James Burbage may be in serious trouble for allowing a woman to act out a part on the stage. And he thinks now he may not perform a play written by one."

"I do not believe you."

"That I cannot help. But I am telling you."

"Then I shall go to Sir Henry. He has offered to help me with my writing. I know he could find a way."

"I think you should not go to Sir Henry either."

"Will, what can be the matter with you? I shall go where I like and do what I like."

"Judith, I have tried to tell you on many occasions that you may not put your trust in Sir Henry. He is not a bad man, yet the fact is that he is a man. And you, dear sister, are a woman. If you do not choose to be his whore. . . ."

"Will Shakespeare, you know I would be no man's whore. And you are an evil person to think such things. Sir Henry is interested in my poems. In my plays. He has said that he will help me."

"How could he help you, Judith? The law is the law. And I am sure of what I tell you. I have seen his eyes when he looked at you. And I have reason to believe that he has kissed you. That you have lied to me. . . ."

Judith felt herself blushing, but knew she would not confess to her brother. For it would never happen again. She knew now there would be no more kisses.

"Do you think I will stand here and let you talk to me this way?" she asked when she had gathered control. "It is your own mind, Will Shakespeare, that you choose to insinuate onto others. It is you who can think of nothing but country matters. I will hear no more. If you will not help me send a message to Sir Henry, I will arrange for it myself. I have servants now. I can do as I like."

"Judith, I am tired. I am hungry. I can argue with you no more for this night."

"And you think I am not tired?"

"Then rest yourself, dear sister. I shall go below and arrange for a room for you and for food to be brought up to you."

"Indeed you shall not. I can make my own arrangements. I am sure the Farleys will be pleased to see me. And since I am dressed as a boy, I am sure I can eat below if I choose."

"Ay God, Judith, eat below. Eat above. Eat on the rooftop if it will please you. But I am beginning to understand our father's displeasure with you. You will not be led, Judith. You will not be what you ought to be."

"And what exactly is that?"

"I sincerely pray you will find out before it is too late."

Judith knew that she could take no pleasure in a meal that night. Nor did she desire to be in her brother's company. She spoke briefly to Mistress Farley in the kitchen, then let herself out the back door and walked slowly toward the stables.

"Snark," she called when she neared the stable door. "Launcelot."

The two of them bounded out of the stable door, looking somewhat guilty.

"What are you two doing?" she asked. "I know it is something for I can see by the look in your eye."

"Tis nothing," said Snark. "We were only grooming the horses after our journey."

"Tis nothing," said Launcelot. "The small matter of it is that we are late with our currying because Master Arthur. . . ."

Snark poked Launcelot hard in the rib cage. They blushed and would not speak another word.

"Are you telling me that you have seen Arthur Amboid?"

The boys looked at the ground and shook their heads in such a way that Judith could not see if they were saying yes or no.

"Has Arthur Amboid been here?"

When still they would not speak, Judith reached for a long stick that lay beside the stable door.

"If you do not tell me, I shall surely beat you til you do."

"Then, Mistress Judith, I would save ye the trouble," said Launcelot. "Master Arthur was here til five minutes ago, and he will return. By way of speaking, he has never left us. And ye can be glad of it, Mistress, for it was Master Arthur which saved us from the robbers. Ye see, he had followed us all along the way to London to see we came to no harm, and we would be penniless this night were it not for him."

"Arthur Amboid told you this? And you believe him?"

"Mistress, we do," said Snark. "He told us everything we did along the way. If he had not seen us, he could not have known what color doublet ye wore, nor where we stopped at night, nor how ye beat Launcelot when he ate all the lunch."

Judith turned and walked quickly back to the inn. She was near to tears. But somehow she was able to hold them back as she discussed the matter of a room for the night with John Farley. And as she gave direction to Mistress Farley for a small tray. And as Jennie brought the tray and stood watching as she ate it. She managed to give Jennie a description of Wilcome Place and all its occupants. But when she was left alone, she sobbed into her bolster til she fell asleep.

In the morning Judith thought it politic not to come down until she was sure Will had left for the Theater. So that when she had seen him from her window hurrying off down the street, she went below, dressed this day in her best bodice and kirtle. She found Mistress Farley alone in the kitchen, the maids being sent to the cellars or to the attics or to the stables to do their various jobs. Mistress Farley smiled broadly and set at once to toasting Judith a piece of bread.

"We did not expect you back in London so soon, Mistress Judith, but we are glad to see you. Jennie has it from Master Arthur that you may stay here some days with us."

"You would do well to forget what Arthur Amboid tells you. I have discharged him from his post as steward. He can have no idea of what I will be doing."

"I am deeply sorry to hear Master Arthur has lost his post. I am sure he has no idea of it."

"And I am sure he does. I have told him in words which could not be mistaken. Arthur's problem is not that he does not know. His problem is that he cannot be trusted with the truth. He is a liar, Mistress Farley. A liar and a cheat. You would do well to see that Jennie has no further conversation with such as he."

"Mistress Judith, I am sure. . . ."

Mistress Farley broke off in distress as she looked up to see Arthur's face poked round the door to the kitchen garden.

"Ah," he said. "What a picture. What a domestic scene. Mistress Farley and Mistress Judith. And what do you say? You desire me to join you in a small repast. I would be pleased to take a glass of ale. No more than that. But I do have private words with my mistress. If you would walk with me in the garden while the meal is preparing."

"I will walk with you nowhere," Judith replied.

"Then shall you choose to discuss matters of business here in the kitchen for all to hear?"

"There is no one present except Mistress Farley. But there is no matter to that, for I have no business to discuss with you at any time, in any place. I shall go at once to find Snark. I have business with him. I will eat when I come back."

"Then I shall accompany you to the stable so that no rough word may fall upon your ear, Judith love."

"There will be more to fall upon your ear than rough words if you do not leave me."

Judith hurried out the door with Arthur close on her heels.

Judith had no recourse but to whisper her commands in Snark's ear. Arthur lounged about the stable door, listening attentively. And she must stand and wait until Snark had saddled his horse and ridden out lest Arthur confound him and discover his errand. Then she must suffer his company as she drank her ale and ate her bread. And must wait with him at the window of the kitchen until Snark returned.

"His Lordship says ye will hear from him soon," Snark said.

And Judith went quickly to her chamber and bolted the door to wait.

Judith sat by the window, looking down into the street. In her lap lay her play and several new sonnets. She would want them by her when Sir Henry came. And what was she to do when he did arrive? It seemed to her that she must offer him something to eat. Or perhaps a glass of Master Farley's best wine would be worthy of His Lordship's palate. And then they would talk of his travels for a time. But not for long because she would want to ask him for his aid as soon as possible. She would want to hear no more about her tender lips and things of that matter. She twisted her skirt in her fingers, sat forward in her chair and looked up and down the street.

And out of the cross street she saw six horsemen turn and ride slowly toward the Angel. Six men-at-arms wearing helmets, and each in the flame livery of the Wriothesley's. But Sir Henry was not among them.

"Ay God," said Judith. "What can this mean? What am I to think?"

She sat staring at the window, unable to move. Perspiration broke out along her upper lip. Her heart was pounding inside her chest so that she felt it must have slipped loose and was hammering in her ears. When Jennie knocked at her chamber door, she tried to speak but found her mouth too dry for her tongue to form words.

"Mistress Judith," Jennie called. "Do you hear me? Have you died in there? You are wanted below. The Earl of Southampton has sent a guard to bring you to Southampton House."

"But I cannot go," said Judith feebly. "I thought he would come to me."

"And well he should," Arthur broke in, for he had accompanied

Jennie up the stair and stood with her on the other side of the closed door. "I shall go below and tell them you refuse."

"No. Wait. I shall go below myself to tell them."

Judith ran to the door, holding tight to her roll of papers.

"Arthur, you must stay out of this completely. I will handle it for myself."

"As you wish," he said.

Arthur and Jennie followed hard behind Judith on the stairs and into the hallway below. One of the pike men stood at the open front door. He removed his helmet when Judith approached.

"Are you Judith Shakespeare?" he asked.

"Yes. I am she. What business would you have with me?"

"I am to bring you to Southampton House at once. And I am to give you this letter."

"I am grateful for the letter, and I would be glad to see Sir Henry, but. . . ."

"Indeed you are right, Mistress Judith," said Arthur. "It would not behoove a gentlewoman to ride thus through the streets so early in the day. When your brother has come from the Theater. . . ."

"And why do you think I would need my brother?" Judith said. She turned to face Arthur, her fear gone and all the anger she had felt the same moment she had heard of his burning of her letter returned to her. This man would not tell her what to do. No man would tell her what to do.

"I have ridden to London without my brother. Surely I can ride from here to the Strand without him."

"His Lordship has given strict orders that you should be treated with utmost care. You will ride pillion with me, the chief attendant at Southampton House. No harm will come to you though you ride through the streets at this early hour."

"Then I will accompany you," said Arthur.

"I forbid it," Judith said. "I go to Sir Henry to ask his protection for myself and for my play. I shall return as soon as we have discussed these matters."

"Judith, I beg you," said Arthur.

"And I beg you to leave me alone. If you do not, I shall have Sir Henry's man enforce you to it."

"Ay God, Judith," Arthur cried out.

But Judith stepped into the street, mounted behind the guard and was off.

Judith was led through the courtyard of Southampton House, into a low doorway, and up a perilous flight of stairs, sometimes lifted off her feet in the effort of the guards to bring her unharmed to Sir Henry.

On those evenings when she had come with her brother to Sir Henry's candlelight readings, she had never seen such a doorway, never imagined there could be such perilous stairs. When they had come to the ending of the steps, the guards turned into a darkened corridor and waited for her to walk ahead. They passed door after door, hurrying her along. She thought of Will's warning, Ay God, of Arthur Amboid's. And even of her own misgivings.

But when they had walked to the very end, one of the guards opened a locked door and stood aside for her to enter. She straightened herself, expecting to come into Sir Henry's presence, and came instead into a chamber empty of all human company but filled with books. Judith gasped. Could there be so many books? The library at Titchfield Abbey had not had half so many.

"You may wait here," the guard said. "I will send a maid presently to offer you refreshment."

"I care for nothing," Judith replied quickly. "But could you tell me when I will see His Lordship?"

"We have no further orders," the guard said. "When you are sent for, we will return to bring you to him."

"Thank you," Judith said.

As soon as the door was closed behind the departing guards, Judith thought about the letter from Sir Henry. She broke the seal and read it at once.

Dear Judith,
Only to think that in an hour I will have you in my arms. I long to sit as we did in the past when you would read to me from your most excellent poems. I have engaged a printer so that we may assemble some number of them into a book. And it may be that you have completed the play you spoke to me about. I have many plans, dear Judith. Many plans.
                    Yours,
                    Sir Henry Wriothesley

Judith laughed and clapped her hands. At last. So then she was right to come. Sir Henry only wished to be her patron. She would dedicate all her poems and plays to him. His name would be as famous as hers, and hers as his.

"Ay God," she sighed. And went straight to the shelves, chose a book, and sat down to read.

Some two hours later, Judith came to herself enough to wonder what could be keeping Sir Henry. But she was drawn back to the page almost immediately and knew nothing of present time and space until the door opened and a bearded guard stepped into view.

"Come with me," he mumbled so low and with such a strange accent that she could scarcely be sure of his message.

"What did you say?" she asked.

Again he muttered some low words and proceeded into the room. He came so quickly, moved so deftly that before Judith could resist he had tied both her hands together with a stout rope, and for good measure twirled the rope twice about her waist.

"What are you doing?" Judith hissed. "Let go of me."

Judith could feel him breathing against her neck where he leant down to do his work.

"Have you lost your senses? Be sure I will tell Sir Henry how you have treated me."

Visions of a dungeon rose up before her eyes. Darkness like the cellar at home in Stratford when her brothers locked her inside one day because she had called them stupid dolt heads. But if there were a dungeon at Southampton House, it would be monstrous huge and no one would hear her call out. They would not discover til too late that this deranged guard had made off with her.

She opened her mouth to scream but the guard covered her mouth with his hands. The sound she made would not have carried across this one room let alone through stone walls. Still she continued to scream, and jerk and pull until the guard was obliged to pick her up in his arms in order to move her across to the door.

The guard looked both ways, then proceeded into the corridor. He ran back along the way Judith had been ushered two hours before, gained the stairs and began to descend. When they had come to the bottom, the guard stopped and put her down. He removed his hand from her mouth. He untied her hands and rubbed her wrists. For a moment Judith was too stunned to move. She looked uneasily about her and than at the man. At his red beard, his bushy eyebrows that half covered his eyes. At his hair where it lay tangled along his forehead and across his ears. She could see that in no way did it match the beard.

"Ay God," said Judith. "Arthur Amboid."

She reached out, grasped the beard and pulled. It came away in her hands. Arthur licked his lips very slowly, staring all the time at Judith's face. He lifted one fingertip and then two, as if he were counting, His lips moved but no sound came. And then he seemed to come to himself and he smiled.

"Yes, Judith love, it is even I."

CHAPTER XIV

Judith looked around her at the dingy gray stone. It was dark in the stairwell. Had she not been standing close to Arthur, she would not have seen his features so clearly. He was peeling himself out of his uniformed livery to expose beneath, the green furze jerkin he had worn as her steward. While he was thus busied, not looking in her direction, she took the occasion to step backward up two steps, the better to make her flight.

"Stay where you are, Judith," Arthur said, not turning his head.

"You have no right to tell me what to do. You have no right even to be here. And since we are at the question, how did you come to be wearing the Wriothesley livery?"

"A fat purse, my love, paid to one of the regular guards. I expect he is having a fine morning in the stews."

"But why would you do such a thing?"

"To be with you. I am always wanting to be with you, Judith love."

"But why? Why should you want to be?"

"Who can say, Judith love? Who can say? It may be that I am after your money. Yet for all that I think we may not tarry here. Let us be off quickly."

"That I will not. I have come here to see Sir Henry, and I will see him."

Arthur stared at her in disbelief.

"Judith love, your incomprehension stuns me. I have paid my last penny to get myself into Southampton House. I have risked my life to get you out of it, since His Lordship has said he wishes nevermore to see my face. And you will not leave this wretched place?"

"I never asked you to come here. Indeed if your memory serves, you will know that I too have told you that I do not wish to look upon your face. Now go. And this time be sure you do not meddle into my affairs again."

Judith drew her skirts about her knees and bounded up the steps two at a time. When she had reached the top she stopped and looked ahead of her into the dim light. The door to the library chamber was the last one on the left. She prayed that she would find it still unlocked, for she must be waiting within when Sir Henry sent for her. She was rushing along the hallway, still holding her skirts above her knee when the door opened and Sir Henry, accompanied by two guards, came out.

"Thank God, tis Sir Henry at last," Judith said.

Sir Henry strode quickly toward her, smiling broadly.

"I thought I had lost you again," he said. "I am sorry I have kept you so long, but I had arrangements to make which I will tell you of as soon as we are closeted in my chamber."

"She shall not go into your chamber," said Arthur who came running up, still tying himself back into his livery. "As long as there is breath in this body, she shall not go."

Sir Henry turned to Arthur, his smile changed now to pure wrath. Arthur bowed low.

"Arthur Amboid," said Sir Henry. "I believe I have ordered you never to set foot in Southampton House again."

"Indeed, sir, you have, but I am here as knight protector to this lady. I will not leave until she leaves with me."

"Indeed, Your Lordship, he is not. I have expressly asked this man never to come near me again."

Sir Henry motioned to the guard at his left hand.

"Take him below," Sir Henry said. "Search him to see he has stolen no valuable. Undress him of our livery. Then set him on the street."

"I protest. . . ." Arthur said, but Sir Henry turned away.

"Come, Judith," he said. "I have much to tell you."

Judith did not look back in the direction of Arthur and the guards, but neither could she look at Sir Henry. She felt strangely weak, tired, she knew not what.

When the guards had led Arthur away, protesting loudly, Sir Henry took Judith's hand and led her into the finest chamber she had seen. There were wide tapestries on four walls, and chairs with satin cushions. A multiplicity of tables and desks. And laid about on these tables were lutes and flutes and silver jugs and Venetian glass flasks. And several books with bindings of crimson leather.

"I can wait no longer, Judith," he said as soon as they were inside. "I am not used to such waiting. I will have what I desire, and that is you, Judith Shakespeare."

He took her in his arms and held her and kissed her tenderly. Yet all the while Judith felt this strange weakness growing in her legs and in her arms.

"I shall buy you dresses, my sweet, and jewels. And I have just come from the small house I have bought for you. I was able to secure the last of the furnishings this morning. Nothing will prevent your moving there immediately."

"But Sir Henry. . . ." Judith said.

Sir Henry put his finger on her lips.

"Hush. Be still. We must be about our present business."

He took her face in both his hands and turned it until she was looking at a bed, a huge bed, marvelously carved with flowers and running vines, and hung with sheer scarlet silks. Judith could scarcely breathe with his hands so close to her nostrils for his fingers were delicately scented with a musky perfume.

"Sir Henry, I. . . ."

"Does my bed please you?" he asked with great assurance.

"It is a very fine bed I am sure. But I have come here to talk of my plays and poems."

Sir Henry laughed softly.

"There will be time for that later," he said.

He took his hands away from her face, then grasped her shoulders and pressed her tight against him.

"Judith, I have longed for you. I can wait no longer. Shall I undress you here or shall I wait til we are in bed?"

"Undress me? But surely, Your Lordship, you can not mean that we should. . .that I should. . . ."

She drew back from him, scarcely believing that he should speak so to her.

"I did think, sire, that you found pleasure in my poems," she said.

"And I do. Did I not tell you that I have gone to a printer to talk with him about printing them into a dear little book? Judith, I have so many plans for you. I shall fill your house with books and pictures and silks and every comely thing."

"Sir Henry, I do not need a house with silks and things. I have come to you this day to ask you to be my patron. I ask that you will help me to find acceptance for my plays. As a woman I. . ."

"Yes, Judith, it is as a woman that I sought you. I want to kiss your sweet lips. I want to touch your small breasts with my fingertips until they tingle. Til they send messages throughout your sweet body."

Sir Henry reached for her again, but this time Judith pushed hard against his chest to free herself. Her head swam. Her breathing was hard and quick. And inside her burnt such a pain as she could scarcely believe.

"Judith," he said. "I was sure you understood me."

Judith looked up at Sir Henry, her eyes brimming with tears. "Not until now," she whispered.

She turned and walked slowly toward the door. Each step required great effort. She was dizzy. She had to breathe in deeply, breathe out slowly to keep from fainting dead away.

"Judith, I command you to stop," Sir Henry said. "Stand where you are."

She walked on.

"Judith, I say you must come to me. I have paid your brother for you in many silk purses of coin."

Judith walked on until she had reached the door. There she stopped and looked back at him. Straight into his eyes.

"Then tis a pity, Sir Henry," she said, "but you have bought my brother and not me."

Will's mind had been strangely uneasy all during the morning. He had no part in the play they were presenting that afternoon, and so he thought several times that he might walk quickly to the Angel and have a word with Judith. Only to reassure himself that she was safely chatting with Mistress Farley in the kitchen. Or in the garden with Jennie. Each time some small matter would claim his attention. And so the play was half done when Snark came knocking at the stage door, crying out for Master Will. Will knew then that his uneasiness had foundation. He ran the whole way with Snark panting beside him, too out of breath to answer questions.

The door to Judith's chamber stood open. Will pushed ahead of Snark, out of breath. And found his sister reclining on a bolster, staring straight ahead of her, her eyes filled with intense pain and sadness. Arthur sat beside her holding her hand. She paid no more attention to him than if he had been below in the street.

"What have you done to my sister?" Will asked.

Will had never seen Judith so still before. So quiet. Her bodice had a large dark stain on the front, and her hair, even for Judith, was fearful. Arthur rose quickly, took Will by the shoulder and ushered him out of the room.

"I have done nothing to your sister," Arthur said when they were out of Judith's hearing. "But I fear that others have broken her heart."

"What do you mean broken her heart? Judith was not in love. How could her heart have been broken when she was not in love? Arthur, do you swear it was not you? Do you swear you have not dishonored my sister?"

"Ay God, Will Shakespeare, what do you think? I love her with all my soul."

For some minutes Will stood looking incredulously at Arthur. How could such a thing be? He would never have guessed it. Yet Arthur had in his face the look of a man who has confessed the deepest secret of his heart.

"Have you said as much to her?" Will asked. "That you love her? Is that perhaps the problem?"

"No. I have told her nothing of my love. Nor must you tell her, for I fear she would send me away."

Arthur looked fearfully back at the open doorway.

"Arthur, you must tell me all that has happened. Start from the beginning.

"Tis a long story which we have no time to rehearse. But briefly, Judith went to Sir Henry this morning at Southampton House. I, knowing her innocence and unable to dissuade her from going, rode with all speed behind her, bribed a guard and gained entrance wearing the Wriothesley livery. I found her and had bodily removed her from the premises when she slipped from me, went back, and this time found Sir Henry. I could do nothing for Sir Henry had me set into the street."

"And what happened then? Did she, Ay God, was she dishonored do you think?"

"Keep your voice down, Will. It were best she did not hear us."

Arthur crept to the door, stood listening for a time, then tiptoed back to Will's elbow.

"I have no knowledge of what happened there. I think there was not enough time elapsed for great harm to be done. In any case, I was waiting below with Jasmine when she ran out, pale as a ghost, stumbling and lurching, and demanded to be taken to James Burbage's house. Not to the Theater, she kept saying. In the fullness of time we found the said abode. This time, I was allowed to accompany her and so I know what transpired."

"Ay God, what?"

"In the beginning Old James was patient with her. He perused the papers of her play for some minutes, then attempted to explain the difficulties he was in on her account, and excused himself from tempting fate with more. He plainly told her he could not play it."

"Nor could he," said Will. "We stand to lose our license if we commit another offence."

"But Judith could not accept this. She became greatly agitated, shouted at the poor old man til he was in tears, and at last was shown the door. And since the moment she stepped across the threshold into the street, she has been as you saw her. She has not spoken, has not looked to left nor right. I have tried to make her laugh, to make her cry, yet she pays no more attention than if I were invisible. Perhaps, Will, you can help her."

Will went into the room and across to the bed. He sat down beside Judith and took her hand. He began to speak to her in quiet tones, pleading with her to look at him. Or to squeeze his fingers. Anything. There was no response.

"Send for strong drink, Arthur. It may be that if we force it through her lips. . . ."

"I have done that. I have baptized her in sherris sack, and yet she will not speak nor move."

"Then we must send for a doctor," Will said. "There is a Frenchman in the next street who is known for his healing. I will go down and give direction to Snark and Launcelot. You remain close beside her, Arthur. If she grows worse, call at once."

In no more than ten minutes the doctor appeared, a round faced man with a bald pate, a set of glasses wired onto enormous ears, and encompassing large, staring eyes. His body was shaped something like a pumpkin, set beneath a long sweeping cloak.

"By Gar, I come," the doctor said, and hastened to the bed

where Judith sat. "Wheech ees her husband? You?" He pointed to Arthur. "Or you?" He gestured to Will.

"Neither of us," said Will. "I am her brother."

"And I am her steward," said Arthur.

"And who ees her husband? Where ees he?"

"She has no husband," said Will, "yet what does that matter? I fear she may be ill."

"That she ees not," the doctor said. "I think she has suffered the shock. To be well she must suffer a second one."

"What do you mean?" asked Will and Arthur together.

"I mean you are too kind to her. Eef she had husband to beat her, she would be well soon."

The doctor bent over her, looked intently into her eyes. He turned her face from side to side. He shook her by the shoulders. And then he stood back, raised his hand and slapped her face hard.

Judith blinked, gasped, then glared wildly up at the man.

"Why did you do that?" she asked.

She looked around the room until she came to Arthur who was smiling broadly.

"Arthur, why did you let this man slap me?"

The doctor bowed low and took Judith's hand and kissed it.

"By Gar, she ees a most lovely maiden. She need food. She need rest. But most of all she need husband."

"Listen to me," thundered Judith. "Get this man out of my chamber. I have suffered enough today. I do not need food. I do not need rest. And above all, I do not need a husband."

She paused and looked from Will to the doctor, then finally to Arthur.

"Arthur," she said. "You must arrange for us to go to Wilcome Place. Tonight. I will not stay another moment in London."

"But, Judith. . . ." Will began.

"Do not tell me it is too late in the day, Will Shakespeare. We will ride all night tonight if we have to. We will ride all day tomorrow and the next day and the next.

"She ees too weak to ride," said the French doctor. "She must not go for three days."

"Which she is this you are talking about? If it is I then I am plainly here in front of you. Speak to me if you have anything to say about weakness."

"I weel not leesten to such talk. Pay me my fee and I leave you weeth this woman. But one thing I tell you, she need the husband."

"I need no one," Judith said. "Arthur, pay the man so he can leave us. Then go below and make ready. And another thing, you may send Mammet back to Sir Henry. I shall ride behind you on Jasmine. Now go."

Arthur started to the bed but she waved him back.

"Go," she said, and turned her face to the wall.

"Ay God, yes, Judith love, I go."

On the last day of the journey to Wilcome Place, perhaps an hour after Judith and her company had paused to eat the bread and drink the ale they had brought with them from the inn at Banbury, it began to rain.

"I think we should return to the village we passed a mile back," Arthur said. "Your hands are like ice, Judith love, and I fear you will catch a chill."

"Ride on," she said. "I would be at home."

She would say no more, but each time they rode past a shelter, Arthur would again suggest they stop. Judith would only point into the road ahead of them.

They arrived at Wilcome Place in the late afternoon. Judith was soaked to the skin. At Old Sallie's coaxing, she changed to a dry shift and went straight to bed. She ate hot soup and drank a toddy which Arthur had made. Launcelot came with dry logs to keep the fire burning brightly throughout the night. And Maryanne slept by the hearth to feed the fire. By morning Judith said she was feeling quite well.

"I fear you have a cough," Arthur said. "I was sure I heard you coughing in the night."

"And I am sure you did not," Judith replied.

There is no doubt that an argument would have ensued immediately except that Old Sallie came to announce that Master John was awaiting them below. Judith hurried down with Arthur at her heels.

"Father," Judith said as she stepped through the parlor door. "How did you know I was back from London?"

"Back from London?" he asked. "I never know you had gone."

He looked at her curiously, and frowned at Arthur who lounged in the doorway.

"Business required our little journey," said Arthur. "But we are glad we are here to receive you."

"I have no business with you, Arthur Amboid. I wish to speak to my daughter alone."

"As you will," said Arthur and vanished.

Judith came to her father who stood warming his backside at the fireplace. She gave him a nod that would pass for a bow, then went to sit in the carven chair.

"Do you care to sit down, Father? Or might I send for a warm drink? I am sure that Arthur is still hiding in the hallway within sound of my voice. Arthur?"

Arthur came smiling into the room.

"I think you could bring my father a hot drink. He has ridden four miles in the cold this morning. . . ."

"No," John said. "I thank you, but no. You may leave us, sir."

"It is my position to dismiss my own servants, Father. Arthur may leave when I tell him to."

Arthur looked strangely in Judith's direction, but said nothing.

"Then," said John Shakespeare, "I hope you will dismiss him. I have business."

"Very well. Arthur, you may go to the stable and see that my father's horse is well cared for. I shall watch from this window, and I expect to see you appear there shortly."

Arthur bowed and said nothing. And went out.

"Now, Father, what is your business?"

"Judith, I have come to see that you are a woman of property, and thus you have, to some extent, the right to manage your own affairs. I, your father, who have given my life for my family, seek nothing for myself. However, I have reason to believe. . ." and here he lowered his voice til he had looked out of the window and seen Arthur sauntering across the yard. . ."I have reason to believe that Arthur Amboid is not to be trusted. I have made inquiries as far as Coventry, and, at Coventry, I found several who knew Arthur in the past. He is a cheat and a liar."

Judith leaned forward, listening intently now.

"And for this reason I took it upon myself to go to Sir Thomas Grevel, who indeed does have your interest uppermost in his thoughts, and I poured the matter before him."

"I see."

"He agrees with me that you should discharge Arthur immediately. And he suggests that you do not hire a new steward. Instead he makes an entirely different proposal."

"And what is that, Father?"

"Sir Thomas in his wisdom, since his land adjoins yours in every particular, suggests that his land and your land be linked together in tillage, that his steward be your steward. And since he has for these weeks since the death of Old Henry Wilcome been invested to take charge of your moneys, he suggests that your moneys be joined with his in investment and management."

"But. . . ."

"Now hear me, Judith. There is one final element. Sir Thomas, since a wealthy young woman is a prey to fiends and vultures of every stripe, offers his hand to you in marriage."

Judith gasped.

"It is arranged. Knowing that you looked favorably on Sir Thomas, I have agreed that the nuptials may take place on Sunday. Your mother is even now planning the festivities. You may have nothing to fear for their excellence."

"Indeed, I do fear nothing. But you, Father, have much to fear, for you will have the trouble of canceling the festivities, and of breaking the news to Sir Thomas that I will have none of it. I am sick to death of love and of marriage. And of lying and of cheating. I shall go to my bed, and it may be that I shall never rise again. Good day, Father. And if you do not have better word than you have brought to me today, then never show yourself here again."

Judith broke into tears, ran out of the room, up the stairs and into her chamber.

Judith remained in her room for two weeks. She would admit no one but Old Sallie. Launcelot would bring logs to the door of the chamber, but Old Sallie would have to bring them to the hearth one at the time, standing them on end until their turn to feed the fire.

And during those days and hours Judith spent in solitude, all the matters she had shut away during her last hours in London and on the ride to Wilcome Place rose up before her. She would see Sir Henry's face with his eyes half closed and his nostrils flared like a horse. Indeed, like a stallion ready to mount a mare in the stable lot. And this was what Will said would bring the inspiration to great poetry. Love of a man for a woman.

Yet what if it did? What reason did she have ever to lift pen to paper again? She would see Old James Burbage in his chair by his hearth fire, straining to read the words, nodding and crying. And she could hear herself screaming at him. "You promised me. You promised me."

There were no promises in this great world and wide that men had intention to keep toward women. Judith rose from her bed and stared into her own blazing fireplace. The little flames were like supplication. They were begging her for something. She thought she heard them speaking to her. "Give me. Give me all you have."

"Then I will do it," she said.

She ran to her table, her bare toes tangling among the floor rushes. She searched among the papers scattered there until she found a neat roll tied in a scarlet ribbon.

"I shall burn it," she said. "Page by page. The fire will enjoy it though no man else does."

She ran back to the hearth, pulled the joint stool close and sat down. Slowly she untied the ribbon, threw it into the flames and watched it burn. And then she took the first page of ROMEO AND JULIET and dispatched that. It burst into flame, as though the lover's bodies might be cast upon a funeral pyre. She waited until it was consumed entirely and then she took up the next sheet. But her fingers would not release it. She thought she was trying to open her fingers, to let it go, but they remained clamped tight along the page.

"Old Sallie," she screamed. "Old Sallie, I need you."

She sat screaming and rocking until she heard her old servant's feet on the stairs. And then she loosed the page and let it fly.

"O God, no," she said then.

And fell to her knees and reached into the flame and took the paper again. When Old Sallie came into the room, Judith was holding the burning page close to her lips and she was blowing at the flame.

"Mistress," said Old Sallie. "I pray ye do not seek ye own destruction."

She grabbed the burning page and threw it into the flames. She took Judith's hand, insistently pulling until Judith got to her feet. She guided her back to the bed.

"Lie ye down, Mistress. And give me now what papers ye have. Lord help us, tis ye little play. Why would ye burn ye little play?"

"Because Old James Burbage will never play it. He said so. No one will ever play it. No one will admit to me that it is better than my brother can write."

"But there ye be wrong, Mistress. I heard Master Arthur mumbling to himself the other day that very matter. He said that ye little play were better far than any he had played in his days on the boards as he called it."

"Did he so?"

"He did indeed. And he said he had undertaken to have it by memory, but have not completed that."

"You say he has it from memory?"

"He says he has some great part of it by memory."

Judith sat up for a moment. She looked toward the table, started to get up, then fell back against the bolster.

"It would do no good," she said. "What does Arthur matter? He is not like the others. He could do nothing. Even as I could do nothing. Leave me, Old Sallie. I am not company worth the keeping."

And she began to sob wildly.

That very day Arthur sent Snark to London with a note for Will.

> Dear Will Shakespeare,
> You must come at once. I fear that Judith is deranged. She keeps to her own chamber. She will see no one save Old Sallie. She cries at all hours of the day and night. And worst of all Old Sallie says she has burnt some pages of her play. I fear for her life. You must help me.
>
> > Your Friend,
> > Arthur Amboid

Snark was waiting in the stable when Will returned from a late afternoon tryst with the Lady Clarise. Will was somewhat red faced and worn out from his exertions. His temper flared in spite of his best efforts.

"Holy mother of God, what can be the matter now?" Will asked.

"Tis a pitiful matter indeed," Snark said. "And I have a letter here to reveal it to ye, Master Will."

"Ay God."

Will suddenly felt the need for strong drink. He could not accept what tidings there might be without it.

"Go to the kitchen," he told Snark. "Tell them I said you must be fed at my expense. I will give you a reply when I have dined and recovered myself.

Will refused all offers of company. He went to a far table, and when Jennie had brought him a cup of strong wine and he had drunk heartily from it, he read the letter. He drank heartily again and read it over. He sighed. He put his head in his hands and deliberated. In his heart he knew it was some trick of Judith's to get her way. But this time he could not help her. What she wanted was beyond his power to give.

He ate his salad and pasty without appetite. It tasted bitter in his mouth. He could not get it down unless he washed it down with more strong wine. When he had eaten all he could, he rose unsteadily and climbed the steps to his chamber, neither looking at nor speaking to those he passed. Once in the chamber, he lit a candle and took up his pen and wrote.

Dear Arthur,

It is with regret I write these words. My regard for my sister remains the same. I love her. I respect the talent she was given by God above. But there is nothing further I can do for her than I have done. It is impossible that I should come into the country at this time. I suggest that she give up all idea of writing both poems and plays. In time her faculties will return to her. Meanwhile, I think you must tell her of your love for her. If she would marry you, her life might prove to be as normal as any other woman. Perhaps a child would fulfill her dreams. In any case, Arthur, she is yours. You must do with her as best you can.

Your Friend
Will Shakespeare

CHAPTER XV

Arthur came clattering into Judith's chamber bearing a log of wood in one hand and a tray of food in the other. Judith roused, looked across the room at him, and frowned deeply.

"Leave me," she said. "I desire service of no one except Old Sallie."

"And would you desire Old Sallie's back to break? The woman is old, Judith love. I have noticed that she stoops lower each day as I meet her on the stairs, coming and going with your food. With your jugs of water. With every necessity for your luxurious living."

"I do not live luxuriously."

Judith pulled the covers tight under her chin and closed her eyes. Arthur stood looking down at her, his own eyes creased with worry.

"You are right there," he said. "The fact is, I think you are not living at all. It would seem to me that my companion of the highroad has fallen into indolent ways. Judith love, let us face it. You are no longer interesting."

"Then leave me. Go back to where you first came. I can do well without you."

"Of course you can if all you choose to do is mope in your chamber."

"What else is there for me to do? If I cannot be a player nor write plays, I should sooner die."

"And what gives you the idea that you can no longer be a player nor write plays? Are your hands tied with ropes? Has your tongue been slit from your mouth?"

"Arthur Amboid, you know well that I am exiled from London. . . ."

"From London, yes, but London is not the sole circumference of the versal world."

For some moments Judith neither moved nor made reply. Then

suddenly she sat up and slung her bare legs over the side of the mattress. Arthur tried manfully to avert his eyes from them, but they were riveted tight to those slim, curving extremities.

"Do not stand there staring," Judith said. "Give me the tray since you are here. And make up the fire. I am cold."

"Indeed, Your Ladyship, I shall do that very thing. And may I say you are sounding much more like your old self. Excellent."

Arthur set the tray on the bed beside Judith, then retreated to the fireplace. He waited, poking about in the burnt logs, on tenterhooks lest she lapse back into silence. As soon as she had drunk from the warm mug of ale and chewed and swallowed an enormous bite of Old Sallie's good bread, he was rewarded.

"Arthur, what exactly did you mean just now? When you said that London was not the circumference of the versal world?"

"I meant this," and he paused and lifted the log he had brought and lay it quickly on the irons. "I think it can be said that I am the greatest actor in all England."

He paused again to give one final stir with the poker.

"And you, Judith love," he went on, "are the second greatest."

"You the greatest? What makes you think you are greater than I?"

"Hear me, love, for the sake of argument. Now to proceed. It may also be said, and truly, that you are the greatest writer in all England."

Judith smiled.

"Therefore, I would suggest that you and I throw together and form a small company of players. We could play individual scenes from whatever plays you may have written. I could set your poems to music and sing, accompanying myself on the lute."

"You have no lute of your own."

"But you, Judith love, have money. You could buy me one. And you could buy fine costumes. I shall require three new doublets, one of which must be black. You cannot imagine how well I look in black. Tis my color."

Judith stood up now, dressed in nothing but her shift, and met Arthur at the hearth. She was deep in thought. She glanced from her writing table to the press where her few articles of clothing were kept. Her frown deepened.

"What is the penalty of unlicensed players if they are caught?" she asked.

"A small fine, I think. Nothing more."

"And would there be an audience hereabouts?"

"There is always an audience for the greatest players in England. And we could travel to distant places as it became necessary."

"As often as we are caught, do you mean?"

"Ah. . .You could put it that way. But what glorious sport between times. What do you say, Judith love? Shall we make a try of it?"

"Yes, Arthur, yes. Even if they catch us and put us in jail. If they take all my money. Whatever may come, let us be players together."

Judith shivered, hugged herself, and drew nearer to the fire. And then she sank down on the joint stool at the hearth and put her face in her hands.

"O, Arthur, I have burnt two whole pages of *ROMEO AND JULIET*. Two very long pages."

"Then are you not a lucky woman to have so clever a steward, for I have at least three pages from memory."

Judith jumped up and threw her arms around Arthur. It was now his turn to shiver as his hands touched the thin fabric of her shift, and her firm, small shoulders beneath.

From that moment the house at Wilcome Place was turned into chaos. Arthur and Jasmine made constant comings and goings to Stratford, and to Coventry to buy props and fabrics, and as far away as Oxford to buy the coveted lute. A seamstress was installed in an upper chamber, where she sat by a window stitching all day. At night she would move to the hearth where Launcelot kept the fire bright til late at night.

Judith spent much of her time at her writing table, composing new scenes and adapting older ones so that she and Arthur could play them. The words came flying into her brain, sometimes faster than her fingers could move to write them down.

Whenever Arthur was able to remain at Wilcome Place long enough, Judith would call him into the parlor, and there they would rehearse. And Judith would know that Arthur had not lied to her this time. Even as she had known at Titchfield Abbey she knew again, he was the greatest actor in all England. Richard Burbage had never spoken with such warmth. Nor had he ever engendered such feelings in her breast. Ay God, when Arthur spoke the love words she had written for Romeo, she thought she must surely be Juliet and she did love him. He touched her hand and she felt his passion.

"Ay God, Arthur, I think I may not kiss you on the lips," she told him once, a little breathlessly, as they stood by the hearth, practicing the first balcony scene.

"Why did you write such powerful words then if you did not plan to kiss? I think, my sweeting, that a kiss may be required."

"Yet I cannot think it well to kiss when we rehearse. When you have found a hall that we may play in. . . ."

"A hall to play in?" Arthur said. "Judith love, I think we must be strolling players who play on street corners, in inn yards, at horse fairs, anywhere a crowd may gather. Are you too proud for that, Judith?"

"No. I am not too proud. It was only that I thought. . .I know not what I thought. I am. . . ."

Judith blushed. She could not remove her thoughts from Arthur Amboid's lips. They were parted slightly, and she could not help but see his pink tongue lick over the bottom one. She thought she would like to taste that tongue with her own. Ay God, she would do it. She had taken the first step toward him when Jane Bigsby came running in.

"Mistress, I would not bother ye for the world, but a letter have come from ye father. I thought ye would want it at once."

"Thank you, Jane. You may put it on the table. Master Arthur and I have important business."

"But it requires answer," Jane said. "The boy says if ye do not give answer ye father will come at once to see what all this riding about and spending moneys is for."

"How does he know what moneys I am spending?" Judith asked.

"Judith love," said Arthur, "You might as well read the letter and answer him. It is time for my fitting with the seamstress anyway. We must keep at work on our costumes."

Judith took the letter, read it, then threw it into the flames.

"Go to my chamber and bring paper, ink, and a pen. I will make quick work of my answer. Arthur, see you return as soon as you are done."

In the late afternoon Arthur and Judith were in the parlor rehearsing the orchard scene when another messenger arrived from her father.

"Arthur," she said as she took the letter from Jane Bigsby, "You are fortunate to have escaped from your family. I would I might escape from mine."

"I do not think you mean that, Judith love. You will come to terms with them."

"I do not see how."

She tore open the letter and read it quickly.

"Father says he knows every shilling, every ha'penny which has left my hand."

"He is a worthy father to know so much about his daughter."

"And further he says that he is instituting a civil suit against Sir Thomas, against me, and of all things, against you, Arthur."

"A father does have certain legal rights in view of the fact that you have no husband. I think according to law he may tell you what is best to be done with your property."

"I shall do as I like with my property. Say no more on that score. And I shall not reply to his letter. Let him sue to his heart's content."

Judith looked toward the door where Jane Bigsby stood waiting.

"Tell the messenger there is no reply. Tell him he may wait all night if he chooses, but there will be no reply. And when you have done that, Jane, bring wine for Master Arthur and me. I am tired from all this haggling."

When the girl had gone Judith settled herself in the carven chair and smiled wearily at Arthur.

"Tell me about your family," she said. "I have a great curiosity to know what manner of people they are. This time, tell me the truth."

"The truth? What is the truth? I have small regard for the truth myself. But if you desire it I shall endeavor to discover it, and impart it to you as best I can."

Arthur settled himself on a joint stool and stared into the flames for some moments. Then he turned to Judith and smiled.

"I, my love, was conceived by a female puff of smoke, and was blown like a zephyr into the world by the fireplace bellows."

"Pretty words, Arthur, are still lies. Tell me the truth."

"Some day I will. When I have strength to remember. Yet I think you must accept me as I am."

"That is the problem, Arthur. I can never tell what you are. I think you are my true friend."

"I am that indeed."

"I know you are a great actor."

Arthur made a mocking bow, then sat down again.

"You always know the answer to any question I ask. Therefore I might think you are a scholar except that I know you are as indolent as a courtier."

"Being a courtier requires more than indolence. A man must work hard to be a courtier. And he is often required to spend all that he has in the service of the queen."

"Unless the queen spends all she has on her courtier."

"Ah," said Arthur. "Unless she does. For that we must wait to see the ending."

Judith slept fitfully that night. She dreamed of Arthur Amboid's face, disembodied, huge. His eyes were two bright skies. His hair was golden sunlight playing through shade. His chin a grassy hillside. And lying between all this his mouth, a gleaming river of words, his lips the opened pages of a leathern book which she could read forever. Yet when she reached for the book, she could not take hold of it. It dissolved and reformed just out of her reach. She cried out and wakened. And knew she would sleep no more that night.

She lit a candle and went to her table to write. When morning came, she looked up from her papers to see that the fire had gone out. The room was cold and she was shivering. Her head ached and her throat felt raw when she swallowed.

"I have no time for sickness," she said.

She dressed quickly in her warmest bodice. She threw a shawl around her shoulders. And then she went below.

"I have need of a warm toddy," she called to Maryanne. "Launcelot, make up the fire in the parlor."

She pulled the carven chair close beside the hearth. And started to read over her night's work.

When Judith had eaten her bread and drunk her morning ale, she felt somewhat better. She sent Jane Bigsby to the barn to find Arthur. He came at once, and they proceeded with the rehearsal.

"But soft! What light through yonder window breaks?
It is the east, and Juliet is the sun!

Arise, fair sun, and kill the envious moon,
Who is already sick and pale with grief. . . ."

Arthur stopped his speech and bent to look at Judith.

"Judith love, can it be that you are sick though not with envy? You do look pale. And I think you are trembling."

"Go on, Arthur, I am not sick. It is only that I could not sleep and so I wrote throughout the night. Go on."

"Who is already sick and pale with grief
That thou her maid art far more fair than she.
Be not her maid, since she is envious;
Her vestal livery is but sick and green. . . ."

Arthur stopped again. He touched Judith's cheek with his fingers.

"Judith love, you are cold as ice. Here, I will bring you a warm toddy, a special concoction of the Amboid's which has been known to bring life to the dying for three generations. Sit down and rest til I am back."

"I shall not sit down, and you will prepare me no concoction. I remember a certain concoction you prepared for me on the night we met with my father. . . ."

"That was a different thing indeed. That night my aim was simple, to keep you safely in the upper chamber."

"And I am safely here and will have none of it. Tis a cold morning, that is all. Now go on with your speech."

"But. . . ."

"The speech, Arthur, the speech."

Arthur nodded solemnly.

"Her vestal livery is but sick and green
And none but fools do wear it; cast it off.
It is my lady; O, it is my love!
O that she knew she were.
She speaks, yet she says nothing. What of that?
Her eye discourses; I will answer it.
I am too bold; tis not to me she speaks.

"Master Arthur," called Jane Bigsby from the hallway beyond.

"Snark says I must give ye a message since Old Sallie will not let him come in with stable manure on his shoes."

"What is this?" said Judith sternly. "Have you not all been told that you cannot disturb Master Arthur when he is rehearsing?"

"But tis a matter of some importance, if ye please, Mistress. Snark says it will not wait. That is, he says there is a gentleman here to see Master Arthur and the gentleman will not wait."

"Who is this gentleman?" Arthur asked.

"I know not and neither do Snark nor Launcelot neither. But Launcelot do secretly think it be a gentleman of the law. He thinks ye have no choice but to come."

"Do not go, Arthur," Judith said. "Tell the man to wait til we have finished this scene."

"I think I cannot do that, Judith love."

"So you take orders from others and refuse my wishes? Is that what it has come to?"

"It has come to nothing, Judith, except that I must go into the yard for a few moments and have a word with some gentleman or other of my acquaintance. It will take only a moment."

He turned to go.

"I say you may not go until we have finished."

"Do not be unreasonable," Arthur said.

"I am not being unreasonable. It is a matter of what you consider important. To me there is nothing as important as this play. But I can see it means nothing to you. So go ahead."

"Judith love, this play means everything to me, but there are other matters that must be considered too. I am going into the yard. I will return in a few moments. You must accept that."

"I must accept nothing. I will go to my room now, and I give warning that you will see my face no more today. So you may save yourself the trouble of knocking at my door. Go. Do whatever business you have. It may be on another day I will deign to give you time to rehearse."

"Very well. If that is how you feel. I will go."

Launcelot had still neglected to make up the fire in Judith's chamber. Yet she was too proud to come down again, and so she stood by her window, shivering and staring into the roadway.

In a short time Snark opened the gate to the lot and out rode two horsemen. One was Arthur Amboid with his cloak pulled tight around him against the cold. The other was a man of middle years, dressed in bright green livery with a matching cape flying loose about his shoulders. Judith leaned against the window the better to see.

"Ay God," she whispered. "I think it may be the sheriff. I think he may be taking Arthur off to jail. O mother of God, what have I done?"

Old Sallie came up at midmorning to find Judith standing shivering by the window. The room was stark cold.

"O, Mistress," Old Sallie had cried. "Ye will catch ye death of cold in such a place."

Old Sallie ran to the door and called below.

"Launcelot. Launcelot Gobbo. Come up this minute with logs and with fire coals from the kitchen. Ye have let the mistress' fire go out, and here she stands shivering. Now ye must come with me, Mistress Judith to sit by the parlor fire til this chamber be warm. Then ye may come back to do ye little writings."

But Judith had written no more that day. She had moped throughout the following day, staring out of windows, holding open the front door and searching up and down the highroad until her teeth rattled from the cold.

"If he must needs leave, he might have come to tell me goodbye. He might have rapped at my chamber, might have whistled through the window."

"But mistress," said Launcelot, who was making up the parlor fire. "Ye told him ye would speak to him no more that day. I heard him mumbling about it. He were sore distressed to leave ye without word, but he had no choice. The gentleman were somewhat forcible to make him go off quickly."

"O Launcelot, I fear it was the sheriff. I fear Master Arthur has been taken off to jail."

"It may be, Mistress, I know not. But the man were forcible."

Judith stared most strangely at Launcelot, then turned away to pace the parlor floor.

On the fourth day, Judith took to her bed burning hot with fever. She would eat nothing. All through that night her fever had grown worse so that often she did not know where she was, nor even who cared for her. Yet she had not ceased to call for Arthur

Amboid, and would cry most piteously when he did not come.

Old Sallie would not leave her mistress. She called orders down the stairs to Jane Bigsby and Maryanne, bade them bring up milk and ale and what breads the two of them could cook. She herself ate little, and Judith ate less. And every other moment she would run to the bed and stare darkly into Judith's face.

"What is it, mistress, do ye think? Do anything hurt ye?"

"Here," Judith said, and touched her hand to her heart.

"'Tis cold settled in the chest, most likely. I shall make another compress."

"Not another compress," Judith told her. "But tell me this, do you think Arthur is in prison?"

"No, mistress. Master Arthur be much too fine a gentleman to be kept in prison."

"Then why does he not come back?"

"I cannot tell ye that, Mistress."

"And you say he left no word for me?"

"None, as I have told ye this four hundred times. But now, Mistress, Jane Bigsby has brought up something of sustenance and ye must drink it so ye may be well when Master Arthur returns."

Judith shook her head, then pushed at the cup. Old Sallie had no choice but to take it back to the hearth to keep it warm.

While Judith slept, Old Sallie sat at her bedside. She loosened her beads from around her neck and began to pray. She did not care who might see her. She cared for nothing but that Judith would be well again.

Ten minutes had not passed before Judith waked and turned her head aside as though listening intently.

"Is it Jasmine?" she asked. "Do I hear the approach of her rattling bones? Look, Old Sallie. Run to the window and look."

"No, mistress, it be too dark to see Jasmine. Still all ye be hearing is me beads clicking up their little prayers to the virgin."

"Prayers? Do you say prayers, Old Sallie?"

"Ay, mistress, that ye may be well again."

"Yet pray beside that Arthur may not be in prison."

Late on the afternoon of that same day, just before dusk, and even as the first snowflake fell softly down, there was heard a rattling all along the wind. Snark and Launcelot came out of the stable and stood waiting. Old Sallie ran to the window to look up and down the highroad. And in only a few moments, Arthur and Jasmine came to view.

It could be seen even from that distance, that a change had come to Arthur Amboid. It may have been his clothing, for he wore a black doublet with lace at the ruff, and buttons that shone like diamonds down the front. Beside which he wore not his usual dagger, but a sword with stones set in the hilt. Beside which a long black cape that fell from his shoulders and lay along Jasmine's backbone. Beside which he wore a wide black hat with dancing plume.

But it may have been more than that. For Arthur rode like a man of decision. A man with coin in his saddle bag. A man with the remains of a library in his box tied on behind. Books for his lady love. He came to her no longer as a vagabond player, but as a man of substance.

Yet if Old Sallie knew none of this, she knew he was the man in all the world she wished to see. She ran to call him, her feet somewhat splaying apart, her knees knocking together, which did not foster speed. And so Snark and Launcelot were first at Arthur's side. They stared slack mouthed at the master's splendor. At the snowflakes like jewels on his shoulders. They inspected the outline of the bulging saddle bag, and peered around at the box strapped at the top curve of Jasmine's back.

"Ay God, lads, tis good to be home," said Arthur, which somewhat freed them from the spell of his great possessions.

"O, Master Arthur, tis good ye have come," Snark said.

Launcelot broke into great sobs.

"Tis all my fault," he said. "If it had not been that I had forgot to make up the mistress's fire. If it had not been that I could wait no longer to take Jane Bigsby to me bed, and so we slept all night together in the hay loft, though to speak truly we neither slept a moment."

"What is this? Launcelot, get ahold of yourself."

But Launcelot could not. He sobbed and bawled and could say nothing more.

"Snark," said Arthur. "What is this all about?"

"The mistress be near death or departed already. We know not. . . ."

"Do not say such a thing," said Arthur. "It cannot be."

He jumped from Jasmine's back and ran to meet Old Sallie.

"O, Master Arthur," she called. "It be well ye came this moment. Stay not, I pray ye, for I know not how long she may live. And she will have no priest. . .And will not send for her father."

"Is it true then?" he asked. "Is our mistress. . . ."

The word stuck.

Old Sallie could only shake her head. Arthur left Jasmine and the bulging saddle bags and ran to the house. He took the stairs three at a time and ran straight through Judith's chamber door. Ay God, if she should be dead already.

She lay so still that his heart failed him. She was propped against snow white pillows like those flakes that gathered already outside on the window sill, that had turned the grass almost to white, they came now so thick and fast. Her hair was combed out on the pillow so that it framed her pale cheeks and forehead. She was so tiny, so like a child stuffed beneath the covers.

A sob broke from his throat and his eyes were moist with tears. Judith opened her eyes. He moved into their view and waited.

"Arthur," she said. "I am so glad to see you. I thought you would not ever come back."

"Of course I would come back," he said.

He approached the bed and took her hands in his.

"I longed to see you, Arthur, and I feared that I had been so unkind to you. And then I feared that you would be restrained so that you could not come back even if you wanted to."

"Not come back to you? S'wounds, Judith love, I must always come back to you, for we have much yet to do. I have made arrangements that we shall play at the inn at Bitford on Wednesday of next week. And I have brought you presents. Shall I go to bid the lads bring them up?"

"Do not leave me, Arthur."

And then she looked at him in that old demanding way she had. Her eyes sharpened and penetrated.

"Ay God," she said, "Where did you find this clothing? You have not stolen it, I hope."

"Judith love, you wrong me. You truly do. It is only that I have come into my inheritance."

"Inheritance of what description? And where have you been? Whose liveried servant came for you? And how could you leave of a sudden with no word for me?"

"Hist. Lie still. You must save your strength, Judith love. O, I have so much to tell you."

They looked into each other's eyes and said no more, but their fingers clung tight, one to the other.

"Tell of your inheritance then," said Judith.

"Yet if I do, you must be quiet."

Judith nodded, and so Arthur, in turn, pulled the chair close to the bed and leaned upon it to bring his face closer to hers.

"Ah, then, my inheritance, Judith love. That liveried servitor who came with the message came indeed from my father's house, and bearing, it must be said, bad news. News of my father's decease."

Judith shivered and tears came quickly to her eyes.

"Ah, but, Judith love, you must not be sad. It seems, dear one, that my father was one hundred and eighteen years old, had not eaten in ten years, nor breathed in fifteen."

"You lie," she said, and smiled.

"And so I must tell you that since the death of my old father, I am become nobility. From this moment, you must call me Sir Arthur Amboid, Thane of Thisbe."

Judith laughed aloud.

"And I must tell you of my castle, Judith love, where I shall take you when you are well."

He looked at her closely to gauge his effect.

"My castle, Judith love, has within it three hundred and sixty five rooms. One for each day of the year. And we shall set foot in neither chamber save on the same date, once a year. Every day a new chamber, Judith love. And we shall dine on newt's toes and onion milk."

"Arthur, say no more. I am worn out with laughter."

"Then you must not laugh but cry, Judith love. Does it feel better to cry? I will sing a sad song."

When Judith closed her eyes for a time and she could not see him, the tears stood out bright in Arthur's eyes. He brushed them quickly away.

"Shall I bring the lute and sing to you?" he asked. "For I am here to entertain and play the fool if you like."

"No," she said. "You must tell me truly of your inheritance."

"Must I?"

"Yes, Arthur, you must. I know you meant only to cheer me, but I would far rather have you speak the truth."

"Then, Judith love, in truth, I tell you, my father was an aged man and has died. These clothes you see, the books and jewels in my box and bag are my inheritance."

"Proceed."

"My father was a learned man, greatly prized for his learning in the household of Sir Robert Ruskin. He served Sir Robert all his life, from the day and hour he left the university. And Sir Robert gave him many gifts which are now mine. But I do not deserve them. I broke my father's heart many years ago when I left the university and ran off to be a player."

"But, Arthur, it is a fine thing to be a player. I am sure he wronged you to say it broke his heart."

"He wronged me, in truth. Yet I cannot speak of it."

"You must, if it is true."

Arthur paused, looked long across to the window.

"You must, Arthur."

"Ah, then, if I must. My father wronged me in that my mother was the serving girl who cleaned his chamber. He wronged me in that I lived among the servants til I was five years old and it was discovered I had taught myself to read. And then. . .then. . . ."

Judith felt, she knew not what. Was this man Arthur? Was this the truth at last?

"Go on," she said.

"I was like a play monkey then, dandled by my father and Sir Robert. I was made to lisp and read and recite whole pages to the wonderment of the assembled company."

"Arthur, you have suffered too."

"Yes, Judith love."

He bowed his head to recover himself. Then he looked up and smiled.

"So. . .this is my inheritance. We shall not speak further of it. Now we must plan what yet shall be. First, I think our future must contain food, for I have had nothing since daybreak. And you too, Judith love, must dine on peascods and dandelion drops. Peascods and dandelion drops are marvelous strengthening foods for famous players."

"Then I shall try," Judith said. "For it is certain that we two are famous players."

Judith seemed to be stronger then as they ate and talked of

their travels. She looked to see the books as he held them close before her. And then she grew so tired that she slept. She did not rouse as Launcelot brought in wood and stoked the fire. Nor as Snark came only to look. Arthur did not send them away, and so they joined Old Sallie who sat in the passage, clicking out her prayers.

The wind blew and the snow drifted against the house. Arthur sat throughout that night, a candle at his side so that, at every moment, he could see Judith's face.

The sky might have shown some light except for the flying snow, when Judith stirred and wakened.

"Ah, Judith love, tis a good sign when a patient sleeps so well. Do you feel better?"

"No. The pain in my chest is fearful. And I am cold. I am so cold."

"Then I shall call Launcelot to make up the fire."

Yet the fire roared like a lion in the grate.

"It will not help to kindle the fire," she said. "Yet go below and bring me Old Sallie's beads. My fingers crave them. And tell me if your father had a Bible among his books."

So he went into the passage and brought back the rosary. And found a worn copy of the Holy Word. And read it for some time til Judith lifted her head and began to sob.

"What is it, Judith love? How may I help you?"

"There is no help for me. I shall die and I know it. And I am so afraid to die," Judith said.

Arthur slipped his arm beneath her head to raise it. The coughing stopped.

"There," he said, struggling to hide his laughter. "I think you will not die for some long years, my Judith. But you must rest now, and when you are well, we shall begin our tour. Old Jasmine is good for many more miles. I say we must begin on the route where our friendship started. First we shall ride forth as far as Wodstock inn where we will play beneath Ben Doyle's windows til he fall into distraction. Then we shall fly with all haste to the inn at King's Langley."

"And shall my father come there to seek us and to bring us back so that he may have my money?"

"Indeed he shall, brave Judith. But I shall say you are my young wife, too shy to show your face."

"And shall I be that. . .your young wife?"

"Ay God, Judith love, for all your life, you shall be."

Judith smiled very broad and closed her eyes. And Arthur talked on in his great happiness, seeing nothing else.

"O, Judith, I have wanted to speak. That word of words has been so often in my mouth. But I knew you could not abide it and so I was silent. Now I must talk of it. I shall say it, Judith, the very word. Marriage. And I shall add that I do love you and have loved you all so long."

Arthur stopped then and looked to see what answer Judith might make. How should she reply to his rapturous love? Judith opened her eyes.

"I am content, so thou wilt have it so," she said.

"But do you love me, Judith?" Arthur asked.

"I am too fond," she said. "And therefore thou mayest think my 'haviour light; But trust me, gentleman, I'll prove more true Than those that have more cunning to be strange."

"Say it in your words, Judith."

"They are my words. I wrote them every one."

"But say, if you mean it, the simple words I love you."

"I love you, Arthur Amboid, and I shall marry you. And we will travel to the end of England together, playing many sets of lovers."

"But I will love you more than all of them. I will love you more than any man has ever loved."

"And I too," she said.

Arthur kissed her lips, her eyes, her hair all along the forehead.

"Judith," he whispered.

"Here," she said. "Lie down beside me. Hold me in your arms that we may rehearse."

Arthur laughed aloud.

"Yet still I think I may not lie down in my best doublet and hose."

"Remove them then," Judith said, and she laughed too.

"Ay God, I will."

When he had finished his untying, he lay down beside her and stopped her words with a kiss.

EPILOGUE

For many years two vagabond players rode throughout the north of England. They played in inn yards, in the great halls of many castles, at fairs, at feasts, at weddings. They were accompanied by five servants, who sometimes could be made to play certain clownish parts. But it was the two lovers for whom the audiences whistled and stamped and clamor clapped. It was the two lovers whom churchmen denounced and sheriffs chased through lanes and byways. Then on to the next town. Always moving.

In Stratford the name of Judith Shakespeare was never spoken. It was as if she had vanished from off the face of the world. Or as if she had never been. Yet John Shakespeare throughout his remaining years continued in a civil suit with Sir Thomas Grevel til no man remembered the source of the contention.

In London, when Old James Burbage had died and the player Richard Shakespeare was quite forgotten, The Lord Chamberlain's Men presented the most lamentable tragedy of *ROMEO AND JULIET*. The play was advertised as being written by their foremost playwright, Will Shakespeare.

In later years, three other plays were delivered to Will Shakespeare by a red bearded messenger, the pages rolled tight together and tied with a ragged ribbon. Attached was a short note. "Will, I beg you, play these as your own. Never let any man know the truth. J."

Will Shakespeare loved his sister. And he was a man of honor.

Doris Gwaltney served as coordinator of the Christopher Newport University Writers' Conference for eight years. She presently teaches writing in a continuing education program and she lives in Smithfield, Virginia with her husband of thirty-seven years. They have three children.

She is a lifelong student of the plays of William Shakespeare and has passed this knowledge on to her characters, who quote most liberally from his writings.